STILLMAN'S GUN

Ben Stillman 13

PETER BRANDVOLD

WOLFPACK
PUBLISHING
— EST 2013 —

WOLFPACK
PUBLISHING
— EST 2013 —

Cover photography by Rick Evans Photography

Published in the United States by Wolfpack Publishing, Las
Vegas

Wolfpack Publishing
6032 Wheat Penny Avenue
Las Vegas, NV 89122

wolfpackpublishing.com

Paperback ISBN 978-1-64119-726-7
eBook ISBN 978-1-64119-725-0

Library of Congress Control Number: 2019946666

STILLMAN'S GUN

Chapter One

Sheriff Ben Stillman poured himself a fresh cup of hot black coffee and returned the beat-up old flame-scorched tin pot to its hook over his cook fire. Staring down into the steam rising from the coal-black liquid speckled with a few bits of gray fire ash, the tall lawman lifted his salt-and-pepper mustache with a smile.

Was there anything better than sipping hot coffee on a cold Montana night by a warm, snapping fire lacing the air with the smell of charred pine resin?

Stillman lifted the cup to his lips, blew ripples on the surface and took a sip. Swallowing, he stared into the cup and gave a rueful chuckle.

Yeah, there was one thing better than drinking coffee by a dancing fire on the trail of cutthroats south of the Two Bear Mountains on a chill Montana night. That thing would be sipping the coffee at his own oil-cloth-covered kitchen table with his wife and his little boy nearby.

The boy on his lap, say. The boy *and* his mother on his lap, even better.

Stillman snorted a sheepish laugh.

It used to be he preferred the out of doors, the thrill of the outlaw chase.

Times had changed. Stillman was no longer a bushy-tailed, glittery-eyed young deputy U.S. marshal who lived for running down outlaws of every stripe, of sleeping under the stars and drinking his coffee so strong it could float a six-shooter.

He still preferred his coffee strong. But he was married now to a woman he loved more than life itself. He and Fay had a boy now, Little Ben, and Stillman preferred drinking his coffee and sleeping under his own roof with them—his bastion against old age and loneliness.

He wasn't a young man anymore. He'd be damned if he wasn't fifty.

Fifty!

How in the hell had that happened?

He chuckled again. He was no longer afraid of the years. He had a family he loved, a family who loved him. He was a happy man—a happy, aging man. The only problem was he was in the line of work none too friendly to men who'd set their sights on living into old age.

That thought had barely shaped itself in his mind when, still staring at his coffee, the cup exploded in his hand.

Coffee sloshed over that hand, burning through its buckskin glove.

Stillman was a seasoned lawman. Still, for a full second, he stared down in shock, the cup now blasted from his hand, that hand now steaming as hot coffee met cold air. As the report of the rifle reached his ears, echoing shrilly, Stillman came to his senses. He kicked dirt on his fire with a single scrape of his spurred boot and, grabbing his Henry rifle leaning against the oak to his left, threw himself right.

As he struck the ground and rolled, another bullet hammered the oak. Stillman rolled into the brush beyond the fire. He fetched up against a blowdown box elder ensconced in shrubs, and swept a wing of hair from his left eye. He'd lost his hat in the roll.

Now he lifted his head, trying to gain his bearings.

He thought the shots had come from the southwest, to his right. But now another bullet buzzed eerily through the air over his camp, and the following report originated from the opposite direction of the first, to the northeast. Three more quick, angry reports followed, the bullets ripping into the ground around Stillman's fire which, after his hasty, haphazard dusting, continued glowing a soft umber, a few small flames tonguing up around the charred, dust-and-pine needle-covered wood.

Those shots had come from the east, the opposite side of the camp where Stillman hunkered behind the blowdown.

The lawman waited, drawing deep, slow breaths, his right hand wrapped taut around the neck of his prized Henry rifle, its stock boasting an inlaid pearl bull's head. His own anxiousness ebbed. In the heavy silence that had fallen back over the night, he sensed the frayed nerves of those who'd bushwhacked him from the cover of darkness.

That pleased him. It also told him he was dealing with a trio of fools. Desperate fools. He still had to be careful. Desperate fools could be even more dangerous than curly wolves who knew what they were doing.

Stillman held perfectly still, kept very quiet. From the dark wood over his left shoulder he heard his bay gelding, Sweets, whicker softly. Stillman had tied the mount to a short picket line about twenty feet away from his camp and near the branch of a creek winding around that side of the camp. Sweets stomped a foot, blew. Stillman heard the sharp rustling sound in the silence as the horse whipped its tail.

After maybe five long, tense minutes, a voice called from the darkness to Stillman's right: "Ben?"

Stillman felt a grim smile touch his mustached upper lip.

He waited, counted slowly to ten, then called in a voice pitched with feigned agony, "You got me, Ace." He gave a grunt. A soft one. He didn't want to overplay it. But, then, he'd wanted the bushwhackers to hear it, too. He was no thespian, but he wanted to convince his assailants he'd taken one of their bullets and was no longer a threat. If they were all like Ace Darden, a man he'd once called his friend before Ace had taken to the outlaw trail, they were fools.

Maybe fool enough to fall for his game of 'possum.

They might be fools, but it was dark out here, and they were three against one. Three desperate fools against one lawman who'd been shadowing their trail for two days through some of the loneliest, wildest country north of the Yellowstone.

"You hit?" Darden called after several minutes of private musing.

"Yep. Took a ricochet, dammit." Stillman winced. Had the "dammit" been too much?

"Why don't you throw your rifle out and step into the camp where we can see ya?" Darden called.

"I don't know where the Henry is," Stillman returned, pitching his voice to imitate that of a badly wounded man. He groaned. "I dropped it. I can't move around overmuch, I'm afraid."

"Where'd we get ya?" another man's voice called from the darkness directly across the camp from Stillman.

"Belly."

"Nah!" said the third man, to the northeast. He sounded skeptical.

"Yep," Stillman said.

He let the three bushwhackers think over his words for a minute then said, "You boys are on your own if you help me onto my horse. I reckon I'll be riding back to town now." He paused, lowered his voice further, again hoping he wasn't overplaying it. "You got me damn good." He gave a wry chuckle. "Pretty damn good...you sure as hell did..."

Silence.

Stillman kept his head low. The night dark and cold, but the stars shone bright, and his eyes had adjusted well enough that he could see a good way into the forest around him. His stalkers might be able to see his silhouette, possibly his breath pluming in the cold air around his head.

"I don't believe him," said the man to the east. He had a low, almost guttural voice with the odd cadence often heard in Indian-accented English. That would make him Billy Three Moccasins, a half-breed from Alberta. "I don't think we hit him."

"I don't believe him, either," said the man to the northeast. Since Ace Darden was off to the west, this one must be Clinch Kingman.

"I think we did," said Darden. Raising his voice, he said, "Ben, how bad you hit?"

Stillman didn't say anything. He was done talking. He'd wait and let the ambushers move to him. He was betting he had more patience than they did.

The three men were carrying thirty-four thousand-dollars in coin and greenbacks they'd stolen from the bank in Winifred, a little town nestled in the territory's belly, near the Big Snowy and Little Belt ranges. A posse led by the Winifred marshal and the Sheriff of Custer County had given pursuit as the gang headed north, but their quarry had split up after ambushing the posse near the White Cliffs of the Missouri River, killing three men and wounding the sheriff.

Winifred Town Marshal Ralph Sanchez had gone after the half of the gang that had continued northwest; while Stillman, who'd been alerted by telegram, had gone after the three who'd been last seen heading northeast, toward his neck of the prairie in Clantick, in the north-central reaches of the vast territory. He'd spotted the three two days ago, and he'd been tracking them as they'd headed east through the rough country along the south side of the Missouri River, probably trying to make it into Dakota Territory before slipping over the border into Canada.

When they'd spied Stillman on their back trail, they'd started heading south, likely hoping to lose him in that rough, remote country between several isolated mountain ranges.

At the moment, Darden, Kingman, and Three Moccasins were rich men. They wanted to be free to spend their money, for it was believed they'd absconded with most of the loot, the posse not having given them time to break it up before the ambush.

No, they weren't as patient as Stillman. He'd ridden in this rodeo before. In his twenty-odd years of lawdogging, he'd learned the discipline of patience. It was cold out here. Even colder if you didn't move around to keep your blood moving. But Stillman would wait them out, gambling that his wait wouldn't be a long one.

"I say we shoot him out of there," yelled Three Moccasins.

"No." Darden was maybe sixty yards off to the southwest, but his voice was clear in the cold, quiet night. "We can't spare the ammo. Besides, he's an all-right sort, Ben is."

Ah, Stillman thought. They're low on firepower.

In his telegram, Ralph Sanchez had mentioned the gang had popped off a lot of rounds, and that they might be low on ammunition. It sounded like the town marshal's guess had been right.

Good to know...

"We can spare a little," said Kingman, his voice filled with irony. "And a lawman is a lawman. I like 'em better dead." He chuckled.

A rifle flashed in Kingman's direction—a red-orange lap of flames.

As the rifle belched, the bullet stitched the air to Stillman's right before thudding into a cedar. Kingman fired again, and then Three Moccasins threw in with him. A sporadic burst of rifle fire followed, the flashes coming from ahead and on Stillman's left and straight out away from him.

Stillman pressed his chin into the ground as bullets screeched and thudded around him, a couple snapping twigs from branches within inches of his position.

Ace Darden joined the fusillade, adding five or six rounds to the onslaught. So much for past friendship...

Stillman gritted his teeth and resisted the urge to return fire. Best to play 'possum. Let them consider the possibility he really was dead. Eventually, they'd either get tired of the waiting game and leave, or they'd move into scour him off their trail once and for all. Also, the possibility existed that the damn tinhorns would shoot each other, firing from three directions as they were.

When they finally moved in on Stillman, they'd be carrying less ammo than before.

Fortunately, he'd tethered his horse far enough away and in thick brush and timber. Bullets likely wouldn't strike the stallion. If the outlaws knew where the horse was, they'd kill him to make sure Stillman had to continue on foot. But Stillman doubted they knew.

At least, he hoped they didn't...

The shooting tapered off. Kingman fired one more round; it spanged off a rock ringing the fire—a shrilly wicked screech that rang in Stillman's ears for nearly a minute after silence had descended over his camp once more.

Anger burned in him. The anger of having his life threatened. Of having all he ever was, was now, and ever would ever be taken away from him by a few ounces of fast-moving lead triggered by scum. He could feel fury in the heavy thuds of his heart inside his chest pressed taut against the ground.

He waited.

Finally, Kingman yelled to the others, "All right, hold your fire, fellas! Let's close on him slow."

"Not a good idea, Clinch," called Darden. "Ben's wily. We'd best wait till morning. We can't see a damn thing out here."

Clinch cursed. He muttered something to Three Moccasins Stillman couldn't hear. One of them laughed. The two men, Kingman and Three Moccasins, moved toward Stillman, their boots crunching dead leaves and grass, occasionally snapping fallen twigs. Gradually, they drew near enough that Stillman could hear them breathing.

Slowly, he lifted his head to peer out across the blowdown before him.

He saw two silhouettes moving toward him—inky black, vaguely man-shaped shadows approaching slowly from ahead and on his left. Kingman and Three Moccasins were maybe twenty feet apart.

More footsteps sounded over Stillman's right shoulder. That would be Darden. The others were moving in, so he was, too, though Stillman knew Ace didn't like it.

He'd known Ace back years ago, when Darden had come up to the Montana country from Texas. Ace was roughly Stillman's age, and, like so many men on the frontier, the winds of fortune hadn't always blown his way. A large rancher had run him out of the ranching business in the Powder River country, so he'd gone on to other things.

Most of those things had soured, as well, so here he was now, wanted for bank robbery and murder, or at least accessory to murder, moving in on a lawman he'd known for years, with the intention of murdering him in cold blood.

Stillman would have felt a little more sympathetic for Darden's plight had not his own life been on the line.

Damn fool.

If Ace died here tonight, he'd get as shallow a grave as Stillman would dig for the others.

Chapter Two

Stillman's fifty-year-old body began cramping up as he hunkered low on the cold, late-autumn ground.

He stared straight ahead of him, over the top of the blowdown. The silhouettes of Kingman and Three Moccasins were approaching—thirty yards away...twenty-five...

Stillman glanced to his left. It took him a few seconds to pick Darden's shadow out of the tangled woods. Ace moved more slowly, cautiously. Starlight winked off the barrel of the rifle he carried.

Stillman turned to the two men approaching from straight beyond him. He raised the brass-breached Henry. He'd already seated a cartridge in the action. He winced as he slowly, quietly raked the hammer back with his right thumb.

Kingman and Three Moccasins just then

approached the dim red light cast by the finger-
ling flames licking up from Stillman's fire ring.
Kingman stepped around the left side of a tree
ahead of Stillman and on his left, while Three
Moccasins—a short, bandy-legged man in a
rabbit fur coat and fur hat with the earflaps dangling—came around the right side of a large box
elder near where Stillman had sat when one of
his stalkers had blown the coffee cup out of his
hands.

His right, gloved hand was still wet. Wet and
cold. That hadn't improved his mood any...

Kingman stopped ten feet ahead of Stillman.
Tall and lean, he wore a red muffler under his
floppy-brimmed, black felt hat. The light from
Stillman's fire shone in his thick cinnamon beard.
Firelight glinted off Billy Three Moccasins' two
silver front teeth as, also looking around, Billy
said, "You see him?"

Stillman straightened his back, lifted his head,
and raised the Henry to his right shoulder. Quietly, so as not to cause more alarm than necessary,
he said, "Drop 'em or you're wolf bait."

Kingman cursed and swung his rifle toward
Stillman.

Stillman's Henry thundered, the flash lighting
up the bivouac and showing his hiding place to
Three Moccasins, who brought his own Spencer
repeater to bear.

The Henry crashed again, and Three Moccasins cursed as he stumbled back into the brush, triggering his own carbine into the ground around his dancing boots.

Instinctively, Stillman lowered his head as Ace Darden fired a shot from his hard right and from about thirty feet away. The bullet ripped a small branch from a bough over Stillman's head. Stillman heaved his still-lean, if aged, body to his feet, wheeled, and, aiming the Henry from his right hip, fired and cocked, fired and cocked.

He fired one more round at the silhouetted figure dancing in the woods before him, then seated another round, eased his finger on the trigger, and scowled through the gray powder smoke wafting in the air around him like ground fog.

Brush thrashed and wood snapped as Darden stumbled, then dropped with a thud and a groan. "No! Stop! You got me, Ben!" He cursed. "I'm done!"

Stillman felt like sending a couple of more rounds Darden's way just to make sure, but he resisted the temptation. He looked at Kingman, who lay on his back unmoving. Three Moccasins was running away, cursing and groaning. Stillman caught brief glimpses of the retreating halfbreed's silhouette as he stumbled away from the camp. The night began swallowing him as well as his cacophony.

Again, Stillman resisted the urge to pop another cap or two. These men had tried to kill him from ambush. Still, he couldn't shoot a fleeing man in the back. He hoped he wouldn't pay later for his misplaced sense of decorum.

These days, with owlhoots running wild across the frontier and there being too damn few lawmen to bring them to rein, you occasionally had to shoot a man in the back. What difference did it make—the back or the front?

The worms they'd be feeding wouldn't care which side the bullet had gone in.

Stillman stepped from the brush he'd gone to ground in. his knees and hips stiff from being hunkered down so long on a cold night. He was glad the owlhoots hadn't made him wait longer. If they'd waited till morning, he'd likely have been so stiff, he'd have been little better against them than a corpse.

Fifty! How in the hell had that happened?

He walked straight south of his camp and into the woods, where he still heard Darden grunting and cursing. He didn't think the man was faking it. Stillman had heard Ace yelp when a bullet had hit him, and a man couldn't fake a sound like that. There was no feigning the sound a man made when a bullet violated his flesh.

Stillman saw Ace moving in some evergreen shrubs.

He stopped to gaze down at the man, down on all fours, trying to rise. The man's Winchester carbine lay on the ground to his left, well out of reach. Its bluing glistened in the starlight.

Stillman crouched to pull Darden's Merwin & Hulbert .44 from the holster thonged on the man's right thigh, and tossed it into the camp. The man wore a Bowie knife in a buckskin sheath against his back. Stillman threw the pig-sticker away, and said, "Got any more on you?"

Ace shook his head and sagged on to his left side.

"How bad you hit?"

"Bad."

"You gonna die within the next few minutes, or do I have to haul you back to my fire? I'm cold."

"What's the matter—just as soon dig my grave right here, Ben? Or maybe you'll just leave me to the wolves."

"It'd be no better than what you deserve, Ace."

"Hell, I know that." Darden waved a hand. "Leave me." He was breathing hard, grunting. "Just leave me here. Go on home, Ben. You did your job. Go on back to your wife. Heard you had a boy now, too. Ain't you the proud poppa? Go on home to your boy, Ben. I'm done."

"Ah, hell."

"What?"

"You're not done, Ace. A dead man ain't as full of horse fritters as you are. Christ, ladies at a temperance committee meeting don't talk as much you just did." Stillman reached down and grabbed the man's arm. "Come on!"

"Ow! Dammit, Ben, I'm wounded here!"

Stillman half-dragged and half-led the man through the brush and around blowdowns. The stocky, pot-bellied Darden ran to keep up and to keep from falling and further injuring himself. He dropped to his knees twice, cursing indignantly. Both times, Stillman jerked him back to his feet, finding no sympathy in himself for the man's misery.

When they reached the camp, he shoved the outlaw down by the fire burning again quietly, a few growing flames licking at the oxygen oozing down around the dirt and gravel Stillman had kicked into the ring.

Straightening, Stillman stared off toward where Three Moccasins had fled. He considered going after the wounded man but nixed the idea. Too dark. He was liable to get bushwhacked again. There was also the possibility it wasn't necessary. Stillman was sure he'd plunged a bullet nearly dead center into the half-breed's hide. If Three Moccasins wasn't dead by now, he probably would be by morning.

The sheriff would scour the area after sunrise tomorrow.

He looked at the balding, bearded gent writhing on the ground before him. Darden stretched his lips back from his tobacco-stained teeth in pain, sucking sharp breaths. Blood shone on the front of his ragged yellow blanket coat. Not as much as Stillman would have expected for a belly shot.

He dropped to a knee beside the man he had once called a friend. "Let me have a look."

"No. Forget it. I'm a goner." Darden looked up at Stillman. "You got any whiskey?"

"Let me have a look, dammit."

Stillman slapped Ace's hands away and unbuttoned the man's coat. He spread the coat flaps away from Ace's bulging potbelly covered by a blue plaid shirt. Opening Ace's shirt, Stillman exposed his blood-soaked longhandles. The bullet had carved a long furrow across the outlaw's abdomen from just above his belly button to his far left side.

Stillman ran his finger through the furrow.

Ace threw his head back and yelled in misery. *"Godalmighty—what're you tryin' to do to me, you madman!"*

Stillman winced, shook his head. "I got bad news, Ace."

"Just tell me straight!"

"You're not dyin'."

"Huh?"

"I've cut myself worse peeling potatoes for Fay." Stillman held his gloved index finger in front of Darden's face. Only the tip of the finger was bloody. "See that? That wound is about as deep as my fingernail is long. It's a graze."

Ace frowned in befuddlement, skepticism. "Pshaw! The way this hurts? Why, my guts must be hangin out..." He let his voice trail off as he looked down at the bloody line the bullet had drawn across his middle and probed it with both of his own gloved hands. "Damn...I thought for sure..."

"No, unfortunately, you're not dying. Which means, I suppose, I've got to not only tend your wound but take you all the way across the belly of the territory to Winifred."

Darden continued to stare at his belly. "I'll be damned—I could've swore I was about to saddle a golden cloud and play a harp."

"I wish. Not that I think you could carry a tune, but..."

Stillman rose and walked to where his saddlebags lay near the rock he'd been sitting on when Darden and his cohorts had ambushed him. He dug out a bottle he used strictly for medicinal purposes, for after his bout with the tangleleg several years ago, he'd promised Fay he'd steer clear of the forty-rod. He had a beer now and then, but he traced a wide path around the who-hit-John.

He tossed the bottle to Darden. He followed the bottle with a torn rag. The outlaw caught the bottle in one hand, the rag in the other.

"Tend yourself," Stillman groused. "Be quick about it. Next, you'll be turning your friend Kingman under with my traveling shovel."

"You expect me to dig a grave tonight?" Darden scowled at him angrily. "I'm wounded, Ben!"

Stillman chuckled.

———————————

"What happened to you, Ace?" Stillman asked a half hour later, as Darden slowly dug a hole for his friend, Clinch Kingman, at the north edge of the camp. "I mean, I've seen men go bad before. Plenty of 'em. For some reason, I didn't see you as bein' one who'd drift as far off the straight and narrow as you did."

He stared into his coffee cup, swirling it. Miraculously, his coffee pot had avoided one of the lead bumblebees Darden and the other two cutthroats had sent buzzing through his camp.

Fortunately, he'd packed a second tin cup. He'd filled it with the piping hot brew still hanging from the tripod over the fire.

Sitting against his saddle, ankles crossed, he faced his prisoner. His Henry rested across his thighs. He'd warned Darden that if he tried anything with the shovel, or tried running off into the darkness, he'd get a couple of blue whistlers between his shoulder blades for the down-and-dirty deed, and he'd meant it.

"Well," Ace said, kicking the shovel into the ground with his right foot, then grunting as he hoisted out the dirt, "I lost the ranch, you know." He paused in his work to cast Stillman a hard look. "No, I didn't lose it. It was taken from me. Right out from under me—*illegally!*"

"Oh, I know, I know. Nightriders burned you out—I know that. Happened a lot back in the Powder River country in those days."

"They called me a nester. I was a *homesteader,* Ben. I filed that claim legal at the land office."

"Yep, you did. I'll vouch for that. And masked riders sent by one of the larger ranches burned you out. Like I said, it happened a lot back then. I tried to get to the bottom of it…"

"But you came in too late."

"I got sent in too late," Stillman corrected the sullen man. "I'd been off trying to run whiskey runners off the Crow Reserve. By the time I got the order to check out your situation, those nightriders' trail was cold, and the Powder River Stock Growers Association wouldn't give me the time of day. Their doors were shut tighter than a Masonic Lodge. Didn't want to give away one of their own."

Darden resumed digging, wincing against the pain from his bullet burn. Steam rose from his body as he worked up a sweat in the chill night, and his breath frosted around his head. "Then... well, you know...Lilly died after we moved to town."

Stillman sipped his coffee, nodded. "I was sorry to hear that, too. She was a good woman."

"Only woman I ever loved. Only woman I'll ever love." Darden tossed another shovelful of dirt away with a grunt. "Expected to have a big family, her an' me. Out on our ranch. I got a job ridin' shotgun for the Powder River Stagecoach Company...and, well...you probably heard what happened there, too."

"Yeah, I heard you took a bullet in your leg. Laid you up for a while."

"By the time I healed, they'd done hired somebody else."

"All right—then what?" Stillman asked.

Ace tossed away another shovelful of dirt, then

leaned against his shovel and glared over his left shoulder at Stillman. "Go to hell, Ben. Just go to hell, will you!"

Chapter Three

"Do you have to ride so damn fast? I'm on foot here!" grouched Darden the next morning at sunrise.

Stillman had cuffed his prisoner's wrists in front of him and tied a long lariat around his waist. Stillman, riding his bay, held the other end of the lariat in his right hand.

He was trotting the horse through the high blond grass of the open prairie, heading for a ravine just ahead. Darden jogged along behind, stumbling and cursing, moving awkwardly because of his tied wrists. The bullet burn across his belly had probably tightened up on him, as well.

Glancing over his left shoulder, Stillman checked Sweets down to a halt. He chuckled as Darden shambled to a stop then dropped to his knees, breathing hard. "Sorry, Ace. I got to payin' more attention to Three Moccasins' blood trail than I was to you, and I reckon ole Sweets took advantage of my distraction."

"Sweets," Darden raked out, gulping breaths. "What kind of name is that for a lawman's hoss?"

"I don't know, it seems to fit him." Stillman leaned forward and patted the fine gelding's shoulder. "Fits me, too, truth be known...as I'm getting on in years."

"Mellowed some, have you? I hadn't noticed."

Stillman chuckled. "Besides, I didn't name this hoss. A young lady friend of mine, Crystal Harmon, turned him over to me when I first moved up to the highline several years back. Sweets belonged to an old friend of mine—Milk River Bill. Sweet man, Bill." Stillman drew a fateful sigh. "I went up to the Highline country to investigate his murder. And I stayed."

"I done heard about that," Darden growled, and spat. He brushed his cuffed hands across his sunburned nose. He added sullenly, "My lucky day when we crossed paths again, after all these years."

Stillman swung down from his saddle and shucked his Henry .44 from the saddle scabbard. He leveled a grave look at Darden, still on his knees in the buffalo grass rising nearly to his shoulders. "It didn't have to be this way."

Darden scowled at him, then spat again. "Can I have some water?"

Stillman grabbed his canteen off his saddle, reached into his saddlebags for some leg irons, then walked over to his prisoner. He gave Darden the canteen then knelt before him. Ace studied the leg irons uncertainly.

"What're them for?"

"I'm gonna leave you here while I go down and scout your camp and, hopefully, retrieve all that sweet-smellin' loot you stole from the Winifred bank. Might even retrieve your pal Three Moccasins, too, if he's around. That blood trail says he is. Or at least, he was as of early this morning."

Stillman glanced at the blood-splashed grass a few feet away. The grass still shone where a man had staggered through it within the past several hours. At least as of late last night or early this morning. The blood had dried and turned a rust-red color. There was quite a bit of it splashed along Three Moccasins' trail from Stillman's camp, a half mile away.

That the half-breed had shed so much blood told Stillman he'd pinked him good. Probably a mortal wound soon, if it wasn't already. Stillman didn't expect a man who'd lost that much blood to be able to put up much of a fight.

"No need for those. I'll stay here. I promise."

"Let's make it simple—shall we, Ace?"

"Don't trust me?"

Stillman gave a caustic laugh as he closed one of the irons around one of his prisoner's ankles, clicking it locked. He locked the other one and said, "Ace, I wouldn't trust you as far as I could throw you dripping wet uphill against a Dakota cyclone."

Darden told him to do something impossible to himself.

Stillman pulled a handkerchief from a back pocket of his denims.

"What's that for?"

"I'm gonna gag you, so you don't call out a warning to your pal."

"That ain't necessary."

Stillman gave an impatient chuff. "Let's make this simple—shall we, Ace?"

When Stillman had tied the handkerchief around Darden's head, he rose, grabbed the canteen from Ace's hands, and took a drink. He gave the flask back to Darden, then shouldered his rifle. "Sit tight. I'll leave Sweets so's you don't get lonely."

"Thrush-putt," Ace chewed out through the gag.

"Don't mention it."

Stillman dropped the bay's reins, then strode

straight out beyond the horse, heading to the ravine cutting a curving line through the prairie a hundred yards beyond. He glanced cautiously around him, squinting against the lens-clear morning light under a clear, blue, cold-scoured Montana sky.

Just because Three Moccasins was wounded didn't mean he wasn't dangerous. He still had his rifle and likely a pistol or two, possibly a Bowie knife. He could be holed up licking his wounds and ready to exact some payback for that blue whistler probably lodged in his belly. He might not be in a condition for a prolonged fight, but he might still trigger a deadly shot or two.

Stillman followed the blood trail to within ten feet of the ravine. He got down on his hands and knees and crawled until he could see over the lip and into the cut, through which a narrow stream meandered, glinting in the sunshine.

The canyon was maybe a hundred feet deep. On the other side of the stream, on the inside of a sharp horseshoe bend, lay the outlaws' camp. The stone fire ring was mounded with cold, gray ashes. Gear was strewn around the ring. Stillman couldn't see the outlaws' horses right off, but after some scrutiny, he spotted a black horse switching its tail behind a thin screen of poplars about twenty feet beyond the camp.

One of the men must have been trying for a fish sometime last evening, for a cane pole angled out of the water from the stream's far side, propped against a large chunk of pale driftwood. The line, beaded with water winking gold in the sunlight, moved back and forth in the stream, slackening then drawing taut, slackening then drawing taut again.

Looks like the fisherman had had some luck. Too bad he hadn't made it back to camp, having fulfilled his dastardly mission, to eat the fruits of his labor.

"Well, they were confident—I'll give them that," Stillman said.

Stillman looked around carefully. He didn't see Three Moccasins. What he did see was sign the half-breed had made it back to the camp. There were only two saddles and two bedrolls arranged around the now-cold campfire. The third saddle and bedroll were missing. That this was the outlaws' camp there was no doubt. Darden had told Stillman where he'd find it, and the blood trail corroborated the information.

Having taken off his tan Stetson to make himself a smaller target from below, Stillman set the snakeskin-banded topper back on his head, rose, and stepped over the ravine's lip and onto the slope dropping toward the canyon floor. It wasn't an overly steep drop, but he saw the broken, matted brush where Three Moccasins must have fallen and rolled. The half-breed had left a broad swath of bent brush liberally splashed with now-brown blood.

The outlaw had rolled to the bottom of the canyon. And when he'd stopped, he'd left more blood. Enough to fill a soup bowl.

Stillman clucked. "You gotta be damn near dry, Billy."

He looked around again. Still no sign of Three Moccasins.

Stillman followed the man's bloody trail across a beaver dam stretched over the stream. On the other side, he climbed the low, gravelly bank and stopped at the edge of the cutthroats' camp. He lowered the Henry from his shoulder, pressed the butt against his cartridge belt, aiming straight out before him.

One of the horses, apparently tied behind the screen of poplars, had just whickered.

Stillman cocked the Henry. "Billy?"

Again, the horse whickered.

Three Moccasins staggered out from behind one of the poplars. His face was drawn and pale, his eyes wide and glassy. A pair of saddlebags hung over his left shoulder. Gritting his teeth, he swung the Spencer in his hands toward Stillman.

"Don't do it, Billy."

"Hell," said the half-breed in a strangled voice. "I'm already dead!"

Just before Three Moccasins leveled the Spencer on him, Stillman squeezed the Henry's trigger. The resolute belch of the sixteen-shooter sent a half-dozen crows lighting from a dead birch to Stillman's right, cawing angrily. The bullet punched through Three Moccasins' chest, clipping the large silver cross he wore from a chain around his neck, making it bounce.

Three Moccasins said, as though astonished, "Oh!"

He dropped the rifle and the saddlebags as he flew straight back and went down, kicking high both his moccasin-clad feet. He rolled onto his belly and sort of tried to crawl away, though he didn't make it even a few inches. He sobbed and quivered as he died, which didn't take long.

Stillman walked over to him. He turned the body over.

The half-breed stared up at him, his face a death mask. He looked as though he'd been dead a long time. The first bullet had taken him just above the buckle of his cartridge belt. The second one was a heart shot, straight through the center of his rabbit-fur coat, soot-stained from the smoke of many fires.

Stillman looked at the bulging saddlebag
pouches beside the man. They were smeared
with Three Moccasins' blood. Stillman picked
them up, looked inside each pouch at the hastily
stuffed paper-banded packets of greenbacks and
several canvas sacks of coins. He glanced to his
right. A saddle lay on the ground near a piebald
gelding. Billy had bridled the mount, but he must
have been struggling with the saddle when Stillman finally caught up to him.

Rising, Stillman slung the saddlebags over his
left shoulder. He set his rifle on his right shoulder
and made his way back to the stream. He saw the
bent cane pole on his right and walked over to it.
The line was slack at the moment, but as it drifted upstream, it drew taut. Stillman lowered his
rifle, leaned it against the driftwood, and picked
up the pole.

He drew the line in until a pretty little
red-throated trout glinted in the sunshine,
sharply bending.

Stillman dropped to a knee, carefully removed
the hook embedded in a corner of the fish's
mouth, then walked up close to the stream, and
fell to a knee again. He eased the fish gently into
the water. When he felt it bend its scaled body in
his hands, he let it go.

———————

When he returned to the opposite ridge, Stillman retrieved both his horse and his prisoner. He rode Sweets back into the ravine, leading the handcuffed Darden by the lariat. The prisoner cursed as he slipped and slid and tumbled down the slope, sometimes nearly rolling up under the bay's belly to risk getting kicked.

He cursed his captor like an Irish gandy-dancer on a Friday night at end-of track. Stillman wished he'd kept the gag in Darden's mouth.

When they'd finally crossed the stream, Stillman riding the bay through the water, Darden keeping dry by crossing the stream via the beaver dam, the lawman swung from the bay's back and unstrapped his folding traveling shovel from his saddle.

"Looks like you got another compadre to throw some dirt on, *amigo.*"

"Ah, come on, Ben!" Darden dropped to his knees, groaning. He lifted his coat with his cuffed hands to reveal his bloody shirtfront. "Look there—my little shave nick, as you call it, done opened up. I'm bleedin' like a stuck sow. I gotta lay up and let it close, or you'll be trailin' a dead man back to Winifred."

"That'd be a cryin' shame."

Stillman peered at the man's shirt. He had bled quite a bit. Besides, Darden looked so damn pathetic and worn out, not to mention old, that Stillman couldn't drive himself to force the man to dig another grave.

Not that Billy Three Moccasins deserved one. Still, Stillman had a hard time leaving the body of even the nastiest of cutthroats exposed to the carrion eaters. Dead, all men sort of seemed equal in a way, somehow deserving of at least a rudimentary internment.

"All right. You can build a fire and brew some coffee. You know where my gear is stored."

While Stillman removed his coat and his hat as well as his cartridge belt and ivory-gripped Frontier Colt .44, and piled everything near where he'd leaned his Henry rifle against a poplar, he got to work with the shovel. He kept an eye on his prisoner, who'd set to work gathering dry wood for a fire in his hangdog fashion, cursing under his breath—cursing Stillman and his fate and the world in general. Darden looked like a man who wished he'd never been born.

Stillman felt no sympathy. Well, maybe a little, but only because he'd known Ace when he'd been a better man. Good men went bad, though. Stillman knew that well enough. There were just too damn many temptations for some men, exploiting some inner weakness they'd likely been born with. Stillman didn't really know. He'd got out of the business of trying to figure folks out about the second year after he'd pinned his deputy U.S. marshal's badge to his shirt, all those years ago.

By the time Darden had a pot of coffee gurgling from the iron tripod, Stillman had dug a roughly body-shaped hole about a foot and a half deep. The ground he'd chosen for Billy Three Moccasins' final resting place was loamy and sandy, and made for relatively easy digging.

Stillman wouldn't dig the hole any deeper, however. He wanted to get back on the trail to Winifred. From here, it was a good three-day ride. It would take four additional days to ride back to Clantick, which meant he wouldn't get home to his wife and boy for over a week the way it was.

He didn't want to shilly-shally here over the grave for a man who didn't even deserve one. Rocks were scattered nearby, churned up by previous spring floods. They would serve to keep the predators from digging up Three Moccasins and scattering his bones to Kingdom Come.

Stillman dragged Billy, wrapped in his bedroll, into his grave then shoveled a layer of dirt over the body. He tossed away his shovel and glowered over at Darden lounging by the fire, leaning back against his saddle, scowling into a cup of coffee.

Catching Stillman's gaze on him, the outlaw grinned and raised his cup in mock salute of Stillman's toil.

Stillman opened his mouth for a harsh retort but let the words die in his throat. He'd seen something in the corner of his right eye. Now he turned his head to stare up the ravine's southern wall.

Three riders galloped across the shoulder of a low hill maybe two hundred yards beyond. Stillman couldn't see them well from this distance. They were just three men on three horses, and they were heading away from him.

Probably just ranch hands working the fall roundup.

Still, caution rippled through the lawman.

He looked at the loot-stuffed saddlebags on the ground near the fire.

"What is it, Ben?" Darden asked.

"Nothin'."

"Oh, I see it." Ace was gazing to the south, where the riders just then dropped down behind the hill. "Riders, eh? Three of 'em?"

"Don't worry about it."

Stillman cursed, then walked to the rocks, grabbed one, and hauled it back to the grave.

"Oh, I ain't worried," Darden said. "I ain't the one to be worried. You're the man with the money, now, ain't ya?" He smiled. "A lone lawman out here with twelve thousand dollars in loot. Free for the takin'." He winked. "Once they get past you."

"Give your mouth a rest, Ace," Stillman said, carrying another stone to the grave.

"You're all alone out here, Ben. I wonder if word of the bank robbery could have come all this way north by now. Hmmm. Lots of hungry men out this way."

"Shut up, Ace."

"All right, all right. I was just ponderin' aloud, is all."

Chapter Four

By the time he'd piled a half-dozen rocks on the grave, Stillman was ready for a rest. He leaned back at the waist, planting his fists on his hips, stretching and grimacing.

"What's the matter, old man?" Darden said, and took another sip of his coffee. "Gettin' tired?"

"A little stiff is all. My back..." Stillman stretched again.

"Ah," Darden said. "I heard about that. Some years ago, wasn't it? A whore, right? In Butte, wasn't it? Shot you in a whorehouse."

"Virginia City. The whore was drunk. She was trying to shoot the devil I was arresting and got me by mistake." Stillman snorted at the old joke of fate and shook his head.

"Nasty luck."

"Wasn't no luck in it."

"I heard you was laid up for a time."

Stillman walked over to the fire, dropped to a knee, grabbed a leather swatch, and removed the coffee pot from the hook. He filled a clean cup, the steam wafting up to bathe his face and brace him with its heady aroma.

Nothing else in this world smelled or tasted like a good cup of coffee, or so effectively filed the edges off a weary body and tired mind.

He said, "I had to retire my deputy U.S. marshal's badge. Couldn't do the job. The pain was miserable there for the first few months. Doctors couldn't get the bullet out without paralyzing me. I licked my wounds for a good, long time in a boarding house in Great Falls. Fells into the bottle, I sure did."

Stillman set back against his saddle and shook his head at the memory.

Darden closed one eye, narrowed the other one at him, and said, "How'd you get out of it?"

"Well, first a young man looked me up to help him find out who killed his pa. That was Milk River Bill's son, Jody. So that helped me crawl out of the bottle—traipsing around the Two Bear Mountains, looking for a killer and getting to know some good folks. And then a woman…"

Stillman smiled fondly at the name inside his head, and at the beautiful image it conjured: *Fay…*

"Ah, that rancher Alexander Beaumont's

daughter from the Powder River Country...
That's who you married, you old goat?"

"That's who I married. That's who gave me my
son, little Ben."

"Well, damn..." Darden sipped his coffee.

So did Stillman.

"What about the whore's bullet?"

"Doc Evans in Clantick knew a sawbones in
Denver who had come up with a procedure for
spinal surgery. It was risky—chances for success
were about sixty-forty. I had no choice, as the
scar tissue was growing against my spine, and
I was gradually losing the feeling in my legs. So
that Denver surgeon dug the bullet out of my
back...and here I am."

He smiled and raised his smoking cup in a
mock salute to Darden.

Ace chuckled, wagged his head. "Ain't that just
my luck? But good luck for you, I reckon, Ben."

Stillman squinted at him through his coffee's
steam. "Sometimes we make our luck, Ace."

"Hogwash. Some folks it tumbles to, some it
don't."

"Oh, hell, Ace."

"Oh, hell, nothin'. After that bullet ripped into
my leg and I couldn't ride the stage anymore, the
only job I could get was swampin' out the Red
Rooster Saloon in Glendive. For room and board

only. I didn't even have enough money for cards. I had to beg for extra. When I got tired of beggin' like some legless old Confederate…"

"You robbed the place."

Darden grimaced and rolled his head around with a sheepish expression. "Heard about that, did ya…?"

"Bill Olney told me, after I'd taken the county sheriff's job up in Clantick. He was ridin' through inspecting stock brands. I bought him a beer one night, and we fell into old-man gossip."

"Did Bill tell you I got six months at Deer Lodge?"

"As you sow, so shall you reap."

"You know what happens to a man who's been in prison. Word gets around, and no one'll hire him for anything. Not even room an' board!"

"So you started robbing the stage line you once worked for."

"Sure, I did. Wouldn't you in my position?"

"Nope."

"You yourself had a bad stretch, Ben. You know how it is."

"I fell into the bottle. Believe me, I begged for many a drink and gambling jingle. But I didn't rob saloons and stagecoaches, you cork-headed no-account. I sure as hell never beefed anybody, like you did." Stillman finished his coffee, tossed the grounds on the fire. "Come on. You can help me haul rocks. I'd like to get back on the trail soon."

"I ain't in no hurry to visit the hangman."

Stillman heaved himself to his feet. "Just the same, help an old friend out, Ace. Call it penance."

"I'm tired, Ben. You're dragging me over here like I was some herd-quittin' calf wrung me out. I got a bad ticker."

Stillman walked over to the scattered rocks. "Pshaw!"

"No, it's true. I had a pill-roller listen to it a couple years ago. He said it didn't sound right. He thought part of it was logy. Maybe a logy valve or somethin'."

Stillman picked up a rock and carried it to the grave.

Darden poured a fresh cup of coffee. "I need an operation, but I can't afford it." He glanced at the saddlebags bulging with the stolen bank money, as though the operation was what he'd intended to use his split of the loot for. "Doc says I gotta take it easy. I get tired real fast. I been tired for days now. Long, hard ride, runnin' away from that posse. Me an' the boys never expected Sanchez to form a posse that fast."

"That's too bad, Ace. I'm very sorry you had to work so hard for that loot."

Darden gave an ironic chuckle. "I reckon it was fatigue caused that bullet to hit your coffee cup last night." He smiled jeeringly. "'Stead of you."

Stillman had just dropped another rock on Three Moccasins' grave. Now he glowered over at Darden. "That was you, huh?"

"Yep." Darden continued smiling at him. Then, suddenly, his brows furled as though he were unexpectedly troubled, and he cast his gaze to the ground. "Yes, it was, all right. Sure enough."

He took another sip of his coffee then stared pensively into the cup.

———————

Stillman finished mounding the half-breed's grave with rocks then had one more quick cup of coffee. He kicked dirt on the fire, turned Billy Three Moccasins' and Clinch Kingman's horses loose from the outlaws' picket line, gathered his gear, and threw his saddle on Sweets' back. He made Darden gather his own gear and saddle his own mount.

The prisoner complained about his ticker, but Stillman told him if he didn't saddle his horse, he'd have a long walk back to Winifred.

"If you don't walk, I'll drag you," he threatened.

Cursing and complaining, Darden saddled his

steeldust gelding, then hooked his cuffed wrists around his saddle horn and stepped into his saddle.

"You know, Ben, I got a proposition for you," he said, as they climbed up out of the ravine and back onto the open prairie, heading south. Three Moccasins' and Kingman's horses followed them doggedly from a distance, not wanting to be left alone. Horses were social creatures.

"You do, do you?" Stillman said. "I reckon you're gonna tell me whether I'm interested or not, aren't you?"

"I think you oughta turn me loose."

"Why is that?" Stillman asked.

"Like I said, my ticker's weak."

"It wasn't so weak it prevented you from robbing a bank, Ace."

"Still, though, it took a lot out of me. I don't reckon I'll live out the year."

"Really?"

"You can't hang an ill man, Ben."

Stillman snorted a wry laugh. "You just watch me, Ace."

"Here's one more."

"One more what?"

"Proposition."

"Oh, boy—here we go," Stillman said as they rode side by side toward a dark line of distant mountains. Those would be the Judiths.

Darden glanced at the bulging saddlebags Stillman had draped over his own, over the rump of his horse. "Let's split the money."

"Split the money."

"Think about it."

Stillman looked at him. He'd be damned if Darden wasn't serious. The man smiled devilishly, his gaze probing Stillman's. It was almost as though the man were trying to mesmerize him.

"You think about it a while. Let it tumble around in your brain a few times."

"All right," Stillman lied, turning his head to stare straight out over Sweets' twitching ears.

"You're not getting any younger, Ben."

"Ain't that the truth?"

"You got any money socked away for when you get too old, and you have to give up the badge? Has that county you work for promised a pension?"

Stillman didn't respond to that. It was a soft spot Darden had been probing for.

"No, of course not. Why, you got a younker. A pretty young wife. Neither one o' them things is cheap. What do you bring down as sheriff? Maybe fifty a month?"

Again, Stillman didn't respond. Darden had found another soft spot. Stillman brought in fifty-five dollars a month, which wasn't enough.

Fay used to teach before the boy came along, but now that she had little Ben to look after, she didn't have time to teach. Stillman raised chickens, and Fay sold the eggs in town, but that only amounted to about ten more dollars a month, when the hens were laying well...

"Probably got you a house. A nice big house. Don't you? A woman...a wife...especially a purty young one...wants a house. Gives her more room to move around with the kid, and, besides, women are creatures of status."

"All right—that's enough, now, Ace. Me, I like silence."

"I bet you're still payin' on that house—ain't you, Ben?"

Stillman ignored the man. Or tried to.

"I bet you're still payin' for that operation you had on your back, too..."

Darden paused. Stillman didn't look at him, but he could feel the man's eyes on him. Stillman felt his face warm.

"All I'm sayin', Ben, is think about it. Twelve thousand dollars. Split two ways..."

"I'll think about it if you'll shut up," Stillman lied. He had no intention of thinking about it. That wasn't the man he was. That was the man Darden was. Stillman looked at his prisoner riding to his right, swaying easily with the movements of his gelding. "All right, Ace? We got a deal?"

"All right, all right, Ben," Darden said, grinning, raising his hands, palms out, as if in capitulation. "All right, all right, all right. My, my, my," he added as though to himself. "I'll be damned if he ain't considering it…"

Stillman continued riding in nettled silence. He didn't know why he was feeling so peevish. Darden might have probed a few soft spots, but there'd been no real penetration. He was just older than he used to be, and homesick. That's what it was.

They crossed a dry wash and then climbed a low grade into heavy pine timber. When they came out the other side, Stillman reined Sweets to a halt.

"Hold up," he told Darden.

Ace drew back on his steeldust's reins. "What is it?" He followed Stillman's gaze toward three men riding toward them and said, "Oh."

The three riders were a hundred yards away and making a beeline for Stillman and his prisoner. All three wore heavy furs against the autumn chill, and battered Stetsons. Rifles jutted from saddle scabbards.

Darden glanced at Ben and narrowed one eye apprehensively. "What do you suppose they want?"

"I reckon we're about to find out," Stillman said. "Just keep your mouth shut and let me do the talkin'."

They watched the riders continue through the knee-high brome grass, leather saddles squawking, bridle chains jangling.

"I don't know, Ben," Darden said, quietly. "They look like a tough breed. Maybe you'd better uncuff me and give me my pistol. You might need me to back your play…if they're after the loot."

"Shut up, Ace," Stillman said. "Let me do the talkin'."

"All right, Ben. Have it your way." Darden sighed.

Chapter Five

The three riders drew rein about ten feet from Stillman and Ace Darden.

The three sat their fidgety mounts, reins drawn tight in their fists, eyeing Stillman and his prisoner with a primal belligerence. The man in the middle of the three seemed to be the leader. He was tall and beefy, broad-faced, unshaven, and in his late-twenties. Eyes dark beneath heavy, sandy brows, he wore a knee-length quilted elk hide coat belted at the waist.

He worked a wad of chaw out of his cheek with his tongue and spat it on the ground to his left, then returned his sharp, angry eyes to Stillman. "This is Jinglebob graze. You're trespassin'." He grunted more than spoke the words.

"I think you're wrong about that," Stillman said. "I think this is government graze, open range."

"Yeah, well, you're wrong about that," spat out the man on the left—roughly the same age as the leader but shorter, stockier, and with a full ginger beard. "Who are you and where you headed?"

"I'm Ben Stillman, Sheriff of Hill County. I'm transporting my prisoner to Winifred."

"Stillman, eh?" said the trio's leader. Stillman saw the man's gaze flick to Stillman's buckskin coat. As the men had approached, the lawman had slowly lifted the flap above the .44's ivory handle. He noticed now that the leader of the trio had his own guns sitting free and easy, as well. The walnut grips of two revolvers poked out of slits cut in the side of the man's coat at each hip.

The ginger-bearded man now quickly lifted the flap of his own fox fur coat above the gutta-percha-gripped handle of a Russian .44. The third man seemed to be having trouble keeping his horse settled, so he didn't have time to free his own weapon. His pinto appeared startled and pranced in place, looking as though it wanted to bolt.

Darden's steeldust lifted its head and gave an uneasy neigh. "Jesus Christ, fella, settle your hoss!" Ace said, pulling back against his own mount's reins.

The lead rider gave the man on the unsettled horse an impatient look then turned back to

Stillman. "Heard there was a run on the bank down in Winifred." He glanced at Darden, and grinned with one side of his mouth. "This one of the runners?"

"It is," Stillman said.

"He's packin' the money," Ace said with a coyote grin, canting his head toward Stillman. "We took down twelve-thousand dollars, and he's packin' the whole load in them saddlebags."

"He is, is he?" said the ginger-bearded man with interest, glancing inquiringly at the leader.

"See them bulgin' saddlebags?" Ace said, now tilting his head toward the rear of Stillman's bay. "That's them, all right. Say, I know. Why don't you shoot him? All that money'd be yours that way. You could turn me loose"—he held up his hands to show the three men before him the handcuffs—"by way of thankin' me for the information. You might even—oh, I don't know—cut me in..."

He chuckled.

Anger climbed up Stillman's back like mercury in a thermometer. He glanced at Darden sneering at him just off his right stirrup, and hardened his jaws as he returned his gaze to the three men before him, regarding him now with renewed interest.

Stillman smiled without humor. "I wouldn't

put much stock in anything this man says. He took his own advice, and look where he sits. You don't want to end up in the same condition…or worse."

"Twelve-thousand dollars you say?" asked the ginger-bearded man.

"Twelve thousand, give or take," said Darden with a smile.

The third man had finally got his pinto checked down, but he had to hold the reins taut to keep it still. He was a small, wiry man with long, red-blond hair and a scraggly mustache and chin whiskers. His eyes were cobalt, and they shone in the light of the high-country sun. He whistled and cut his gaze toward the leader sitting his mount between him and the ginger-bearded man.

"We could do it, Jed," he said. "Who'd know? We'd bury him deep. Who'd know?"

"Forget it, Willie," Jed said after a couple moments' unsettling hesitation. At least, they were unsettling to Stillman. "We're here for Mr. Conyers." He looked at Willie and hardened his voice. "We ride for Mr. Conyers!"

Willie scowled. "Yeah, but…"

Jed looked at Stillman. "We're lookin' for a woman. One with a boy. You seen her?"

Stillman stared back at him, trying to read the

state of things here. All he could see, however, was a good bit of turmoil in Jed's eyes.

"What woman?" Stillman asked. "What boy?"

"The woman who stuck a knife is Byron's belly. She's got a boy with her."

"Byron?" Stillman frowned, curious. "That wouldn't be Byron Conyers, would it?"

"Sure enough, it would," said the ginger-bearded man.

"Shut up, Big Mike," Jed admonished him, keeping his eyes on Stillman. "I'll do the talkin'. A damn whore stuck a knife in Byron's belly. At the Eagle Creek Saloon."

"You don't say?" Stillman said, considering the information. He knew of the Conyers family. They'd owned the Jinglebob Ranch in these remote parts for a dozen or so years. Old John Conyers was a colicky, imperialistic devil, and Stillman had heard the man's oldest son, Byron, was a firebrand.

"The old man's madder'n an old wet hen." Jed spat to one side again. "We ride for him. I'm top hand, second only behind Loco McGuire." He proudly thumbed himself in the chest. "Jed Nordekker. He sent us out for the woman, and we aim to find her. If you see her on the trail south to Winifred, you'd best send word to the Jinglebob—understand, old man?"

The old-man comment only fueled the flames of anger inside Stillman, who shifted his position on his saddle and leaned forward commandingly and said, "You watch your mouth, Nordekker. I might be a tad long in the tooth, but I can still stomp the shit out of both ends of you."

Nordekker opened his mouth to respond, but Stillman cut him off with: "And if you're thinking about exacting vigilante justice on this woman who stuck Byron Conyers, you'd best think again. That's a law-and-order matter. You'd best ride over to White Sulfur Springs and notify the county sheriff there—Buck Reno. Takin' the law into your own hands—or Conyers' hands—is against the law."

Nordekker leaned forward, his broad face red with fury. "You go to hell, *old man!* The crime was committed on Jinglebob graze. The men of the Jinglebob will see that justice is served. Now, *old man,* get your prisoner off Jinglebob graze, or you might just find yourself swinging from a cottonwood. We got quite a few down by the creek that's badly in need of trimmin'."

The others snickered.

Nordekker neck-reined his horse around, said, "Come on, fellas. We got a kill-crazy whore to find!"

He booted his mount around Stillman and

Darden. Chuckling, Big Mike followed suit. The fiery Willie laughed louder, mockingly, at Stillman. He yelled, *"Hi-yahh!"* and gave the pinto its head. The horse traced a half-circle around Stillman and Darden and went buck-kicking off after the others.

Soon they were galloping through the timber, and their crunching hoof thuds dwindled to silence.

Stillman turned to Darden.

Ace gave a sheepish shrug. "Sorry, Ben. I figured it was worth a shot."

Stillman narrowed an eye at him. "Anymore tricks like that, Ace, and you'll be riding Dutch to Winifred." "Dutch" meant he'd be dragged. "And we still have a hundred miles to go."

―――――――――

Later that afternoon, the wind kicked up and clouds moved in.

It wasn't much longer before wind-blown snow began to fall, laying a thin downy covering on the broad prairie between far-flung island mountain ranges—the Little Rockies, the Highwoods, and the Judiths—humping up on the horizon in a broad circle, like brooding storm clouds.

Stillman and his prisoner crossed a couple of

more dry watercourses, then climbed a long, low incline toward the town of Hobbs capping the bench above and ahead of them. They traversed bald, open prairie now, with the gentle swells of a vast ocean. It smelled like dirt, autumn-cured grass, and cattle. Heavy with cattle; the wind blowing the stink of manure from all directions.

There wasn't a tree within sight. If there ever had been any, they'd likely gone to constructing the dozen or so false-fronted, two- and three-story clapboard business buildings of Hobbs, facing each other from both sides of the broad main street in familial silence.

A few more of those trees might have been used to construct the dozen or so shacks and shanties flanking the business establishments, as well as a livery barn with a couple of adjoining corrals.

Stillman knew the town of Hobbs well—better than he wanted to, in fact. He'd once holed up here with Milk River Bill Harmon when they'd been hunting buffalo. Back then the town was no more than a hider's camp, rife with the stench of sour hides. As a deputy U.S. marshal, he'd once had to kill "Big Nose" George Braddock in the Squaw Peak Saloon & Gambling Parlor. That had been a dozen years ago, however. Water under the bridge.

That was one good thing about getting older. There was a lot of water under the bridge. Anyone in town who'd given a damn about Big Nose's untimely demise, choking on his own blood at the base of the long mahogany bar in the Squaw Peak Saloon, with Stillman's .44 round lodged in his bladder, had likely drifted away or gone under the rich prairie sod—wheat-growing and cattle-raising sod.

Water under the bridge.

That didn't mean the river was dry, however, he told himself as he and Darden rode into town, noting several heads swiveling toward them, eyes beneath fur hats or immigrant caps straying toward the swollen saddlebags draped over Sweets' hindquarters. He silently opined that it might have been wiser to spend the night on the prairie, away from prying eyes and wicked intentions.

The problem was, he hadn't expected to be out here for as long as he had, and his supplies were low. He just plain yearned to sleep in a warm bed instead of out on the hard ground. And he could do with a steak and a pile of potatoes, possibly a schooner of frothy ale.

Also, he remembered that Shorty Skinner, who'd run the Squaw Peak for years—and whom Stillman thought still ran it—brewed a tasty ale from his own homegrown hops. He even kept the working beer in big crocks behind his bar, filling the saloon with the comforting, heavy, warm smell of fermenting hops and barley.

Stillman had given up forty-rod, he reminded himself. But he'd made no promises concerning mankind's oldest and most treasured elixirs...

As the snow stitched the gray air, the breeze turning noticeably colder, Stillman swung right around Hawkins's Grocery & Drugs and plodded down a side street to the south where the Inter-Mountain Livery & Feed Barn still stood, as Stillman remembered it, though maybe a little tired-looking, weathered, and in need of a coat or two of fresh paint. The large sign stretched across the hayloft was so badly faded, Stillman doubted he could have made it out if he hadn't already known what it said.

The smaller sign beneath it—R.L. Pogue, Prop.—had weathered the years not substantially better.

The two large front stock doors were closed, as was the man door to the left. A few rental horses stood stock still in the paddock to the left of the barn, two facing the third one from a couple of feet away, only their tails and manes moving as the breeze whispered at them. Feathery snow was beginning to settle on their backs.

Stillman swung heavily down from Sweets' back and dropped his reins. He glanced at Darden, who sat hunkered inside his yellow wool coat, grimacing against the cold breeze, his battered cream Stetson pulled down as low as it would go.

"Wait here," Stillman told him.

Darden held up his cuffed wrists. "Don't worry—I won't abscond with your fancy jewelry."

Stillman walked through the man-door and into the barn, which was as dark as night. It lightened a little as Stillman's eyes adjusted. The strong smell of hay and ammonia nearly pinched off his wind. It was like taking a deep sniff of a horseradish crock. "Christ," he said, looking around but spying no movement. He called: "Robert?"

No response but the wind outside, and the snow ticking against the barn's old whipsawed pine boards.

"Robert?" Stillman called again. "It's Ben Stillman."

Still no response.

Knowing Pogue—or at least the Robert Pogue Stillman had known when he'd last swung through Hobbs—the man was probably hunkered down before the potbelly stove in the Squaw Peak Saloon. Stillman moved to his right, where a door shone in the wall, abutted on both sides by hooks and pegs laden with moldering tack and wool saddle blankets.

Stillman knocked on the door. "Robert?" he called.

He tripped the metal latch, shoved the door wide, then threw himself to his left as a gun exploded just inside the small room, ripping a fist-sized wad of rotten wood out of the door's edge and making Stillman's ears ring like cracked bells.

Chapter Six

Another blast rose inside the small room. It sounded like the thunder of a large boulder crashing against another one.

This bullet caromed through the open door to slam into a ceiling support post five feet beyond it and bedecked with ancient tack and doubletrees. One of the doubletrees dropped to the floor. Dust wafted around the post.

"Hold on, hold on!" Stillman bellowed.

He'd lifted his coat flap and ripped his Colt from its holster. He raised the gun barrel-up and clicked the hammer back.

A weak, froglike voice croaked from inside the room. "Show yourself, dammit!"

"I tried to do that two seconds ago and nearly got cored for my trouble," Stillman said. "Robert Pogue—is that you in there?"

"Who the hell else would it be?"

"It's Ben Stillman."

"Who is?"

"I am!"

"I don't care who you are! What are you doin' skulkin' around out there? You tryin' to get my money?"

"Hold your fire. I'm gonna show myself."

"Do it!"

Stillman depressed his Colt's hammer, lowered the gun, and moved into an open doorway webbed with powder-gray black smoke from the old cap-and-ball revolver the old man sitting in the rocking chair held in his spidery hand.

Stillman scowled. "Robert? Robert Pogue?"

"Yes. What the hell you want?"

The old man in the chair, buried under quilts and animal skins, his head topped with a knitted red cap, and with a dirty cream scarf wound around his neck resembled nothing so much as a big, scalded bird. Long gray hair, thin as corn silk, hung straight down the sides of his face. His face was patch-bearded, and liver spots and warts shone through and between the patches.

Slowly, the man lowered the still-smoking, ancient Walker Colt. Not because he wanted to, Stillman had a feeling. But because he didn't have enough strength to keep the heavy piece raised. He set it atop the hides and quilts somewhere

around his right thigh. Stillman had probably
nudged him out of a deep, old-man's sleep. Maybe
he'd thought Stillman was a scalp-hunting Sioux
warrior from twenty years ago...

The lawman was having a hard time reconcil-
ing his remembered image of Robert Pogue—a
big, strong, vigorous man who stood at least as
tall as Stillman's six-two—with the scrawny old,
long-haired bird in the chair, who couldn't have
weighed much more than a sack of cracked corn
dripping wet and fully clothed. But, then, the
oldster seemed to have a hard time remembering
Stillman, too.

"Robert, don't you remember me?" Stillman
asked, stepping into the room in which the gray
powder smoke still sifted through the shadows.
"I'm Ben Stillman. I used to ride through here as
Deputy U.S. marshal out of Helena."

The old man blinked, scowling. His washed-
out brown eyes probed Stillman, like the eyes of
an old buzzard trying to work up the gumption
to make a play on a tasty meal. "Oh," he croaked.
"Oh...now I remember...I think. Ben Stillman."
He smiled. "You're some grayer, got a few more
lines in your face."

"Yeah, well..."

"Ben Stillman." Pogue had said the name as
trying it out on his old memory, seeing how it

would play, what images it would conjure. Most likely those of a younger man, less gray in his hair and mustache, with fewer lines in his face. "Yeah…yeah…now I remember." What might pass for a smile tugged as Pogue's thin-lipped mouth. "You shot Big Nose Braddock."

Humor glinted in his mud-brown eyes. This was the sparkle that resembled the Robert Pogue Stillman remembered, if nothing else about the man did.

"That was quite a night," Stillman said, lifting his coat flap to return the big Colt to its holster and snapping the keeper thong into place over the hammer.

"That purty li'l Injun whore, Althea Crow, was singin' 'O Would That She Were Here.' I hadn't heard that song in years till that night. The only thing I didn't like about you shootin' Big Nose was you done it right when li'l Althea was in the middle of the final chorus."

Stillman smiled. "Me an' my poor timing."

"I done changed a little, ain't I?"

Stillman flushed. He realized he'd been scrutinizing the old man in the chair with what was probably a frank expression of disbelief.

"Sorry, but…yeah, you've changed, Robert. But then, it's been a good dozen years since I last rode through here."

"Cancer."

"What's that?"

"I had a cancer." Pogue padded the quilt and hides mounded over his belly. "A sawbones cut it out of my guts. Took out damn near a yard of gut with it. He said the tumor looked like a big, liver-colored chestnut hangin' on a big ole tangled vine."

Stillman winced at the image. "That's tough—sorry to hear that."

"After the sawbones sewed me up and I was still breathin' after two weeks, the sawbones confessed he didn't expect me to make it through the surgery. He sorta did it to experiment and because I wasn't gonna live, anyway—not with that big ole ugly nut growin' on my gut. I got so damn skinny because about all I can hold down"—he reached out with his left hand and pulled an unlabeled bottle off a shelf cluttered with airtight tins, pipes, cigars, and tobacco—"is rotgut whiskey old Bill Tattersall distills from corn an' whatnot down by the creek."

He wheezed a laugh and poked out a finger of the hand holding the bottle to his lips. "Don't tell his wife. Ol' Dory'd skin him alive!"

He raised the bottle to Stillman, extending it. "No, thanks, Robert. I had to give it up."

"Damn—that's nasty. Life's too damn short to

give up the squeezin's." Pogue raised the bottle to his lips and took a long, deep pull. His Adam's apple hung like an apple inside the sagging burlap-like skin of his neck; it bounced up and down now as the man drank, like a child's rubber ball.

Stillman felt a cool breeze behind him. He turned to see Ace Darden enter the barn through the man door, shivering. He scowled out from the gray light angling in behind him. "Damn. After I heard the shots, I thought you was dead. Hoped so, anyways..."

"Your bad luck's holding," Stillman said. "Robert's aim isn't as good as it used to be."

"Hah!" Robert wheezed out a laugh and pointed his finger and bottle at Stillman. "I still got the peepers of an eagle-eyed owl. I may not got much else left, but I still got that. No sir, Ben, if I'd wanted to hit ya, you'd be wolf bait."

He wheezed another laugh.

"Is that Robert Pogue in there?" Darden asked.

"One an' the same," Stillman said. "Just a little smaller."

"Who's that out there?" Pogue asked, lifting his head to try to see around Stillman.

Stillman stepped aside to share the doorway with Darden.

"Ace Darden," Darden said. He frowned up at Stillman, who stood several inches taller than he. "I thought you said Robert Pogue was in here."

"Hah!" Pogue laughed again. If a frog could laugh, that's what Pogue's laugh sounded like. "He don't recognize me, neither!" He slapped his thigh, howling his laughter.

Darden gazed at the old man, startled. "Well... I'll be damned."

"How you been, Ace? I remember you from when you rode the stage through here. The old Musselshell River Line. When I used to contract my place out for the relay station, you an' me used to get drunk and gamble and frolic with that good-lookin' Injun whore, Althea Crow, over at Shorty Skinner's saloon."

"Like I said, I'll be damned," Darden said, raising his cuffed hands to shove his hat up off his forehead. "I didn't recognize you, Robert. Why, you're all shrunk up."

"A sawbones in Winifred cut a cancer out of me that size." Pogue held up his hands to indicate something the size and shape of a plum. "Took out most of my guts, too. I shouldn't be alive, but now that I am...two years gone by now since he gutted me like a trout...I take special notice of every day—and you should, too, my friend." The old man narrowed a grave eye at Darden. "You should, too."

"Yeah, I reckon."

"Say, what you got on your wrists there?"

"Ah, hell." Darden's shoulders sagged under the weight of his shame.

"Handcuffs?" Pogue addressed the question to Stillman.

"He robbed the bank in Winifred," Stillman told the oldster.

Pogue's lower jaw dropped several inches. His old peepers turned dark with shock. An angry flush rose in his withered cheeks, turning his liver spots and warts a shade darker. There was a purple splotch on his left temple, and that turned nearly black. "What in tarnation did you that for, Ace?"

"Oh, hell, Robert—I had a run of bad luck."

"Bad luck, huh?" Old Pogue continued to stare at Darden in astonishment.

Stillman heard a soft whistling behind him. He turned as something black winged toward him, startling him so that he jerked back against the door frame and nearly knocked his hat off. He felt the cool rush of displaced air.

"Holy…!" he intoned, as whatever the object was caromed through the doorway, over his right shoulder and over Darden's left shoulder. The winged beast stretched its wings out in the air between Stillman and Pogue, and lit on a wooden perch suspended from the ceiling by a couple of slender wires to Pogue's left. The crow turned its small, black eyes on Stillman, opened its beak, and gave a cackling cry that didn't sound all that different from Pogue's laughter.

"Jeepers!" Darden muttered. He'd stumbled to his right when the bird had flown in. Now, getting his boots set beneath him again, he laughed. "That's a crow! I left the damn door open!"

"No, no—he belongs here," said Pogue. "I leave the loft window open, but he flew through the man-door there, sure enough. This, gentleman, is my only remaining friend in the world—Heinrich."

Stillman and Darden shared a dubious glance.

"Heinrich?" Stillman asked, wondering if the old man's mind hadn't gone as far south as his body had.

"I saved Heinrich from the same damn gold eagle that killed his ma. Eagle killed her and the rest of her brood, or whatever you call a crow's family. Heinrich here was just learning to fly an' couldn't provide for himself. Well, I live on rabbit an' squirrel, an' I fed ole Heinrich bits of rabbit an' squirrel meat so he could keep his strength up for flying.

"He got good at it, too. Flyin', I mean. I never felt so proud as the day I looked up to see him wingin' it all the way from the Lutheran church steeple at one end of town to the widow's walk atop Madame Charlevoix's whorehouse on the other end of town. I waved Heinrich good-bye, but I'll be damned if he didn't show up back here at the barn that night. Showed up every night since. Took up quarters here with me, permanent-like. When he ain't off flyin' an' huntin' an' courtin' and whatever else crows do, he lights there on that perch every afternoon about this time an' don't leave till mornin'.'"

Pogue grinned, tears glistening in his eyes. "He thinks I'm his ma, Heinrich does. I'll be jiggered if he don't. I think he may love me—the last one." He thumbed a tear from the corner of his eye and glanced at the sleek, night-black bird, who'd lifted a wing to groom under it with his beak.

"Ah, hell, listen to me carryin' on over a bird." Pogue took another long drink from his bottle then held the whiskey high in offering to Darden. "Since you're a bank robber, you prob'ly still imbibe—don't you, Ace? Since you're not above the former, you can't be above the latter."

Darden glanced sheepishly at Stillman then walked forward to grab the bottle. "I sure could use somethin' to nudge this chill out of my bones." He took a couple of deep drinks, then returned the bottle to the old man. His face flushing bright red, he said in a high, raspy voice, "My word— that's some mighty strong skullpop, Robert!"

He grabbed his throat as though he were strangling on the stuff.

"It's damn near all I live on. Files the edges off my loneliness. I can't eat much food, anyway. Can't do nothin' like I used to. I just sit here—all alone save ole Heinrich. Most of my friends are dead. My dear wife, Alma—she died damn near ten years ago now. Ten years ago—imagine that! I still think of us as newlyweds! My daughter, she married the banker—little prissy fella who walks with a cane though he don't have a thing wrong with him. Charlotte, she brings me food from time to time, but I tell her to spare herself the trouble. I prefer my own squirrel and rabbit stews. I shoot 'em right out the back door, cook 'em there on that stove.

"My daughter—she wants to me go live in that big house with her an' that fancy-Dan husband of hers, and I told her I'd just get lost in that big house. Or I'd smother her loudmouth brats. No, I prefer it here. Just me an' Heinrich. Nice an' quiet. I got a good stove. I got a boy who helps around the barn and cuts my wood. I'm doin' all right. I stop and take notice of every damn day, though—I'll tell you that. We never know which one will be the last. We're toe-down a helluva long time, you know, fellas."

He hammered the arm of his rocking chair as though to hammer home the pronouncement.

Heinrich gave a corroboratory caw then lifted his other wing to preen under that one.

"Listen to me go on," Pogue said, chuckling. "A lonely old man. I reckon you fellas have some stock that needs tendin'. If so, could you tend 'em an' stable 'em yourself? This cold air keeps me glued to this chair. I'll only charge you a dollar apiece, ten cents extry for feed. The boy I got workin' for me is down with the pony drip he picked up over at Madame Charlevoix's place. Here, I thought he was only chopping her wood. Hah! Oh, Lordy, when it gets bad, you should hear him howl!"

Chapter Seven

It was almost dark when Stillman and his prisoner hiked from the livery barn to the town's business district.

Once back on the main street, Stillman saw most of the shops were closed. Not that there were very many that could have been open. Hobbs appeared to have become stagnant over the years. Unlike towns positioned along the relatively recently laid railroad lines, those that had been by-passed died slow deaths.

Probably the only thing keeping this town running was business from the area ranches. Stillman remembered such spreads to be large and far-flung, home to mostly rough-edged, desperate men, working for men even rougher and more desperate than their employees. In their drive for wealth and power, they'd fight to hold onto their property in a land that remained remote and uncivilized.

The Squaw Peak Saloon & Gambling Parlor lay just ahead of Stillman, on the right side of the street. It stood alone, abutted on each side by two empty lots. Well beyond it and on the left side of the street was the town's jailhouse. Years ago, when Stillman had been riding this country as a deputy U.S. marshal, he'd used the jail on overnight stays when he'd been transporting prisoners—mostly rustlers back in those days. Or regulators hired by the larger ranchers to keep nesters off land they'd claimed as their own—whether the land was their own or not.

He didn't see a lamp burning in the jailhouse. He'd check it out later, as he'd like to get Darden under lock and key for the night. First he'd buy the man a drink and pad out his belly on the government's dime—he'd make sure Uncle Sam reimbursed him, though he dreaded the paperwork—and then make himself comfortable in one of the Squaw Peak's second- or third-story rooms.

"Yeah, I remember the Squaw Peak," Darden said, blinking against the snow the breeze was assaulting both him and Stillman with. "Isn't this where you killed Big Nose George Braddock?"

"While the pretty little Injun whore sang 'O Would That She Were Here'..."

"I need a drink," Darden said as they stepped

into weak light filtering from the saloon's large front window, and could hear the tinkle of a piano from within. "It's colder'n a grave-digger's ass and ole Robert Pogue kinda soured my mood."

"Yeah," Stillman said. "Me, too."

The image of old Pogue wasting away there in his rocking chair was a haunting one, indeed. At least Pogue had Heinrich, Stillman thought as he followed Darden through the saloon's winter door.

He paused, as did his prisoner, to stomp snow from his boots and bat his snow-dusted hat against his thighs. He adjusted the weight of the two sets of saddlebags draped over his left shoulder, one considerably heavier than the other. He'd been carrying his Henry repeater on his right shoulder, but now he lowered it barrel-down, making it less conspicuous.

He looked around cautiously, as was his custom. He'd been a lawman in the territory for a good many years. As such, he'd cut a broad swath. There were likely more than a few owlhoots still willing and able to punch his ticket and claim as reward of admiration of their peers. Also, his second set of saddlebags held thirty-four thousand dollars in stolen bank money, and he had every intention of returning it safely to Winifred.

The old, black Cayuga stove with four lion's

feet was right where he remembered it—near the front of the room. The bar ran along the left wall—an elaborate mahogany affair with a brass foot-rail and zinc top, complete with a scrolled and varnished back bar including a leaded glass mirror etched along the edges with the figures of galloping horses.

The once stylish saloon looked as shabby as the rest of Hobbs, as though it, too, had fallen on hard times. It also appeared smaller than Stillman remembered. More barren. Pictures of horses and landscapes and half-naked women once adorned the painted plaster walls above the wainscoting, but only one remained, and it was badly faded or obscured by smoke and soot. Stillman remembered that every time he'd ridden in off the trail back in those by-gone days, he'd always found a crowd of people here, as if they'd been waiting for him.

There were usually a dozen folks at least in here—men and girls, mostly of the parlor variety—he'd come to know over the years. Men from the ranges as well as the town. Shopkeepers. Swampers. The mayor, Santee Graham, whose dog always sat in a chair nearby and begged for treats from the free lunch counter. There'd been an dipsomaniac lawyer called Smarty McFee. The barber, Ralph Larrimore, who'd get drunk and buy drinks on the house until the house cut him off till he paid up. The liveryman, Robert Pogue, was always here, of course.

Stillman had come to know several of the saloon's pleasure girls on intimate terms because in those days he'd been a young bachelor and, according to some of the fairer sex, rather pleasing to the female eye, with his thick head of dark-brown hair, his six-foot-plus, broad-shouldered, broad-chested, slim-hipped stature, and his sparkling blue-gray eyes and easy manner.

Seeing the place now was a bit of let-down. He had to admit that, like Darden, his visit with Pogue had unsettled him, and he'd been looking forward to the celebratory atmosphere he remembered in the Squaw Peak.

Today's Squaw Peak stood in sharp contrast to the one from the old days, however. There were only six other men in the place—four men in store-bought business suits playing cards at the table up close to the window. Stillman didn't recognize any of them. Two others, clad in rough-hewn range gear including canvas coats and wooly chaps, were bellied up to the bar, sullenly, silently contemplating their drinks.

A young doxie played the piano against the right wall near the base of the stairs. She looked very young to Stillman's old eyes. Too young, too pale and fragile, sitting there with feathers in her long brown hair and a heavy blanket draped around her shoulders, against the room's chill despite the ticking stove. She couldn't play the piano worth a damn. Stillman couldn't even recognize what she was trying to play.

The only other person in the place was a middle-aged Indian woman with long, straight, dark-brown hair liberally streaked with gray. Her face was haggard. That her body had gone to tallow could not be hidden by her shapeless burlap dress or beaded puma-hide jacket. The pear-shaped Indian woman stood at the bar, smoking a loosely rolled cigarette, and regarded Stillman and Darden without expression through her molasses-dark eyes.

She glanced at the cuffs on Darden's wrists then slid her gaze back to Stillman. A faint smile stretched her lips and flickered in her tired eyes. She took a deep drag off the cigarette and exhaled the smoke through her nostrils, saying, "Still at it—eh, Marshal Stillman?"

The overly-painted, far-too-young whore stopped playing the piano to glance at the two newcomers. She turned her head forward again and resumed the banging, which was the only way to describe what she was doing to that poor piano. Stillman remembered the girls here used

to be able to hold a tune. They'd sing and even
dance, and sometimes the mayor would play his
fiddle and his dog would howl.

Stillman smiled at the woman behind the bar.
He didn't recognize her. He frowned curiously as
he moved toward her. "You have me at a disad-
vantage, Miss...?"

"Sure enough—you're Ben Stillman. You killed
Big Nose Braddock right over there." She slid her
gaze toward Stillman's right.

"I know, I know," he said, "while Shorty Skinner's pretty Indian whore, Althea Crow, sang—"

"'O Would That She Were Here'," the woman
finished for him, smiling more broadly now. The
smile almost made her start to look pretty, Stillman silently, sheepishly reflected.

"Now," he said, "how in the hell would you
know that?"

"Because I was the one singing the song, Marshal."

Stillman's lower jaw dropped in astonishment

Her fleshy brown cheeks dimpling, the woman threw her head back and laughed huskily. "I'm
Althea Crow. What—you don't remember me?"

"Ben!"

Stillman found himself welcoming the inter-
ruption. He shifted his gaze to see a man just
then entering through the back door flanking

the stairs. A short, stocky gent, he had an enormous gut bulging out his ragged blanket coat. An armload of split wood in his arms, he drew the door closed behind him with his foot then moved along the bar, heading for the stove near Stillman and Darden.

"Ben Stillman, you old reprobate! I heard you was still kickin'!"

"Shorty?" Stillman said, recognizing the broad, freckled face between the swinging flaps of the man's fur-lined, leather hat. "Shorty Skinner, I was wondering if you were still alive. It sure it nice to see a familiar face for a change!"

He'd no sooner let the tail end of the sentence fly out of his mouth than he felt the burn of chagrin and glanced at Althea Crow. She seemed unfazed by his unintentional rudeness, but only continued smiling wearily and drawing on her cigarette, her eyes squinted against the smoke webbing the air in front of her face.

Shorty dropped the wood in the box beside the stove then waddled up to Stillman, grinning broadly, laughing joyously. "I'd recognize you anywhere, you devil! Not that you haven't aged, though." He rose onto his tiptoes to swipe Stillman's hat off his head with one hand and run his other hand through Stillman's longish hair. "Look at that—you still got a thick head of hair, but there sure is some gray in it, isn't there?"

"A little gray, a little tallow," Stillman said. "A few saddle galls in the mix, as well." He rubbed his behind and winced. "I'll be hanged if my saddle ain't as unforgiving as it used to be, and the ground a whole lot harder to sleep on."

"Or maybe your ass has got softer!" Shorty laughed and slapped Stillman's hat against Stillman's chest. He looked at Darden. "Who's this here? Ah, another prisoner, I see. I heard you was workin' as sheriff up in Clantick."

Darden had had his head lowered, staring sheepishly at the floor, his cuffed hands hanging in front of him. Now he lifted his chin and glowered, pulling his mouth corners down. "How you doin', Shorty?" he asked, his voice droll. "I haven't seen you in a coon's age."

"Ace!" Shorty seemed stunned. He looked at Darden's bracelets again. "What in the hell, Ace?"

He looked at Stillman.

"Tell him," Stillman told the prisoner.

Darden grimaced, looked at Shorty then at Althea and then back at Shorty again. "I ran into some bad luck, Shorty. Fell in with a bad crowd."

That seemed to pain Shorty, who gazed at Stillman's overstuffed saddlebags, then snapped his dentures in reproving disappointment and sadness. "Ah, hell, Ace."

"Yeah, I know."

Stillman stepped up to the bar. "Well, Miss Crow, if it ain't too much trouble—"

"Missus," she said, cutting him off. She rolled her eyes to Shorty. "Somehow, that sawed-off little bastard convinced me to hitch my star to his wagon."

Stillman glanced in shock at Shorty, who rose up on the toes of his hobnailed, lace-up boots, grinning like the cat that ate the canary. "Sure enough! Didn't take much convincin'." He placed a small, thick hand beside his mouth, glanced around, leaned forward, and whispered with mock secrecy, "All I had to do was drop my pants, and she said 'I do'!"

He threw his head back and roared.

"No, it wasn't that," Althea said, taking another deep drag off the quirley, which was so short she now had to hold it between her thumb and index finger. "I married him for his money."

"Hah!" Shorty bellowed. "That's even funnier!"

"As I was saying, uh, *Missus Skinner,*" Stillman said, "if it ain't too much trouble, I'd like a large mug of ale." He glanced at Shorty, who'd set to work feeding wood to the stove. "As long as he's still makin' the finest suds in the territory, that is."

"I am!" Shorty assured him, grunting as, down on his thick knees on the floor, he stirred the fire around with a long, slender split pine log. "Just tapped the most recent batch and had a mug with lunch. With my beer as with my woman, I ain't lost my touch—have I, sugar?" He grinned up at Althea, who merely rolled her eyes and shook her head as she stubbed out her cigarette, then set to work drawing an ale for Stillman.

"I'd like a jug of whiskey," said Darden. "Best bottle you got." He glanced at Stillman. "Since Uncle Sam's payin'."

"What the hell?" Stillman said. He was about to add that the lowly gent probably didn't have many days left on this side of the sod, but held his tongue. Even outlaws who'd tried to kill him—*former friends-turned-outlaws who'd tried to kill him*—had feelings.

Stillman set both sets of saddlebags atop the bar. He leaned his rifle against them and fished in his pants pockets for money. When he'd paid Althea Skinner for the bottle she'd set on the bar before Ace, along with a shot glass; and for the tall, dark ale she'd filled Stillman's thick, dimpled glass schooner with, he picked up the mug.

"Say, old fella," called one of the two younger men in range garb standing off down the bar to his right, "what's in them saddlebags?"

Chapter Eight

Stillman sipped some of the froth off his malty ale, licked his mustache, and turned to the tall, skinny man standing ten feet up the bar on his right. The skinny man's partner was also tall and skinny though not quite as ugly. The man who'd spoken had bulging eyes, sunken cheeks, and a knobby chin. He looked about as smart as an oak knot.

"Say again?" Stillman said, cupping a hand to his ear. "It's hard for this old fella to hear from so far away."

Standing to his left, Darden chuckled.

The first skinny man, who was maybe twenty-two or -three and had the look of a grub-line-riding saddle tramp, probably as worthless off the range as on it, glanced at his partner. Both men snickered, then the first one said, "I asked you, *old-timer,* what you had in them saddlebags."

Stillman scowled and, leaning forward and still cupping his hand to his ear, said, *"What?"*

The four card players near the window chuckled softly. Behind the bar, Althea Skinner smiled as she stood leaning back against the back bar, rolling another quirley.

The skinny, ugly gent flushed a little. He smiled, but the muscles in his face were stiffening.

Raising his voice, he said, "I asked you—*you old, deaf bastard*—what you got in them saddlebags!"

"I'm sorry—I can't hear ya," Stillman yelled, manufacturing a look of extreme bafflement on his craggily handsome features. "The years ain't been kind to this old mossy-horn. Too many guns have gone off too close to my head. Too many whores done screamed their pleasure in my ears. If you want me to hear what you're caterwaulin' about like some chicken-livered coyote stuck on a barb-wire fence, you're gonna have to come closer!"

Standing at the far end of the bar, both hands on the bar top, Shorty Skinner said, "Hee-hee-hee!" and wagged his head at the Squaw Peak's old high-jinx raising its head in the form of the deputy U.S. marshal who used to ride through here regular-like, a dozen years ago and more. Stillman was back, wearing a sheriff's star instead of the moon-and-star of the U.S. marshals, looking more weathered, grayer, humbled by the years, maybe a little sad, even, but still willing to conjure a little of the old fun...

The card players snickered a little louder this time. Stillman couldn't see them, for they were behind him, but he knew they'd paused their playing to watch the festivities. In the corner of his right eye, he could see Ace Darden grinning from ear to ear over the rim of his whiskey shot.

Now the inquiring saddle tramp's face had grown even tighter, and an apple-red flush splotched his jaundiced cheeks. He was being laughed at. Hell, even his partner, leaning against the bar to his right, was snickering into his whiskey glass. Calling Stillman's bet, as though he hadn't been expected to, the inquiring saddle tramp moved slowly along the bar in Stillman's direction.

His molting gray wolf coat was open, and the old Schofield .44 holstered high on his right hip was within a quick reach—if he wanted to go that way. Stillman made a mental note. He'd opened his own coat, though he hadn't yet tucked the flap back behind the butt of his own .44 positioned for the cross-draw on his left hip. Vaguely, he wished he had. The Henry was on the bar before him, to his left, but a tad too far away for quick action...

When the ugly grubline rider was three feet

from Stillman, crowding him, he stopped. He gazed insolently at Stillman for a full half a minute before he shouted, "Can you hear me, now, old-timer?"

"Jesus," Stillman yowled, closing a hand over an ear. "You don't have to yell. I'm just hard of hearing, not deaf!"

That raised more laughter around the room. Althea's smile widened as she scraped a lucifer to life on her thumbnail and touched the match to the end of her freshly rolled quirley. The ugly grubline rider's friend laughed, as well. He turned to face his friend and Stillman, his right elbow resting atop the bar, his half-empty shot glass in his right hand.

Scowling, the ugly man canted his head toward the saddlebags. "I asked you what was in the saddlebags...*old man?*" he added, leaning forward and spitting the last two words out like watermelon seeds.

"Why didn't you say so?" Stillman said. "What's in them saddlebags is thirty-four thousand dollars in cold, hard cash."

He smiled at the skinny, ugly man facing him.

The skinny man's friend whistled. "That's a lot of cash, Pug."

Pug, eh? Right fitting moniker, Stillman silently opined with an inward grin.

"That is a lot of cash," Darden said behind Stillman. "Why don't you fellas shoot this nasty ole mossyhorn an' take it? You don't even need to cut me in. Just take the keys out of his pocket, and take these purty bracelets off. That's all I ask."

Stillman heard the soft jangle of the handcuff chain as Darden raised his hands to show Pug and his friend the cuffs.

Pug smiled at Darden over Stillman's right shoulder. "Now...there's an idea."

"Thirty-four thousand, huh?" said Pug's friend, as though wanting to make sure he'd heard right. "You know, I could work all my life, till I'm eighty years old, and never see that much money."

"That's a nice stake, Pinto," Pug agreed.

Pug and Pinto, Stillman thought. One as brainless as the other. And likely soon as dead, too. If not here tonight, then elsewhere soon.

The room had fallen eerily silent. So silent that Stillman could hear the breeze outside in the street and the softly patter of snow against the saloon's windows. Occasionally, the walls or the ceiling gave a faint creak. The wood stove ticked. Somewhere off in the town, a man called to another man, though he was too far away for Stillman to hear what he said or what the other man's response was.

A faint, amused smile spreading her mouth,

Shorty's wife, Althea, slowly lifted her cigarette to her lips and, narrowing her eyes slightly, took a deep drag, making the coal at the end glow bright red.

Pug was thinking about it. Stillman could tell by the strain in the man's eyes, the tightness of his features. Pug turned his head slightly to say over his shoulder, "You'll back my play, Pinto?"

Pinto smiled over Pug's right shoulder at Stillman. He had long red hair and scraggly side whiskers and mustache. His jade green eyes were set too far apart, on either side of a long, hooked nose. Stillman saw Pinto's hand drop to the pearl-gripped Bisley he wore in a soft leather holster over his belly. The fancy six-gun stood out in sharp contest to his otherwise ragged attire. He'd likely fleeced it off some drunk drummer during a poker game.

"Why, sure, Pug," Pinto said slowly, stretching his lips in a smile revealing several rotten, black teeth. "Why, sure, I will."

Stillman stared blandly at Pug.

Pug stared back at him. Pug's pupils were dilating, and his chest was rising and falling a little more heavily than before. His blood was rising, warming. Sure enough, he dropped his right hand toward the Schofield. Stillman lashed out with his right hand, closed the hand over Pug's, and ripped the Schofield from the ugly man's grip.

With a loud grunt, Pug stumbled toward Stillman.

Stillman slammed the barrel of the revolver against Pug's forehead.

Pug yowled and stumbled backward, falling into his partner just as Pinto started to raise his Bisley. Pug knocked the Bisley out of Pinto's hand, then Pug fell to the floor, Pinto holding one of Pug's hands and staring warily up at Stillman, who now had Pug's Schofield cocked and aimed straight out from his right shoulder, drawing a bead on a heart-shaped cluster of freckles on Pinto's forehead.

"Wait!" Pinto said, releasing Pug's hand and letting his friend drop to the floor. He held both of his own hands up in front of his face. "Wait, now! Wait, now! Wait, now! You *wait!*"

"You listen," Stillman said tightly as he aimed down the barrel of the cocked .44. "If you two dumbasses get anymore smart questions, this deef old man ain't gonna play near as nice as I'm doin' here now. I'm the sheriff of Hill County. That thirty-four thousand dollars is going back to Winifred, and if anyone tries to relieve me of it, or tries to relieve my horse and saddle of *me*, I'm gonna kick 'em out with a cold shovel and leave 'em where they drop. Coyotes gotta eat, too."

"All right, all right, old ma…I mean, *sheriff!*" Pinto corrected himself, glowering and canting his head back as though away from the bullet he was sure would come. "I'm sorry. We was just funnin' with ya, me an' Pug. He glanced down at where Pug had just sat up and was holding his hand over his forehead, looking as groggy as a man waking up after a three-day drunk. "I said, wasn't we, Pug?"

Pug glared up at Stillman. "Damn, you sure tattooed me good!"

"Just tryin' to improve on your looks," Stillman said, aiming the cocked revolver at the man on the floor. "Can't blame a man for tryin'. Maybe you need a third eye, instead."

"No!" Pug raised both hands, palms out. "No! Please! Don't shoot, old ma…I mean, *Sheriff!*"

"Stand up," Stillman ordered.

Grunting and groaning, holding one hand to his forehead, Pug gained his feet. He and Pinto stood side-by-side, regarding Stillman and his appropriated Schofield in wide-eyed consternation.

"Pinto," Stillman said, "set your gun on the bar top."

Pinto grimaced, then reluctantly did as he'd been told.

"You got any more?" Stillman asked him.

"Nope, that's it," Pinto said, again holding his hands up.

"How 'bout you, Handsome?" Stillman asked Pug. "You got any hideouts?"

"No," Pug said sourly.

"You'd best not. I see either of you with one, even if it's not aimed in my direction, I'm gonna shoot you *both*." Stillman shoved both Pug's and Pinto's six-shooters into a pouch of the saddlebags stuffed with the bank loot.

"Hey, what're you doin'?" Pug said, pointing at the bulging pouch. "You can't take our guns!"

Stillman said, "You'll find 'em on the bar here after I've left town tomorrow mornin'." He turned to Althea, who'd almost finished another quirley. "Is Louie Cantrell still the marshal here in town?"

"Louie Cantrell?" This from Shorty moving up the far side of the bar from the end. "Hah! Louie's been dead nearly ten years, Ben. He was found froze-up solid one winter in his outhouse. Heart-attack, the doctor figured. We haven't had a badge-toter in Hobbs since." He glanced at Pug and Pinto, and wrinkled his nose distastefully. "Haven't really needed one. If we do, we send a rider over to Price. The county sheriff has a deputy who lives over there and oversees this area."

"What condition's the old jailhouse in?" Stillman asked.

Althea mashed her cigarette out in a tray on the bar. "The grocer uses it for cold storage."

Stillman tapped a thumb on the bulging saddlebag before him. "I reckon a room will do. You got one you can rent me for the night? One with a lock?"

Louie frowned at Althea. "I think rooms seven an' nine have locks, don't they?"

Althea flushed a little. Staring down at the bar, she said, "Nine is occupied." She looked up at Stillman. "You can have seven."

Louie was drawing himself an ale. "I'll give it to you free for the night, Ben."

"No need." Stillman tossed several coins atop the bar. "Uncle Sam's payin'."

Louie slapped his hand on the bar, grinning. "Just like old times!"

"I'll be hanged if ain't." Stillman walked to the far side of the room.

The little whore had resumed playing the piano, if you could call it playing, after the dust kicked up by Stillman's encounter, if you could it that, with Pug and Pinto had settled. She stopped again to regard the middle-aged lawman skeptically as he crouched down beside a stout ceiling support post.

He picked up a length of chain attacked to the post by an iron ring, and turned to Shorty. "It's still here."

"Guess so." Shorty chuckled. "I'll be hanged if I didn't even forget it was there. Doubt it's been used since you last pulled through town with a prisoner in tow, Ben."

From the bar, Darden frowned at the chain. "What's that for?"

Stillman looked at him and smiled.

Chapter Nine

The key to room seven in his hand, Stillman carried his rifle and both sets of saddlebags up the stairs to the second story.

The soft hum of conversation and the young whore's infernal banging on the piano retreated behind and below him, though he could feel the reverberations of the banging in the floor beneath his boot heels as he made his way down the hall.

He wished the girl would take a break.

There was only one candle bracket lamp lit in the hall, and the flame was guttering with drafts from cold wind blowing in from outside. Stillman squinted as he studied the doors passing to each side of him, then stopped before the one marked 7, though only half of the wooden seven remained. He poked the key in the lock and froze when he heard a latch click farther down the hall on his right.

He was about to drop his gear and reach for his Colt but forestalled the action when he heard the latch bolt click again. Someone had briefly opened and closed the door two doors down the wall on his right. That would be the door to room 9.

Stillman studied the door, vaguely curious, then opened his own door and stepped into room 7. He dropped his gear on the bed and fumbled with a lantern mantle until he got the wick lit. He looked around the room, looking for a safe place to store the thirty-four thousand dollars.

Finally he grunted a caustic snort, and left the loot on the bed. There was only the bed, a single chair, a wash stand, and a few hooks for clothes. The door lock would have to secure the loot enough for one night. Besides, Stillman wouldn't be far away. He'd have supper and maybe another beer downstairs then head up here for a good night's sleep.

He and his prisoner would be back on the trail to Winifred at first light.

Hearing the wind howl, moaning under the saloon's eves, made him shiver. After this blow, tomorrow would likely be an especially cold ride. He hoped it was followed by a Chinook, God's gift to this cold country. One of his few.

He left the room and locked the door. With one

more glance toward the door he'd heard open and close briefly, he pocketed the key and walked back downstairs. Althea was just then serving up the stew he'd ordered from her kitchen, placing the steaming bowls on the table near the post to which the chain was attached. Ace Darden was attached to the end of the chain by way of his handcuffs.

Ace sat at the table now, watching Stillman move toward him. Ace had removed his hat and coat. The hat was on the table near the steaming stew bowl Althea had just set before him, along with a plate of crusty brown bread and some cheese.

Althea turned to Stillman. She seemed to consider him thoughtfully then said, "Is the room all right?"

Stillman tossed his own hat onto a chair at the table he'd picked out for him and his prisoner, and started shrugging out of his coat. "It's just fine, Althea. I'm much obliged to you."

She studied him, hesitating, as though she wanted to say more.

"Everything all right?" Stillman asked her.

She opened her mouth to speak but closed it again when boots thudded on the boardwalk fronting the saloon. She and Stillman turned to see the winter door open and three men file in, all wearing ratty fur coats. Immediately, Stillman recognized the tall, beefy Jed Nordekker followed by the scrawny red-head with cobalt eyes, Willie, and the stocky, ginger-bearded man, Big Mike.

Ah, shit...

That seemed to be Althea's sentiment, as well. She glanced at Stillman, frowning as though in frustration. She muttered, "Never mind," then lowered her tray and headed to the bar.

It being the supper hour, three more men—traveling drummers, by the look of them—had entered the saloon and now sat near Stillman and Darden. Two hulking, bearded freighters had also entered; they stood at the bar tending beers and whiskey shots. The four townsmen were still playing cards by the front window, and Pug and Pinto, both apparently overnighting here in Hobbs, had taken a table near the bar.

They'd both ordered the stew and now sat over their bowls—both in sour moods after the dustup with Stillman. Especially Pug, for obvious reasons, not the least of which was the red goose egg on his forehead.

As Nordekker and his two partners entered the saloon on a gust of cold air, stomping snow from their boots and brushing it from their coats and hats, Nordekker swept the room quickly with his dark gaze. Instantly, his eyes settled on Stillman and Darden.

After the scrawny redhead, Willie, had closed the door on the wind, cursing the cold, both he and Big Mike followed Nordekker's gaze to Stillman. Willie chuckled. Big Mike flared an angry nostril.

"Well, now," Nordekker said, lips slowly spreading an insolent smile. "Ain't it a small world?"

Stillman didn't say anything. He sank into his chair beside Darden, lifted his schooner of ale in mock salute at the three newcomers, and took a sip. Nordekker gave a caustic chuff.

While the other two moved up close to the wood stove, warming themselves, Nordekker stomped past Stillman, keeping his arrogant, belligerent eyes on the lawman, then pulled a chair out from an empty table near the drummers, and planted his right foot on it. Leaning forward with an air of supreme self-importance, he rested one arm on his raised knee and yelled, "All right, everybody—pipe down an' turn an ear!"

Silence fell over the saloon. The whore had mercifully stopped assaulting the piano to help Althea and Shorty in the kitchen off the rear of the place. The only sounds now were the wind and the ticking of the stove. All heads had turned to regard the tall, beefy Nordekker with his deep-set dark eyes and broad, unshaven cheeks.

He removed his hat and ran a gloved hand through his curly, sandy hair, taking his time before he said, "There's been trouble out to Mr. Conyers' Jinglebob Ranch. As most of you know, I'm the Jinglebob's top hand, Jed Nordekker. Mr. Conyers' son, Byron, was viciously attacked two days ago at the Eagle Creek Saloon. His attacker was the crazy woman who ran the place—Olivia Coulter. What I want to know is this—have any of you seen Miss Coulter or that kid of hers?"

"What do you mean—have we seen 'em?" asked one of the beefy, bearded freighters at the bar. "She an' the kid make a run for it?"

Nordekker said, "That's what they done, all right. In all the commotion of tryin' to get poor Byron back to the ranch so that his life could be saved, the men who was with him that night lost track of the woman an' the boy. When Mr. Conyers himself and myself rode over to Eagle Creek, she an' the boy was gone. Lit a shuck!"

Althea Skinner stared coldly over the bar at Nordekker. "You say Mrs. Coulter *viciously* attacked Byron Conyers?" Her words were taut with sarcasm.

"That's what I just said, *Missus Skinner,*" said Nordekker, matching the woman's tone with his own sarcasm. His gaze sharpened, and so did his attitude. "You seen her, Missus Skinner?"

"Missus. Skinner ain't seen her." Shorty Skinner stood in the door that opened into the kitchen, just beyond the end of the bar. He wore an apron around his bulging waist, and he wiped his hands on it as he glared at Nordekker. "Or the boy."

Nordekker studied the proprietor, nodded slowly. He looked around at the other customers, giving Stillman a mocking leer in passing. "If any of you see Mrs. Coulter or that dirty heathen kid of hers, you get word to Mr. Conyers, hear? He's offering a thousand dollars for word of her whereabouts. Two thousand dollars to the man or men who bring her and the boy back to him. *Alive."*

"What's he gonna do to her?" Althea asked. Her voice was sharp, clipped, angry.

One of the freighters said, "Likely give her what she gave to his son."

"Why'd she do it?" one of the four card-playing townsmen asked the Jinglebob top hand. "I mean, I been out to Eagle Creek. I know that Mrs. Coulter's high-headed, downright snooty, for a fact. But a killer—well…"

Nordekker dropped his foot to the floor, straightening and facing the man belligerently. "Yeah, well, that's what she is, all right! If Byron dies, that is, and it's likely he will. She cut him good. He lost most of his blood between Eagle Creek and the Jinglebob, when the other men were riding him home. There's a sawbones out there with him now. The doc gives him a half a chance."

"He was just foolin' around with the woman," Big Mike said, standing with his back to the stove. "He didn't mean nothin' by it, Byron didn't."

"Yeah," Willie added. He'd drifted over to the bar. "She's always got her chin in the air. He was just tryin' to show her that—"

"Shut up, Willie!" Nordekker scolded him, turning to Big Mike and adding, "You, too, Big Mike. Shut up!" He looked around at the others. "Remember that, gentlemen—one thousand dollars for word of her whereabouts. Two thousand for her delivery to the Jinglebob headquarters. Cash on the barrel-head."

He glanced at Althea, and added, "I should say gentlemen and *ladies...*" He gave a lopsided grin.

Althea flared her nostrils and tightened her lips in bald disdain for the man.

Nordekker moved slowly up to the bar, swaggering, kicking out his boots, scraping his spurs across the floor. "We'll be needin' a room for the night, Missus Skinner. We're gonna continue the search tomorrow before headin' back to headquarters."

"And whiskey," Big Mike said, also strolling to the bar. "We'll take that right now."

Althea pulled a bottle off a shelf beneath the bar. Probably the cheap stuff.

Splashing the busthead into three shot glasses, she said, "I have a room on the third floor with two beds in it, and a straw pallet. One of you will have to sleep on the floor."

"Sure, sure," Nordekker said, lifting his whiskey to his lips. "Willie'll take the floor."

Willie and Big Mike argued over who should take the pallet.

Finishing up his bowl of stew, Stillman glanced toward the kitchen doorway. Shorty Skinner still stood there. He gave Stillman a dark look, then, shaking his head morosely, retreated into the kitchen.

Darden finished his own stew and swabbed the bowl with a thick slice of bread. "You know what I think, Ben?"

"What?"

"I think it's stackin' up to be a long night." The prisoner chuckled and shoved the bread into his mouth.

———————————

"I'm gettin' sleepy, Ben," Ace said about an hour

later, when he'd finished nearly half his bottle of whiskey. He yawned against the back of one of his cuffed hands. "I don't know about you, but I'm ready to head upstairs. Can't wait to tumble into the ole mattress sack."

Stillman was nursing his second beer. Ace's yawn made him yawn. He stretched, throwing his arms out to his sides and then behind him, moving around in his chair. "You ain't goin' anywhere."

"Huh?"

"After the stunt you pulled at the bar…on top of the one you pulled earlier…you're gonna sleep right here in your chair. Or curl up on the floor. You're staying chained to that post."

"Ah, come on! I can't sleep in my chair!"

"Like I said, curl up on the floor. You'll be warm, anyway. That stove really puts out the heat. There's no stove up in the room. My *own private suite.*" He lifted his mug again, smiling.

"You can't hold it against me that I told them two to shoot you an' set me free!" Ace slapped the table, leaning in close to Stillman, his face flushed with exasperation. "That ain't fair. What's more, I don't think it's legal! I got rights!"

"Out here, you have as many right as I wish to recognize. By *frontier rights,* I oughta haul your raggedy ass out into the country tomorrow, shoot you, say you tried to escape, and bury you right there. *In a very shallow grave.* Then I oughta ride back home to my good wife and son and my warm house, and cable the sorrowful news of your tragic but well-deserved demise to the county prosecutor in Winifred."

Stillman turned to Ace, his blue eyes grave, his voice hard. "Not one person would shed a tear. Well, maybe the hangman. He'd be out his fee for hangin' you."

Ace slapped the table again, cursed Stillman roundly. A few of the fellas sitting around them turned to see what the commotion was about. Most, however, were involved in private conversations or cards.

There were a few more folks in the place than before. Since it was getting on toward mid-evening, several had come in for a drink and stew, and gone—a few saddle tramps, more drummers, a market hunter, and a couple more townsmen whom Stillman didn't recognize. Most of the people he'd known in Hobbs were either dead or had pulled their picket pins, and a few others had moved in to take their places in a dying town.

One of the suited townsmen who'd been playing cards by the window earlier just then walked down the stairs at the rear of the room, having had himself a tussle with the doxie, Miss Sarah, upstairs. He carried his coat over one arm, his hat in his hand. One tail of his pin-striped shirt stuck out of his pants. The whore walked down the stairs beside him, one of her arms hooked through one of his, and they were talking and laughing and the townsman was blushing.

Laughing but still somehow looking bored, the little blond whore moved awkwardly in her high-heeled, purple shoes that appeared a size too large for her. Clad in a purple gown, also a size too large for her, she carried a moth-chewed blanket around her otherwise bare shoulders. Despite the stove Shorty kept stoked, the saloon was a drafty building, and a chill kept swirling around the room.

Stillman decided to have a smoke, then go out back to tend nature before heading to bed. He was enjoying his ale and the warmth from the stove.

He dug out his makin's sack and had just started to roll himself a cigarette when the girl gave a yell. Stillman spilled some of the tobacco he'd been sprinkling onto his Black Fox rolling paper, and turned to see that one of the three Jinglebob hands—the scrawny redhead, Willie—had just pulled the little blond whore onto his lap and was nuzzling her neck.

She seemed none too pleased with Willie's attentions. She kicked and tried to squirm her way off of Willie's lap, yelling, "Let me go, Willie. I'm not entertainin' you ever again. You know what you did to me last time!"

"Ah, come on, Miss Sarah," Willie said, laughing as he tried to kiss the girl writhing in his arms. "You know I never meant nothin' by it."

"You gave me one hell of a shiner, Willie!" With a grunt, she struggled free and rose to her feet.

As the other men around them, including Nordekker and Big Mike, laughed at the high jinks, Willie grabbed an end of the blanket around Sarah's shoulders and drew her back down to his lap. "I didn't mean nothin' by it, Sarah," Willie said. "I was drunk!"

"Yeah, well, you're drunk now, too, so let me go!"

"Hey, Willie!" This from Althea Skinner, who glared at Willie from behind the bar where she was drawing an ale for a big, shaggy-haired man with the arms and chest of a blacksmith. That man had turned to face Willie and the girl, and he, too, laughed at the display.

Nothing like bedeviling a whore to make a sporting night out of an otherwise dull one...

"Willie, you're not allowed with Sarah!" Althea yelled above the din of laughter and the girl's pleas. "I told you—she's off-limits!"

That made Nordekker and Big Mike laugh all the louder. All three men were three-sheets-to-the-wind, Stillman saw. They laughed with drunken abandon, their eyes bright and glassy.

If Willie had heard Althea, he didn't act like it. Sarah clambered off of him once again, then wheeled to slap him across his face. The slap was like the crack of a pistol shot vaulting over the din of laughter and conversation reverberating throughout the room.

The slap instantly wiped the smile as well as the laughter off the young firebrand's face. He sagged back in his chair, eyes suddenly dark with anger.

As the other men around Willie laughed even louder, the whore wheeled and strode away from him, heading toward another man who'd risen from his chair, as though indicating his turn with her upstairs. Willie sat staring at the whore's retreating back, his face reddening, nostrils flaring.

No, no, no, Stillman thought. *Don't do it, Willie.*

Willie did not heed Stillman's unspoken warning.

Ah, hell.

Chapter Ten

The young redhead leaped out of his chair like a mortar from a cannon. Just as Sarah reached the burly freighter who'd apparently announced his turn with her, Willie grabbed her arm and spun her around to face him.

The girl screamed. It was a short scream, for just then Willie grabbed her, crouched, and hoisted her up over his left shoulder.

Wheeling, he headed for the stairs with the girl draped over his shoulder like a fifty-pound sack of potatoes.

"No!" she cried. "No, Willie! You're *crazy!*"

Her lashing feet kicked over several bottles and beer glasses as Willie strode between tables toward the stairs.

Shorty Skinner moved out from behind the bar to block the redhead's route to the stairway. "Willie!"

Willie stopped and drew the Colt from the holster on his left hip. Cocking the weapon, he aimed it straight out from his right shoulder, screeching, "Get back, you sawed-off little devil, or I'll blow your head off!"

Nordekker and Big Mike laughed louder.

By now, they were the only two still laughing. The others in the saloon—a dozen or so men and Althea Skinner—had fallen silent, regarding the young man and the girl struggling on his shoulder with open-mouthed, wide-eyed apprehension.

Shorty raised his hands, palm out, and backed away.

Willie lowered his pistol then started up the stairs, taking the steps two at a time, grunting angrily with every lunge.

"Help me!" Sarah cried. "He'll kill me! *This time he'll really kill me!*"

Stillman cursed and gained his feet. This wasn't his jurisdiction, of course, but that had never stopped him from intervening in such a situation before. Someone had to help the poor girl.

As he started away from the table, Darden said, "Hey, Ben—take the cuffs off, dammit! What if he kills you up there?"

Ignoring his prisoner, Stillman gained the bottom of the stairs just as Willie and the sob-

bing girl reached the top. Shorty had retrieved a
sawed-off, double-barreled shotgun from under
the bar and, Althea flanking him, he headed toward the stairs, as well.

Stillman waved him off.

"Stay here, Shorty."

Shorty lowered the shotgun. "Be careful, Ben.
That's one poison-mean little devil."

"Yeah, be careful, old man!" Nordekker called
as Stillman climbed the stairs. "Shorty's right—
that's one poison mean little devil. You don't
wanna mess with Willie when he's had a few."
When Stillman continued climbing the stairs,
Nordekker closed his hands around his mouth
and yelled, "Don't say I didn't warn ya!"

He and Big Mike pounder their table and
howled.

Stillman got to the second floor and paused.
He heard the girl crying and struggling behind
the first door on his left. The door wasn't latched.
Stillman nudged it open and stepped inside.

Willie and the girl were on the bed. Willie was
on his knees, straddling her, laughing maniacally.
He swung his right arm back behind his shoulder,
his fist clenched, intending to punch the howling
doxie. Before he could swing the fist, Stillman
grabbed it and pulled it farther back and down,
twisting it hard.

Willie yowled.

Stillman reached around with his left hand, pulled the kid's .45 from its holster, and tossed it to the floor.

Willie cursed shrilly, raging.

Keeping Willie's right arm twisted behind his back, wrenching it with such venom that he could see the shoulder bulging from its socket, Stillman dragged the kid off the bed and through the open door. Willie was on his knees, screaming, when Stillman got him onto the stairs.

"I'm gonna kill you, you old bastard!" Willie screeched at the tops of his lungs. "I'm gonna kill you slow. Oh, I'm gonna gut-shoot you and listen to you—*no, no, WAIT!"*

Stillman had picked the younker up by the seat of his pants and the scruff of his neck. He heaved him forward and let him go.

Screaming, Willie struck the stairs about a third of the way down. He landed so hard, the entire staircase shuddered. Yelping, Willie rolled wildly, bouncing off the left rail and then the right rail and plunging ass over tea kettle until he piled up on the floor below.

He lifted his red-faced head, mewling and clutching his right arm, which hung askew at an odd angle. The hothead's face was a mask of pain and agony. "My arm!" he cried. "My arm, you old devil!"

Obviously, the arm had been jerked out of its socket.

Standing at the top of the stairs, Stillman looked down at Jed Nordekker and Big Mike. Both men stood at their table, staring down in hang-jawed shock at their hot-blooded young partner.

Nordekker and the ginger-bearded Big Mike turned to glare up at Stillman.

Nordekker thrust an angry arm toward Willie and bellowed, "You had no call to do that!"

He and Big Mike began to reach for their side-arms.

Stillman whipped his Colt .44 from the holster on his left hip, aimed, and fired twice. The bullets shattered two beer glasses on the table before the two Jinglebob riders. A glass shard must have cut into Big Mike's cheek. He lifted his hand to his face, cursing. He dislodged the shard, slammed it down on the table, and glared at Stillman. Blood leaked from a cut just above the big man's ginger beard on his left cheek.

Stillman walked down the stairs, keeping his smoking Colt aimed at the two men, but keeping the raging and writhing Willie in the corner of his right eye.

While Stillman had been upstairs, much of the saloon's clientele had fled the premises. No one wanted to catch lead poisoning, and the night had suddenly seemed to be shaping up for a bad bout of it. The two big freighters remained, however.

So did Pug and Pinto. They sat not far from where Ace Darden sat alone at his and Stillman's table. Shorty and Althea stood near the end of the bar. They all regarded the lawman coming down the stairs, revolver extended, with wary interest.

All except for Nordekker and Big Mike, that was. They'd been splashed with the beer Stillman had shot out of their mugs. Big Mike had a nasty cut on his cheek. They were angry. Drunk and angry. Rage fairly flung razor-edged cavalry bayonets from their eyes.

"My arm, my arm," Willie moaned. "Ohhh... my arm!"

Gaining the bottom of the stars, Stillman crouched over the kid. "Here, let me help."

"Nooo!"

Stillman grabbed Willie's right hand, jerked the kid to his feet. He heard the crack and saw the sliding bulge through Willie's shirt as the shoulder ball rolled back into its socket. The lawman pivoted to the left, throwing Willie across the left side of Nordekker and Big Mike's table, knocking what remained of their beer mugs off the table as the kid hit the floor on the other side, and rolled, howling again like a gut-shot coyote.

Stillman had holstered his Colt to throw Willie like a bundle of straw across a loft. Nordekker and Big Mike again reached for their pistols. Again, Stillman beat them to the draw. Before either could raise his revolver, Stillman drilled two more rounds into their table, perilously close to both men's belt buckles.

Big Mike dropped his gun and leaped back with a yelp.

"Hold on!" Nordekker said, lowering his own uncocked Colt to his side and holding up his other hand, palm out.

Stillman glared at Nordekker through wafting powder smoke. "I'll take that."

"What?"

"Set the gun on the table. I'll be confiscating it. You too, Big Mike. Pick up your gun and set it on the table. Nice an' easy."

Nordekker's eyes sparked. "You can't take our guns!"

"See—that's what he does!" yelled Pinto, gaining his feet unsteadily, drunkenly, and thrusting an accusatory finger at Stillman.

Snickers rose from the others around the room, though little of the previous crowd remained.

"Sit down before you fall down, Pinto," Stillman said.

Pinto collapsed into his chair beside the scowling Pug with the large, red, egg-shaped bulge in the middle of his forehead.

Stillman glanced at the Colt Nordekker held down low by his right leg. "On the table...or the next one's going through your belly button!"

"All right, all right!" Nordekker tossed his Colt onto the table. It slid toward Stillman.

"You, too, Mike!"

When Mike had picked his own revolver off the floor and slammed it onto the table before sliding it toward Stillman, Stillman shoved both weapons down behind his own cartridge belt.

"Crazy old man!" Big Mike spat out.

"This crazy old man has had his fill of you fellas," Stillman said. "I don't want to hear another peep out of you this evening."

Stillman sheathed his Colt and turned to the bar.

"What about our weapons?" Nordekker said, sullenly.

"I'll set 'em on the bar when I leave tomorrow mornin'. I got a feelin' I'll be up a whole lot earlier than you fellas."

"Mr. Conyers is gonna hear about this!" Nordekker threatened, pointing at Stillman, who only smiled and bellied up to the bar.

"Althea, I think I'd like a fresh beer to help send me to the sandman."

"Comin' up." Althea drew him a fresh, frothy ale, set it on the bar before him. "On the house… old man." She smiled, winked.

Stillman returned her smile and then trudged back over to his table, drew his chair toward him with his boot, and slacked into it. He set the beer on the table and picked up his makin's sack once more.

Ace chuckled and shook his head. "You sure know how to make friends. If you make it to Winifred in one piece, I'm gonna be mighty surprised."

"You better hope I do."

"Why's that?"

Stillman troughed a wheat paper between the first two fingers of his right hand, and gave Darden a wolfish grin. "Because if I go down, I'm takin' you with me."

———————

The saloon emptied out a half hour later.

Pug and Pinto shrugged into their torn canvas coats and headed out through the front door, casting sullen looks at Stillman. They'd likely look for a pile of hay to bed down in. Apparently, they didn't have the jingle for a room even here in the humble Squaw Peak.

The freighters and drummers drifted off to their own rooms, and then so did Nordekker and Big Mike, both of whom helped the groaning and generally miserable Willie up the stairs. They cast Stillman looks similar to those of Pug and Pinto.

Ace chuckled again, shook his head. "Yep, you sure know how to make friends. You better hope none o' them have another gun squirreled away somewhere. You might catch a blue whistler in your sleep."

Stillman wasn't worried. His enemies were disarmed. No doubt they'd get their hands on another weapon if they wanted to badly enough, but they were so drunk, all they probably wanted now was a good night's sleep. Even more than revenge. At least for tonight.

When Stillman and his prisoner were the only ones left in the saloon, with Althea and Short clattering around in the rear kitchen, cleaning up and putting their range to sleep, Darden said, "I gotta pee."

"Hold it till mornin'."

"I can't hold it till mornin', Ben. Now, dammit—I gotta *pee!*"

Stillman was just funnin' with the man. When he'd finished his beer and his cigarette, he uncuffed Ace and led him out back to the privy.

Stillman evacuated his own bladder in the freshly fallen snow while his prisoner did the same in
the privy.

It was a cold, windy night, but the snow appeared to have stopped. Only an inch or two had
fallen. Tomorrow's ride would be a cold one, but
the horses shouldn't have trouble getting through.
And there was always the promise of a Chinook.

Stillman yawned.

He led Ace back into the saloon, cuffed him
to the chain, and left him slumped on the floor
against the ceiling support post.

"Well, this oughta be a good night's sleep," Ace
said, crossing his boots at the ankles and folding
his arms across his chest, grumbling.

Stillman slogged up the stairs. He went into his
room, washed his face with the chill water from
the pitcher on the washstand, and got undressed.
He lay in bed a long time after he'd turned down
the lamp, staring at the dark ceiling.

He was tired. Dead-dog, old-man tired. It had
been a long day. The ales had gone down well.

Still, sleep eluded him.

"Hell!"

He crawled out of bed. He wrapped his Colt
and pistol belt around his waist, grabbed one of
the quilts off the bed, and a spare pillow, and, clad
in only his longhandles, socks, and six-gun, went

downstairs. The saloon was dark, lit only by the snow glowing beyond the windows. Althea and Shorty had gone to bed.

Darden snored softly in the darkness. He was not so deeply asleep that he did not hear Stillman move up to him. The prisoner, leaning back against the ceiling support post, knees drawn up to his chest, looked up, his eyes glinting in the blue light pushing through the windows.

He was hunkered down deep in his coat, as though chilled. The fire in the stove had nearly gone out, and the saloon was cold and would be getting colder.

"What is it?" Ace asked.

"Here."

Stillman tossed him the blanket and the pillow. He stoked the stove, adding several split logs, then closed the door and went back to bed.

Chapter Eleven

Stillman was dead asleep when someone tapped on his door.

He cursed and grabbed his .44 off the chair he'd shoved up beside the bed. He clicked the hammer back, aimed the barrel toward the door that was a pale rectangle in the darkness to his right, and said, "What?"

He tightened his finger against the trigger and waited for a bullet to chew through the door.

"Ben? It's Althea. Please, let me in." Her voice was low, urgent.

Stillman threw the covers aside, rose, and lit the lamp on the dresser. He turned the wick about halfway up, spreading the weak light into the shadows. He walked to the door. Always wary, he kept his gun cocked and ready as he drew the door open six inches.

Althea's thick, pear-shaped body stood just beyond the door. Her gaze met his, communicating the desperation that had been in her voice. Stillman lowered the Colt, depressing the hammer. He drew the door open and stepped back. When she was inside the room, he closed the door, latching it softly.

A little embarrassed about his state of undress, he said, "What's the matter, Althea?"

"I need your help. Or...I should say...she needs your help. Her an' the boy."

Stillman drew a deep breath, released it slowly. He knew who she was talking about. He'd seen Althea send a couple of covered supper plates up the stairs with the piano-punishing whore.

"Room nine?"

"She and the boy walked here from Eagle Creek." Althea paused. "She's...they're...very frightened, Ben. They know what John Conyers will do to them if they find them. If they stay here, they will be found. Once Conyers' men have finished scouring the countryside, they'll come here." She paused, looked down at her hands. "She has few friends."

"Are you one of them?"

Althea shook her head. "I don't like her. She's very high on herself. But the boy.... I don't want anything bad to happen to them."

"What do you want me to do?"

"You're headed for Winifred, right?"

"Yeah, but…"

Althea closed a hand around his arm. "You could take them with you. They'd be safe with you. At least, safer with you than with me and Shorty. They can't stay in Hobbs. She's from Billings. She can take the stage from Winifred back to Billings. She'll have a chance there."

"Have you considered reporting all this to the county sheriff?"

"Buck Reno?" Althea's round face crinkled in a scowl. "He's in Conyers' back pocket!"

"Ah, hell." Stillman walked to the dresser. He set his gun on it, then ran his hands through his hair.

He turned back to Althea. "How old's the boy."

"Ten, I think."

Silently, Stillman cursed. "Can they ride?"

"They know they'll have to."

Stillman sat on the edge of the bed. He sighed. Nasty situation. He was transporting a prisoner to Winifred, still a two-day ride, in bad weather. Now he'd have a woman and a boy in tow, as well. A woman and a boy with a pack of Conyers' angry wolves nipping at their heels.

That meant Conyers' men would be nipping at Stillman's heels, too. But what choice did he have? Althea was right. If the woman and the boy stayed here, they'd be found and likely killed. Stillman knew Conyers' reputation for savagery. And with Buck Reno in his pocket, the woman had nowhere to turn.

Except to Stillman.

He drew a sharp breath.

"Get her and the boy up before dawn. I'll meet you at the back door with the horses."

Althea smiled, nodded, and went out.

———————

Stillman's inner clock chimed around what he figured to be five a.m. He checked his old Ingersoll. Sure enough. Five a.m.

He'd snatched a few hours' sleep but it didn't feel like enough. He hadn't been on a long horse-back ride through rugged country in a coon's age, and he felt the saddle even when he wasn't sitting on it. This imaginary kak felt as though it were made of iron, and it had grown into his backside.

Times like these, crawling out of bed against his own will, his joints screeching, he wished he were still a drinking man. Nothing like a couple shots of who-hit-John to get the horses hitched. A couple straights shot then one in a cup of black coffee.

Those were the days.

"Stop torturing yourself, fool."

He stumbled over to the washbasin and used his Colt's butt to bust through the rime on his wash water. When the water hit his face, he felt the sting deep down in his loins, even into his toes. It took him a good minute afterwards to draw a breath.

Dressed, encumbered by cold-weather gear, by his rifle and saddlebags and a short night's restive sleep, he stepped into the hall and drew the door closed behind him with his boot toe. He didn't latch it. No point in making any noise, not that the Conyers men could hear it up on the third story, where Althea had wisely put them.

They'd sleep till mid-morning if not later. Especially the wicked little Willie, with his injured wing.

Stillman looked down the dark hall to his left, toward room nine. He couldn't hear anything there yet, and he was glad he didn't. He didn't want the woman and the boy—what were their names again, if he'd been told?—moving around any too soon. No point in them risking betraying their presence before Stillman could bring the horses around.

To that end, he shifted the gear on his shoulders and made his way downstairs. He dumped his collection of pistols onto the bar, but only after emptying them first, and tossing the cartridges into the wood box. He had to gently kick the sound-asleep Darden awake and then practically drag him out the front door, the man's hands once again cuffed before him.

"Damn, Ben—how come we couldn't sleep in another hour?" Ace said as they slogged off through the freshly fallen snow. "It's early yet. And *cold!*" He gave a violent shake.

"You got a date with the hangman, and I got a date with my wi—" Stillman stopped.

Ace ran into him from behind, looked around. "What is it?"

The street was deserted under a sugary layer of virgin snow. It wasn't yet dawn, but a purple light edging toward blue glowed off the snow, limning the dark edges of buildings and showing the dark mouths of breaks between shops.

A cold hand of apprehension spread its fingers across the back of Stillman's neck.

"What is it?" Darden asked again, keeping his voice low.

Stillman drew a breath. "I caught a whiff of cigarette smoke."

"So?" Ace smiled. "Make you want one? Why don't we go back inside, have a cup of coffee and a—"

"Shut up, Ace."

Stillman studied the layout before him. The snow was scuffed in the street to his right. Someone had walked from a corner of the harness shop on the opposite side of the street and ahead a half a block. The person had come this way and stepped into the break between the Squaw Peak and the meat market thirty feet beyond.

Stillman chewed off his right glove, shoved it into his coat pocket. He reached under his coat and drew his Colt. Holding the big popper barrel up before him, his thumb on the hammer, he moved forward until he could see down the side of the Squaw Peak Saloon.

At the near front corner, behind a frozen rain barrel wearing a two-inch cap of downy snow, someone had been standing. The prints in the snow painted a clear picture. The snow was melted where the person who had been standing there had dropped a quirley stub.

The tracks scuffed on down the side of the Squaw Peak to the rear.

Darden had walked up to stand beside Stillman. "Who you suppose that was?"

"I don't know. Cold morning to be skulking around on the street."

"Yeah, well, speaking of that—why don't we—?"

Stillman shoved his prisoner on ahead.

Darden cursed, slipped in the fresh snow, nearly fell, then continued walking. Stillman followed him, looking around, keeping the Colt in his right hand.

It was cold out here. The mercury had to be stuck somewhere not far above zero. Living close to the Canadian line for the past ten years, Stillman had become good at judging the temperature by the texture of the air against his leathery cheeks.

The air this morning felt like rough sandpaper. It burned in his lungs. His hand ached from the cold. Soon, he'd have to put on his glove or lose the feeling in his hand and also its usefulness.

Damn miserable weather. Now he had a woman and a boy to take charge of in addition to Darden. He had to get them all down to Winifred in one piece...

"What's the matter?" Ace asked as they turned east toward the livery barn.

"Huh?"

"You cussed."

"Shut up an' keep walkin'."

"Boy, you ain't a mornin' person—are ya, Ben?"

"Depends on the morning."

They approached the barn hulking darkly before them in the misty blue light, thickening gradually so that the world resembled a black and

white daguerreotype slowly developing before
them. Stillman kept an eye on the snow around
him, looking for more prints, glad not to see any.

He could smell the barn as he and Darden drew
near—the smell of hay, ammonia, old leather, and
horses. It was a familiar, inviting smell, but it did
not relieve the hand of apprehension still spreading its cold fingers against the back of his neck.

A loud cawing broke the morning's silence,
making Stillman's heart lurch.

"Jesus!" Ace said, also giving a start.

Caw! Caw! Caw!

Stillman lifted his gaze to the barn roof. At
the very peak over the loft doors perched Pogue's
crow—a small, inky black shape against the sooty
charcoal-blue of the gradually lightening sky.

"Heinrich ain't a mornin' person, either," Ace
said with a chuckle.

Caw! Caw! Caw!

Stillman shoved Darden through the man-
door to the left of the large stock door, and
stepped in behind him.

A caw-like coughing rose on his right followed
by the ratcheting click of a heavy gun hammer
being eared back and: "Friend or foe?"

It was still fairly dark in the barn, so at first
Stillman could make out only the spidery shape
of Robert Pogue sitting on a small bench near

the open door to his sleeping quarters. Stillman smelled the peppery aroma of the man's cigarette before he saw the quirley pinched between the thumb and index finger of Pogue's left hand clad in a knit glove with the upper halves of the fingers cut out.

In his other hand, clad in a similar glove, Pogue aimed his infernal Walker Colt straight out from his right shoulder.

"You can put the cannon down," Stillman said.

There was the click of the hammer being uncocked. Pogue lowered the big revolver, wincing and placing his left hand over his right shoulder. "I'll be damned if that ain't a heavy gun."

"They make 'em lighter these days, Robert."

"I've never fired anything but the old cap 'n' ball and never will. Did me through the Mexican War, so I reckon it'll do me to the end, which is stormin' closer and closer with every passin' day. Possibly for you, too."

Stillman had started walking down the barn alley, heading for his and Darden's horses. Now he stopped and frowned curiously at Pogue.

"Two men were here last night," Robert said, sliding his gaze toward where Ace still stood near the half-open man-door. "Lookin' for him."

"*Me?*" Ace said, skeptical.

Stillman turned to Darden. "Shut the door."

He moved back up to the front of the barn. "Who was here, Robert?"

"Didn't tell me their names, but they asked— *real polite*—if I'd seen Ace in town. Of course, everybody stables their horses here, so I see most folks comin' an' goin'."

Pogue gave a slit-eyed smile. "I say they asked me real polite because I had the drop on 'em with old Mr. Walker here."

Pogue patted the big Colt on the bench beside him. Cigarette smoke billowed around him. "They didn't tell me who they were. In fact, our conversation was pretty short, them bein' kind of nervous, havin' this big popper trained on their eyeballs. But there was two of 'em, sure enough, and they was askin' for Ace. I told 'em I hadn't seen hide nor hair of that rascal in a dozen years, and I told 'em if I saw either one of 'em skulkin' around my barn again in the middle of the night, they'd be Heinrich feed."

As if on cue, the crow gave its froggy-voiced cry from atop the barn:

Caw! Caw! Caw!

Pogue grinned.

Darden said in a low, dreadful tone, "What'd they look like?"

Pogue shrugged inside his wool coat and the several blankets wrapped around his shoulders.

"I don't know. It was dark, an' they was all bundled up." He held a finger to his left eye. "One of 'em had a dead eye, though. White as an egg."

Stillman looked at Darden, who shrugged. "I don't know. It could be Bob Owens."

"One of your gang?" Stillman asked.

"Uh-huh."

"That means they must have evaded Sanchez's posse." Stillman paused, pondering. "Either that, or...wiped 'em out." He pondered that, as well, a feeling of dread washing over him like a cold, oily wave. "Now they're after the loot."

"I reckon they would be...sure enough." Darden gave a dry laugh, but there was a distinct lack of humor in it.

Stillman looked at him, then brushed past the man. He cracked the man-door and peered outside.

The sun wasn't up yet, but the shadows were thinning. Not seeing anyone lurking around the barn, Stillman drew the door closed and turned to Darden again. "Let's get saddled up. For thirty-four thousand dollars, they'll likely be back."

"Oh, they would be—sure enough." Ace strode past Stillman and down the barn alley, heading for his horse. Stillman frowned at him, vaguely puzzled. Then he turned to Pogue. "Robert," he said, "I'm gonna need another horse."

Twenty minutes later, Stillman stepped out of the barn's rear man-door. Holding his Henry rifle in both hands, he looked around carefully. The sun would be up in another thirty minutes, he figured, judging by how many more shadows had thinned and retreated since the last time he'd peered outside.

He could see no one around the barn, and no sign in the snow.

Relieved, he stepped back into the barn, opened the two big stock doors, and led Sweets outside. The horse he'd rented from Pogue—a short, stocky roan—walked out behind the bay, its bridle reins tied loosely to Sweets' tail. The horses sniffed at the new snow and snorted friskily, the roan nodding its head as though in approval. Ace led his steeldust out of the barn, looking around warily.

"What's the matter, Ace?" Stillman asked, sliding his rifle into his saddle sheath. "Wouldn't you be happy to see your pards?" He was honestly curious about the man's obviously apprehensive demeanor.

Darden whipped his head around to him. "Huh? Oh…" He grinned, feigned a chuckle, then wrapped his cuffed hands around his apple and pulled himself into the saddle.

He glanced at the roan. "Say, Ben—what's the

spare for? You gonna pack extry grub, are ya? Fine by me."

"Seein' as how we're havin' so much fun, a couple more folks decided to throw in with us."

Ace scowled. "Huh?"

"You'll see." Stillman reached up to grab his saddle horn.

Caw! Caw! Caw!

Stillman pulled his hands back down and turned to see Heinrich perched on the near end of the barn roof. The bird stared down at something on its left, to Stillman's right. The growing light flashed like nickel in the bird's black eyes.

Caw! Caw! Caw!

Following the crow's gaze, Stillman saw the man with the rifle moving quickly toward him through the corral on the west side of the barn.

"Get down!" Stillman yelled to Darden.

A half-second later, the man stopped and raised his rifle. As the man's Winchester Yellowboy blossomed smoke and flames, crashing wickedly, Stillman jerked his own Henry from his saddle scabbard.

Ace cursed.

The horses neighed angrily, leaping with starts. Stillman flung himself belly down to the ground, racked a cartridge into the Henry's action, and aimed at the man, who had stopped about two-thirds down from the front of the barn, inside the otherwise empty corral.

He was violently pumping another round into his Winchester's action. A slender, red-faced man in a fox fur hat, he also wore a red-striped yellow mackinaw.

Stillman drew a bead on him, fired.

The bullet slammed into the side of the barn, ripping wood from a log several inches in front of the shooter. The man fired at Stillman. The bullet plumed snow just off the sheriff's left shoulder.

Stillman cocked and fired again.

This time his aim was true. The rifleman flew backward with a wail to lie writhing on the ground, close against the barn's stone foundation.

"Ben!"

Stillman whipped his head to his left. Darden's steeldust was crow-hopping. Over and beyond its arched tail, Stillman saw another man bolt out from around the barn's opposite corner—a big man in a wolf coat and wooly chaps, and wearing round, wire-rimmed spectacles beneath the high crown of his Stetson.

He had a pistol in each hand. He fired one now at Ace, who screamed as the steeldust wheeled sharply to one side.

Ace flew out of the saddle to hit the ground with a thud. He rolled, howling.

As Sweets and the roan galloped out of the line of fire, Stillman fired beneath the steeldust's belly, between its scissoring legs. His bullet punched through the bespectacled gent's right knee. The man screamed as that leg flew out from beneath him, and he hit the ground on his other leg.

Still on his belly, Stillman cocked the Henry again, awkwardly. He aimed just as awkwardly and triggered another round at the bespectacled man. By now the steeldust had cleared out, giving the lawman a better shot.

This bullet punched into his target's left shoulder, rocking him backward at the waist but not felling him. The man bellowed angrily then, gritting his teeth, started to aim his rifle at Stillman once more.

Stillman aimed the Henry again, taking an extra second with the shot. The Henry belched, bucked, lapped fire and smoke.

The bullet carved a round hole through the bespectacled gent's forehead. The man's head bobbed several times, as though nodding in the affirmative. He threw up his hands as though in defeat, tossing away his pistols, and flopped backward at the waist, one leg curled beneath him.

"God *damn!*" Ace bellowed.

Heinrich couldn't have agreed more.

Caw! Caw! Caw!

Chapter Twelve

Powder smoke cleared from the air in front of Stillman, lying belly down in the newly fallen snow.

He stared at the second man he'd shot, who lay slumped on his back, one leg beneath him, the other splayed wide, the knee bloody. He was sort of cocked up on one hip, looking damn uncomfortable, near the barn's far corner. He wasn't moving.

Stillman whipped his head and rifle toward the man who lay against the barn. He wasn't moving, either.

Darden groaned fifteen feet to Stillman's left. He lay on his back in the snow his and the other horses had scuffed up.

"You all right, Ace?"

"Hell, no."

"Hang on." Stillman got up and checked each

of the men he'd shot, making sure neither was any longer a threat. They were not. He recognized neither.

Returning to stare down at Darden, groaning and mewling, he said, "Enough lollygaggin'. Rise an' shine."

"Go to hell!" Ace complained.

Stillman prodded Darden with his boot toe. "If you're not hurt so bad you can't get up, get up."

"Just shoot me, Ben. Put me out of my misery. I'm tired, I'm hungry. I ain't even had a cup of coffee yet today. I just been bucked off my hoss, I ache in every joint and in some joints I didn't know I had, and you got me trussed up like a pig you're fixin' to roast for a Fourth of July barbecue. At the end of this damn trail, some sour-breathed, noose-chewin' hangman is gonna play cat's cradle with my head. Nah, nah. Just shoot me! Do me that much, Ben. For old times' sake, if nothin' else..."

Stillman crouched, grabbed the collar of Darden's coat, and heaved the man to his feet. Ace growled and spat like a trapped bobcat as Stillman led him into the west side corral and along the barn to where the first man he'd shot lay sprawled, gazing opaquely up at the lightening sky through his one good eye.

The other eye was as white as an eggshell.

"You know him?"

Darden cursed.

"Who is he?"

"Bob Owens, all right. They call him Brother Bob 'cause he's a lay preacher. Baptist, I think."

"Well, he's communin' with St. Pete right now. Probably getting taken to the woodshed." Stillman looked around for others of this man's ilk, keeping his Henry raised and ready. "I wonder how many more of your gang are around."

"It wasn't my gang, Ben. Fred Newcastle was the head honcho."

"Don't split hairs with me, Ace."

"Brother Bob's part of the gang, all right." Darden gazed down at Brother Bob, crestfallen. "Leastways…he was."

Stillman led Darden back out of the corral and over to the other man. Robert Pogue, clad in a fur coat and two heavy quilts, a fur hat with earflaps on his wizened head, was on one knee beside the man, going through his pockets. A half-smoked quirley sagged from between the old man's thin lips. Heinrich sat perched on a corral post nearby, lifting his wings slightly as he shifted from foot to foot.

Old Robert gazed up at Stillman, a predatorial glint in his rheumy eyes. "Nice shootin', Ben. I'll bury these fellas fer ya, if I can have what's in their pockets. This fella's got him a nice pair of fur boots. I'd like his boots. Mine got holes in the soles so's when I pull 'em off at night, my feet are more blue than white!"

Stillman looked at Darden. "Who's this one?"

Ace gazed down at the bespectacled gent, whose spectacles now hung down his face, attached to one ear. Blood oozed from a corner of the man's mouth. Darden said, "Craw Engelhardt."

"Engelhardt must not have liked you all that much, Ace. He tried to shoot you."

"Yeah, well…"

"Why would that be?"

"I don't know," Ace said, giving the dead man a light kick then chuckling grimly. "Ask him…"

Stillman sighed. He looked at old Pogue, who had begun counting out some silver he'd pulled from the man's pocket onto the dead man's fur coat, muttering under his breath. "They're all yours, Robert."

Old Pogue looked up at Stillman, his eyes glinting again, and smiled. "Thanks, Ben. You're a gentleman and a scholar." He looked over at the crow. "Fresh rabbit stew tonight, Heinrich. I'm buyin'!"

Heinrich's small, black eyes flashed gold as he regarded his master greedily and shifted his position on the corral post. "Caw! Caw! Caw!"

Stillman led his prisoner off to fetch their horses.

———————

He and Darden rode up to the rear of the Squaw Peak a few minutes later.

The sun was nearly up now. Few shadows remained. He'd figured on getting out of town over a half hour ago, but here he was pulling up to the saloon in the revealing light of morning, with two different factions after him.

At least, one more faction would be after him as soon as the woman and the boy threw in with him and Darden.

"Stay put."

Darden only grunted.

Stillman swung down from Sweets' back. He'd just dropped his reins in the snow when the rear door clicked. Still jumpy from the recent lead swap, his blood quickened, and he'd started to reach for the Henry again but stopped when he saw Althea Skinner poke her head out the door.

Her gaze met Stillman's, and she frowned reprovingly.

"Where've you been?"

"Ran into a little trouble."

"That shooting…" Althea canted her head in the direction of the livery barn. "That was you?"

"Who else?" Stillman grumbled. "That was Ace's bunch, not Conyers." He walked up to the round-faced Indian woman, their breaths frosting in the air between them. "Has Nordekker's group shown their ugly heads yet?"

"Still sawing logs." Althea glanced behind her, then shoved the door farther open and stepped out and to one side.

A woman dressed in a blue wool coat and man's flat-brimmed, low-crowned felt hat moved into the doorway. She wore a thick, red wool muffler around her neck, and she carried two carpetbags and a burlap sack in her black-gloved hands, holding them down in front of her, like someone standing on a rail platform, waiting for a train. She looked around warily, sullenly, the rising breeze touching her hair.

A tall, slender, dark-eyed woman, she had long, dark-red hair. Her pretty, pale, oval-shaped face was liberally splashed with freckles. She glanced at Stillman, and he detected vague reproof—or was it condescension?—in her direct gaze. He judged her to be in the twenties, maybe late.

"This is Mrs. Coulter," Althea said.

Stillman pinched his hat brim to the woman. "Pleased to meet you, Mrs. Coulter. Of course, I wish it was under better circumstances. I heard there was a boy…?"

Mrs. Coulter reached out to her left and pulled a boy into the open doorway with her, draping her arm across his shoulders protectively as well as reassuringly. The boy stood a little above waist-high to her. He was dressed in a bullet-crowned black felt hat, and was bundled against the cold in a butterscotch-colored elk hide coat and black muffler.

The most distinguishing thing about him was that he did not at all resemble his mother. In fact, he appeared to be almost full-blood Indian. His skin dark cherry, his face was sharply defined with mud-brown eyes and high, square cheek-bones.

His hair looked to be short, though Stillman couldn't see much of it because of his hat and that muffler tied over it and knotted, like Still-man's, under his chin. Standing there beside Mrs. Coulter, the boy did not look at Stillman but only studied the toes of his wool-lined elk hide boots rising halfway to his knees.

Stillman saw the woman wore a similar pair of boots—both hand-sewn.

At least they were dressed for the weather.

"This is Daniel," the woman said.

"Hi, Daniel."

The boy said nothing, just stared at his boot toes.

"Well," Darden said, staring at the boy in open-mouthed surprise, "I'll be jiggered…"

Quickly, to cover for Darden's impoliteness and because they needed to get moving, Stillman said, "I want you to know that it's going to be a dangerous trail, Mrs. Coulter. We'll likely not only have Conyers' men dogging our heels, but an outlaw gang, as well."

Althea scowled. "Outlaw gang?"

Stillman jerked his head at Darden, who pulled his mouth corners down in chagrin.

"I'm in more danger here, Sheriff Stillman," said Mrs. Coulter, her frank, intelligent eyes meeting his. "I'd rather take my chances with you than remain here in Hobbs. If you know Conyers, you know…" She let her voice trail off as she glanced down at the boy. "Besides…I have no other way of making it to Billings, and I have nothing left at Eagle Creek. They burned down my saloon. I saw the smoke as my son and I were fleeing."

"I'm sorry to hear that. Knowing Conyers' reputation, it doesn't surprise me. Let's get you mounted. I rented one horse for both you and the boy."

"I'll pay you back."

Stillman didn't know how to respond to that. At the moment, it seemed a trifling concern. She followed him over to the roan. "Yes, that'll be fine."

"Can you ride?"

"Yes."

"The boy?"

"He's a little afraid of horses, but he'll be fine with me."

"Good," Stillman said with some relief. That had been a question in his mind. If she couldn't ride, and relatively well—well enough to elude pursuers—they were all in big trouble.

Not that they weren't already.

Stillman helped the woman onto her horse then turned to the boy. He crouched down, hands on his thighs. "Are you ready, too, young man?" He tried to look into the boy's eyes, but Daniel kept his gaze on the ground. He gave his head a very brief, quick nod.

"Okay, then." Stillman placed his gloved hands on the boy's waist, and eased him up onto the horse behind his mother. "There you go...nice and easy. Wrap your arms around your ma's waist and hold on tight. There you go. You'll be fine."

The boy wrapped his arms tightly around his mother and pressed his head against her back, but turned his face away from Stillman. Most Indians Stillman had known had been shy people. At least, shy around white folks. This boy was shy, too; he was also very afraid.

Stillman couldn't blame him. He felt his heart going out to the boy and Mrs. Coulter. They were as vulnerable as lambs out here, and they had only him to protect them. That responsibility added a lot of weigh to shoulders already weighed down with the prospect of getting Ace Darden and the stolen bank money back to Winifred in one piece.

His ambivalence must have been obvious on his face as he adjusted the woman's stirrups. He was looking around apprehensively, on the scout for more drygulchers, but when he turned to her, she saw her regarding him wistfully.

Quietly, she said, "Thank you, Sheriff. For what you're doing. Daniel and I appreciate it." She said the words as though by rote, without any real warmth. Stillman didn't hold it against her. She was in a world of rough men. She was on the run from several of those rough men. Maybe the worst of them. And, at least in her eyes, he was just another man she hadn't made up her mind about.

Stillman smiled. He tried to make it a reassuring smile, but she didn't seem reassured. She didn't feign a return smile. When he'd finished adjusting both of her stirrups to fit the length of her legs, he walked over to Althea, who stood waiting outside the back door. She clutched a blanket around her thick body.

"Do you know if anyone's living in that cabin along Black Creek? The one the woodcutters for the steamboats built a few years back?"

Althea smiled. "A few years back? That cabin was built over twenty years ago, Ben."

Stillman winced. "Ouch."

"A couple market hunters for the railroad occupied it for a while till last winter. They got drunk and had a falling out over a poker game. Shot each other. Left a bloody mess. Frenchie MacGregor found them a couple days later, on the floor beside the table littered with playing cards. He dragged them out and cleaned the cabin. As far as I know, it's only used now and then by passing travelers."

"All right. I'll head that way."

"It's longer."

"Yeah, but we'd be harder to track through the Buffalo Barrens." Stillman glanced at the sky. "If we get the Chinook I'm hoping for on the tail end of last night's storm, that'll help."

He walked over and picked up his reins. He mounted and turned back to Althea. The former doxie regarded the Indian boy with worry in her dark eyes.

Stillman said, "Next time I pass through, I'd like you to sing 'O Would That She Were Here' for me. I don't think I've ever heard the whole song all the way through."

Althea poked a cigarette into her mouth, and drew on it. "These days I sound like Robert Pogue's crow." She shrugged, smiled, and exhaled smoke out her nostrils. "But if you insist."

Stillman pinched his hat brim to her. He glanced at the sullen Darden and then at the equally sullen-looking Mrs. Coulter and the Indian boy. "All right, then."

He reined the bay around and headed south.

Chapter Thirteen

An hour later, Althea Skinner carried a crate of fresh beer bottles from the storeroom beneath the kitchen into the main drinking hall. She slowed her pace halfway to the bar. There rose the snow-muffled thumps of several riders out on the street fronting the Squaw Peak Saloon.

Dread touched her.

Suppressing a shiver despite the heat the ticking woodstove spread throughout the room, she continued around behind the bar and set the crate on top of it. Not wanting to, for she knew who she would see out there, but unable to stop herself, she tipped her head to the right, so she could see through the window to the right of the door and into the snow-white street directly in front of the saloon.

When she saw the riders milling around, her heart skipped a beat. She gasped, drew a shallow breath, let it out slowly.

Eight or nine men. Jinglebob riders.

She recognized several. They didn't ride through Hobbs often but when they did, they usually stopped for drinks at the Squaw Peak. She'd rarely seen the ranch owner, John Conyers, himself. He was known to be a reclusive old bear all year long. She had seen him a few times before, however. She would never forget the first time she'd seen him.

An array of violent images assaulted her, causing rage to burn up from the base of her spine. She drew a deep breath, trying to calm herself, as she gazed out the window at the ghoulish old man sitting on a cream horse just outside the saloon. Conyers wore a hooded buffalo coat, the hood pulled up over his head, around which he'd tied a red muffler.

Conyers was an ugly, hawk-faced man whose long, sandy-gray hair, thin as the hemp at the end of a frayed rope, trailed out from the hood to flutter down his chest in the breeze that was building now on the tail end of last night's storm. He wore two pistols on his hips, belted around the outside of his coat.

He talked to several of the other men, their breaths hazing the air around them. One of the men he was talking to was his *segundo*, Loco McGuire, a tall cold-blooded gunfighter Conyers had hired many years ago to help Conyers hold his land against rustlers and nesters. Sitting a rangy brown and white pinto, McGuire wore a black bear fur coat and black bear fur hat. The black fur matched his long, black hair and black beard that contrasted with the amber of his eyes.

As Conyers and his men began to dismount their horses and tie them to the two hitchracks fronting the Squaw Peak, violent images continued to hammer at Althea. In the tumult, one stood out—a cabin door being kicked open and two men bulling through it, their eyes glistening from drink. Althea heard her full-blooded Blackfoot mother scream while her father shouted "Get out, you damn dogs!" as he reached for the double-barreled shotgun mounted over the fireplace.

As Conyers and McGuire stepped up onto the boardwalk, heading for the Squaw Peak's front door, the age-seasoned face of each man was overlaid with the face of his younger self. Twenty-five years younger...on a night twenty-five years ago...at a lonely cabin on Three-Legged-Wolf Creek...on a night about this same time of year...early winter...

A savage night that changed Althea's life forever...

"We're not open!" she yelled above the roar of

the gun in her head as the door opened and John Conyers walked in, more stooped and wasted than he'd been twenty-five years ago, but still displaying the same wolfish savagery in his cold gray eyes.

He stopped just inside the door, looked at Althea, and blinked. "You ain't open?"

"Nope. Don't open till eleven."

"Well, hell." Conyers winced in feigned disappointment. He turned to McGuire and the others standing behind him and said, "She ain't open yet, boys. I reckon we're gonna have to go and come back at eleven."

The others stood in a ragged semi-circle around the man, gazing at him blankly. Their eyes were all like Conyers'—flat and indifferent, as opaque as a window crusted with frost. The man had always hired other men just like himself. Coldly brutal, uncompromising. He understood such men, and they understood him.

Conyers turned back around to face Althea. He gave an ironic chuff, flaring one nostril. He walked into the saloon, and McGuire walked in behind him. The others followed—the younger wolves following the two older leaders.

As Conyers approached the bar, looking around and sniffing the air, very much like the human wolf he was, Althea's heart fluttered while her belly turned cold. Conyers turned his aged, patch-bearded, hook-nosed face with close-set gray eyes to her, and she wondered if he remembered her, if he knew who she was.

The few times she'd seen him in town over the years, he'd seemed not to see her at all, even when he was looking right at her. When she'd been whoring, he'd never taken her upstairs, though she'd vowed that if he'd ever tried she would have gelded him and let him bleed to death, howling.

That hadn't happened, which was just as well. She wasn't sure she would have had the courage to go through with it. Althea wasn't afraid of most men. But John Conyers was different from most men.

He'd never paid any attention to her, because to him she was just another dark-eyed half-breed, the fruit of some ill-begotten union between two rock-worshipping savages, despite that Althea's parents had followed the Christian faith. That was how men like Conyers saw those with Indian blood. She knew far too well. His views had made it even easier than usual for Conyers to murder her parents all those years ago, when he'd accused them of "squatting" on his land, though Althea's father had filed a legal homestead claim on their five acres.

Conyers removed his gloves as he approached

the bar. He slapped the gloves down on the bar and then slapped his hand down with a sharp *crack!* that made Althea jump and her heart lurch. Rage rushed in behind her fear, behind her humiliation at her reaction to this savage man's intended terror.

Conyers loved evoking fear. This was as close as Althea had ever been to him since that night all those years ago in her family's cabin, but she could see it in his eyes. She'd seen it then, and she saw it again now.

Nothing gave him as much pleasure as causing others to fear him.

She was convinced he hadn't killed her that night because he'd derived too much enjoyment from seeing the horror in her eyes, after he and McGuire had killed her father then violated her mother in the marriage bed. Laughing, they'd left the cabin, but not before Conyers had pinched his hat brim to the cowering Althea, as though bidding her adieu.

Conyers ran his large, brown, scarred hand around on the zinc bar top, slowly, as though giving it a good cleaning. As he did, he studied Althea closely, but even now she thought he was looking right through her.

"Lookin' for three men," Conyers said. He had an oddly nasal, high-pitched voice that added a chilling weirdness to the smelly, roughhewn body before her. "My men. They were headed this way, lookin' for that bitch who murdered my son."

Murdered? That meant Byron Conyers had died.

"You seen 'em?" Conyers asked.

"They're upstairs."

Conyers drew his mouth-corners down and glanced at McGuire flanking him off his right shoulder. Odd, Althea thought, how McGuire didn't look much older now than he had twenty-five years ago. An oddly ageless creature, maybe just a few gray bristles in his beard, but hardly any more lines in his stupid face that owned the indifferent amber eyes of a bear.

"They was drinkin' here, then?" McGuire asked. He had an oddly lilting voice, like that of a Canadian.

Althea nodded.

"What about the woman?" Conyers asked. "Did she come here? With the boy?"

"No."

"You sure?"

"Yes."

"No, you're not." Conyers studied her, moving his head a little from side to side, frowning. It was as though he were trying to read something that was a little too far away for him to make out.

He turned his head askance, narrowed one eye, and lifted his lip in a crooked grin. "You're not all sure."

Althea tried to keep her composure. "I'm sure."

"How do you know what woman I'm talkin' about?" Conyers smiled.

"They asked about her," Althea said calmly.

Conyers widened his eyes, nodded slowly, pensively. "Ah-*huh.*" He glanced at McGuire. "First things first." Turning to Althea again, he gestured toward the stairs. "Show me where them worthless men of mine are. I'll be havin' a word with them. They was supposed to have met us at Waverly Crossing at first light."

Althea turned and walked slowly down the bar, running one hand lightly along the bar top on her right. Her heart began to slow, her tension easing.

Conyers believed her about the woman. At least, he seemed to. She glanced around the saloon quickly, making sure no sign of either the woman or the boy remained, that they hadn't dropped anything that would identify them, not even a hat pin. That much might give them away.

She stopped at the end of the bar and looked at where Conyers and his men stood where she'd left them, silhouetted against the dull gray windows behind them, watching her in menacing silence. She held her hand out toward the stairs at the back of the room.

Conyers glanced at McGuire again, in silent communication, then strode forward. McGuire followed him, saying quietly over his shoulder, "You men stay here. Stay out of the liquor. Mr. Conyers don't want no one lettin' their guard down on a job so serious as this one."

The men stayed where they were, statue still, staring at Althea and the stairs.

Althea continued to the stairs but stopped when heavy footsteps rose from the kitchen, beyond the doorway to the left of the stairs.

No, she thought. *No, Shorty. Don't come in here now.*

The kitchen door opened and Shorty, who'd been working out in his brew barn, walked into the saloon carrying a stone crock. He was smiling happily as his eyes met Althea's. "Honey, you gotta try this new batch of..."

He stopped in his tracks when, his eyes adjusting to the saloon's thick shadows, he saw the fur-clad men flanking his wife, standing there like wolves pondering prey.

Conyers and McGuire stopped behind Althea.

Conyers said with false joviality, "Well, hello there, Skinner, you old squaw dog. How you been? I hear your ale's as good as ever. Give me a minute, an' I might come down and try me a lick."

The smile faded from Shorty's face as he stared at Conyers and then at the bear-like McGuire. Slowly, he lowered the jug to his side. His mouth tightened and his eyes darkened in gradually growing anger.

When Althea had first come here to the Squaw Peak, she'd told Shorty about that night in the cabin. That's why she'd come to town, after all. She'd needed a home. She'd told Shorty why she'd so suddenly become homeless.

She'd told him *who* had made her so suddenly homeless.

Shorty hadn't taken action, of course. He and everyone else in the county, including the county sheriff, knew you didn't take action against the Jinglebob. Not if you wanted to remain on this side of the sod. Unwitting U.S. marshals had gone out there, investigating the murders of so-called squatters, and were never heard from again.

Shorty stood gazing, red-faced in his helpless frustration, at the savage Conyers and his equally savage segundo, Loco McGuire, who slitted a smile.

"It's all right, Shorty," Althea said, holding her hands palm out toward her husband. "They just want to see their men."

"Yeah, it's all right, Shorty," Conyers said, again pitching his voice with phony joviality. "We just wanna go up an' roust our men, is all. Them brush-poppin' scoundrels went an' got drunk on me. Must be sleepin' off some mighty sore heads...instead of meetin' the rest of us at the stage station at Waverly Crossing last night, an' never showed. Here they were, stompin' with their tails up."

His face suddenly clouded over like the changeable Montana sky itself. He gritted the cracked ivory-yellow stubs of his worn-down teeth. "While my boy is lyin' cold in his grave, gutted like a damn fish."

Althea's spine turned to ice. She looked down, drew a deep, calming breath.

Something bad was going to happen. Something very bad. It was as certain as the screams of her mother and father echoing in her haunted mind.

"Let's go, Squaw," Conyers said, giving Althea a hard shove toward the stairs. "Time's a wastin', now, hang it!"

Chapter Fourteen

As she climbed the stairs, Althea cast a look back over her shoulder.

She and Shorty held each other's foreboding gazes for several seconds, Shorty's eyes rising as Althea rose up the stairs to the second story. She sought comfort and reassurance from her husband's gaze, but all she found was a cold fear like her own.

She turned her head forward as she approached the landing, then crossed the landing and kept climbing, hearing the thuds of the two men behind her, hearing the faint wheezing of Conyers' strained breaths, smelling the old buffalo-robe and chewing-tobacco stench of the man.

The rickety stairs creaked and pitched.

Althea stopped in the dim hall outside the room to which she'd let Nordekker and the other two Jinglebob men. Beyond the door rose a barrage of raucous snoring.

"Stay back," Conyers told Althea.

As she stepped back and pressed herself against the wall, Conyers looked at McGuire, who gave a short nod. Conyers closed his hand around the door knob, turned it, thrust the door open, and stepped into the room. As he did, McGuire leaned a thick shoulder against the door frame and crossed one fur boot in front of the other. He lifted his hat from his head, ran a gloved hand through his long, black hair that had a few more gray strands than Althea had thought, then returned the hat to his head.

Althea peered around McGuire into the room. Two men lay on the bed—one belly-down, the other on his side. Another lay on the straw pallet on the floor to the right of the bed, covered with several blankets. Judging by his small size, that would be the youngest one, Willie.

Conyers stood at the foot of the bed, staring down at the two sleeping men before him. Althea stepped to one side, to better see around McGuire, even though most of her didn't want to.

Conyers didn't say anything but just stared down in silence at the two men snoring on the bed, sound asleep beneath quilts and blankets. The smell drifting out of the room was rife with the fetor of whiskey, sweat and several other unpleasing male aromas.

When Althea saw Conyers move his right hand to the pistol on his right hip, and slide the gun from its holster, a shallow breath rattled across her vocal chords. Conyers raised the pistol, slanting the barrel toward the ceiling, and loudly clicked the hammer back.

Nordekker groaned and stopped snoring.

The man lying next to him, Big Mike, waved a big hand in front of his face as though to shoo away a fly. "Go...go way!"

Nordekker opened his eyes to slits and stared up at the rancher, blinking. When he realized who he was staring at, and who was staring down at him with a cocked pistol in his hand, Nordekker widened his eyes in shock. He gulped.

"B-B-B-*Boss?*"

Conyers said, "My boy wasn't even cold in his grave, and you two were drinkin' an' carryin' on instead of lookin' for his killer."

The other two began stirring now, as well, Big Mike quickly rolling onto his back, an expression like Nordekker's on his rawboned, ginger-bearded face. Willie lifted his head from his pallet with a startled cry, eyes bright with fear.

Slowly, awfully, Nordekker raised his hands, palms forward. "Hold on, now, boss...!"

"You hold this."

Conyers extended the pistol straight out from his shoulder.

All three men screamed, Nordekker shouting, "No, boss...no...*noooo!*"

The last "no" was partly drowned by the crashing report of Conyers' Colt.

Peering around the left side of Loco McGuire, Althea saw the bullet punch a hole in Nordekker's forehead, painting the plain pine planks behind him dark red.

"No, Mr. Conyers!" Big Mike cried. "Please, Mr. Con—"

The Colt spoke again, and Big Mike flopped back against the bed. Conyers fired two more bullets into the man's writhing body, making the bed pitch like a small boat on choppy seas.

Willie howled as he gained his feet, clad in only his wash-worn longhandles. Conyers slid the Colt toward the small redhead and fired.

Willie screamed and flopped back against the wall. Screaming, he bolted forward and rushed past Conyers in a full sprint. Just before Willie reached the door in which McGuire still stood casually, apparently amused by the entertainment, Conyers wheeled and shot Willie in the back.

McGuire stepped to one side as Willie ran through the door and into the hall, his pale face a mask of terror and misery, blood pumping from three holes in his chest. He dropped to the floor just outside the bedroom door and rolled toward Althea, who had pushed herself taut against the wall, trying to make herself as small as possible, ears ringing from the pistol blasts.

Willie wailed and rolled onto his back. He stared up at Althea, placed a bloody hand on her leg, and cried, *"Help me!"*

Another crashing report knocked Althea back against the wall.

Willie yelped as another bullet slammed into his back. Slowly, his hand slid down Althea's leg to the floor.

Shorty's voice thundered up from below: *"Althea?"*

Althea trembled. As she looked at both Conyers and Loco McGuire standing before her, she turned her head to yell, "I'm all right, Shorty! Stay there!"

"There," Conyers said, scowling down in disdain at the dead Willie. "That takes care of them gutless curs. Serve as an example to the others. When I say no drinkin', I mean *no drinkin'*, by god…"

He turned to stare down the hall. Several doors had opened, and the drawn, startled faces of the Squaw Peak's overnight guests stared out into the hall now hazy with the gray of billowing powder smoke. When Conyers' turned to the guests, doors slammed abruptly.

Conyers glanced at Althea. "She here?"

The Indian woman drew a breath, shook her head.

"She *here?*" Conyers bellowed. "She is, ain't she? This is the only place she *could* be!"

Althea stood with her back tight to the wall, eyes closed, slowly shaking her head.

Conyers glanced at McGuire. "Help me here, Loco."

Both men walked down the hall. Conyers kicked open the doors on the hall's left side. He didn't need to kick them in. None were locked. He kicked them in anyway, as Loco McGuire kicked open the doors on the hall's right side. As they busted into the rooms, the men inside the three occupied rooms yelled brusque responses to the shouted question: *"She here? She here?"*

"Hell, no!"

When Conyers and McGuire had made it to the hall's end, they turned to face each other in silent discussion, then stomped back to Althea. They were breathing hard. McGuire wore a grim smile on his amber-eyed, black-bearded face. The tall, stooped Conyers was grim, his eyes cold and dark.

He grabbed Althea's arm and squeezed painfully. "Come with us, Squaw!"

Althea cried out as he jerked her along behind

him. He, Althea, and McGuire descended the stairs to the second story. When they gained the landing, Althea saw Shorty standing near where he'd been standing before, staring up at her in mute terror.

Conyers' other men stood closely around him, hands on their gun butts. Shorty had a shotgun behind the bar, but he'd never make it...

"Wait here!" Conyers shoved Althea against the wall.

He and McGuire went down the hall as they'd done on the third floor, kicking in doors and yelling, *"Where is that murderin' she-devil?"* or *"Where is she, dammit?"* Althea felt the reverberations of the men's violent thunder through the wall against her back. The Squaw Peak's lone whore screamed when Conyers kicked open her door. When the rancher had scoured the doxie's room, he stomped out and continued to the next one, leaving the whore sobbing in the room behind him, terrified.

Althea stood holding her breath as the two men made their way down the hall. She hadn't put any lodgers except Stillman and Mrs. Coulter and the boy in any of the rooms on this floor, so Conyers and McGuire were finding only empty rooms. Althea hoped, prayed, that when Conyers reached the last room on the hall's left side, he would find nothing to indicate the woman and the boy had been in there.

Althea had scoured the room. She'd even made up the bed. She'd made sure no trace of either Mrs. Coulter or the boy remained.

Still, her heart lodged in her throat.

It edged a little higher when Conyers kicked the door in.

Althea pressed her back tighter against the wall. Her heart thudded in her ears as Conyers stomped around in the woman's room. McGuire stepped out of the room on the opposite side of the hall from the one in which the boy and the woman had stayed last night. He stood staring into that room.

Conyers had fallen silent. No sounds issued from the room. Still, Conyers did not emerge.

He'd found something...

Althea had no idea what he could have found. She'd scoured the room herself, finding nothing.

Her heart kicked when Conyers emerged from the room and stopped just outside the open doorway. He held a pillow in his hands. He looked at McGuire regarding him darkly, that grim smile still on the *segundo's* lips. Conyers turned toward Althea. He raised the pillow to his face and took a deep sniff.

A cold, sharp-edged spur rowel of dread dropped in Althea's belly.

Conyers lowered the pillow, opened his eyes to look at Althea again, and then slowly exhaled, his shoulders drawing down as he did. "She's been here." He raised the pillow again, gave it a shake. "That's woman-smell. Not a man smell. Not a cheap whore's smell. That there's the smell of a *refined* woman."

He dropped the pillow to the floor, kicked it aside, and strode slowly toward Althea. He was like a human thunder cloud moving toward her, dark with danger. Her mind froze with terror. She remembered that horrific night so long ago, and suddenly it didn't seem long ago anymore. She had the cold, dark feeling she was about to relive it, and that it would turn out even worse this time.

Conyers grabbed her arm. "This way, Squaw!" Althea cried out in pain as he pulled her toward the stairs and then led her quickly down to the first floor where Shorty stood as before, eyes wide and glassy with worry.

He grunted and stepped toward her.

"No, Shorty! Stay there!" Althea moved her feet as quickly as possible beneath the hem of her plain, burlap dress, so she wouldn't fall.

"Come on, Shorty," Conyers said when he and Althea gained the first floor. He flung Althea into a chair at a near table. She nearly fell over backwards in the chair, but quickly grabbed the table for balance.

Conyers turned to Shorty and beckoned broadly with one arm. "Come on over here, Shorty. Bring the jug, you sawed-off little son of a buck. Let's taste that new brew of yours…and have us a powwow."

Conyers sat at the far end of the table. Althea was on his right, on Shorty's left. Shorty stood staring at the man, frozen in place. Loco Mc-Guire moved down the stairs then stood beside Shorty, and placed a hand against the back of Shorty's neck, squeezing until Shorty winced and glowered up at the killer.

"Leave him alone!" Althea cried. "Leave Shorty alone. He didn't do anything to you, Conyers!"

"Leave him alone?" Conyers stared at her with a look of mock astonishment. "Why, I ain't done nothin' to the man but ask him to sit down an' have a drink with me." Turning to Shorty, he said, "Come on over here, you old squaw dog. Bring the jug. Let's have us a drink and a palaver here with your squaw."

Chapter Fifteen

Althea looked at Shorty.

Shorty looked back at her.

Enraged, Conyers slapped his hand on the table—hard. "I said, fetch the jug an' let's palaver over here with your squaw, Shorty!"

Althea gasped at the man's sudden fury, and jerked back in her chair, again almost knocking it over.

Shorty swung around and grabbed the jug off the bar. He slammed the jug down on the table. "There's the damn jug!"

Conyers arched his brows in mock shock. "Shorty, you raised your voice to me!"

Behind Shorty, Loco McGuire chuckled.

Shorty leaned forward, his fists on the table. He glared at the old rancher, red-faced with his own fury.

"What?" Conyers asked. "No glasses? Were you raised by wolves, Shorty?"

Shorty didn't move. Althea sensed the rage in her husband. She also sensed that if he didn't check it soon, it would get him killed. She hadn't realized it before now, but she loved this squat old man. He'd taken her in. Yes, he'd put her to work upstairs, but he'd taken her in when no one else would have taken in a plump, plain-faced, sixteen-year-old half-breed girl.

He'd started out treating her like a daughter. Later, like a husband. A very kindly, respectful older husband...

"I ain't here to serve you, Conyers," Shorty said tightly, his nostrils swelling. "You come in here and throw your weight around, abuse my wife, kick in my doors, disturb my guests..."

Keeping his mild, vaguely amused gaze on Shorty, Conyers said, "Loco, fetch three glasses from the bar—would you, please? Obviously, Shorty here was raised by wolves."

McGuire gave a wry snort then walked around behind the bar. A few seconds later, he returned to the table holding three dimpled beer schooners. He set them down on the table.

"Do the honors, will you?" Conyers asked, glancing at the crock jug.

"Be my pleasure, boss." McGuire yanked the cork out of the crock's mouth and slowly filled the three glasses with the dark ale, building a nice, thick milky head on the butterscotch surface. McGuire slid a glass over to his boss. He set one in front of Shorty, the other in front of Althea.

"There...that's the stuff." Conyers lifted the ale to his nose, sniffed it. He glanced up at Shorty, who still glowered down at him. Conyers frowned with mild reproof and said, "Have a seat, Shorty. We can't have a proper palaver with you standin' up an' me an' your lovely squaw here sittin' down."

Shorty drew a deep breath, keeping his angry gaze on the rancher.

Althea slid a chair out beside her with her foot. "Sit down, Shorty."

Shorty let out his breath and plopped into the chair. He leaned back and folded his thick arms on his broad chest, continuing to glare at the rancher, who seemed impervious to Shorty's disdain. Or more amused than offended by it.

Conyers tipped the glass to his lips and took a couple of large gulps. He set the glass down, the froth running down the inside of it, and smacked his lips. "That's the stuff! Now, that's the stuff! Shorty, I done forgot how good you was at brewin' beer!" He licked his lips again and slapped his hand down on the table, making Althea jerk with another start. "Damn righteous ale!"

He glanced at the eight other men forming a ragged semi-circle between him and the door. "Fellas, I'm sorry you're on duty and can't try this. You'll have to come to Hobbs on a day off and indulge yourselves. You will not regret it—no, sir!"

They all just stared, dark-eyed, blank-faced, like wolves at the edge of firelight.

"I for one am gonna do just that," McGuire said, standing a few feet behind Shorty, his hands resting on his pistols' grips. "Next day off…"

"You'll be well rewarded for the ride," Conyers assured his *segundo.*

Conyers took another big drink of the beer, set his glass back down on the table, swallowed, and glanced at Althea and then at Shorty. "Ain't you two gonna try it? It's every bit as good as you thought it would be, Shorty. Go on—have you a sip. No? Well…okay, then."

The rancher reached behind his back and set a horn-gripped Bowie knife on the table beside his glass. "Since your thirst seems to have dried up, let's get down to business."

Althea looked at the Bowie. It was as long as her forearm and as wide as one of Shorty's. She could see the razor edge, the wickedly upturned tip that resembled an eagle's beak, fashioned for cutting and tearing. The blade glistened like newly polished nickel in the gray light from the windows.

Althea shuddered.

He's going to kill us, she thought. If there had been any doubt since the moment he and Loco McGuire walked in here, there wasn't now. She looked at Shorty and sucked back a sob. She wasn't as sad for herself as for Shorty—a good man if there ever was one. He didn't deserve this. Althea had been the one who'd convinced him to let the woman and the boy stay...

Conyers looked pointedly at Althea. "Where is she?"

Althea just stared at him. Fear...terror...was a wild horse inside her.

Conyers said, "I'm gonna ask you one more time, real polite-like—where is she an' that heathen dog of hers?"

Althea looked at Shorty. Shorty looked back at her. It was hard to read what he was thinking but not what he was feeling. Her husband's terror was as poignant as her own. He was more terrified for her than for himself, she knew. Just as she was more frightened for him than herself.

Shorty leaned forward and looked sharply at Conyers. "Get out of my saloon, Mister. You got no right to come in here and..."

He let his voice trail off as Conyers slid the knife across the table, to the far end. It slid past Shorty's right arm.

Conyers looked at Loco McGuire. "Loco, pick up that Bowie."

"You got it, boss." McGuire picked up the knife, ran his thumb across the blade. "Ouch—*sharp!*" He chuckled.

He stepped behind Shorty, holding the knife up so that the blade glinted in the gray light from the window. He grinned menacingly down at the stocky man in the chair before him.

Conyers turned to Althea. "Where's the woman?"

Althea glanced at Shorty.

Sweat had broken out across Shorty's broad forehead. His eyes were adamant, however. He shook his head. "Don't tell him."

Conyers sighed, glanced up at McGuire. "Loco, cut his left ear off."

"No!" Althea cried, lurching to her feet.

Laughing, McGuire shoved Shorty's head down on the table. Holding the man's head against the table with one hand, he slid the knife to Shorty's left ear.

"No!" Althea cried again, throwing herself at McGuire.

Laughing, he gave her a hard shove. His greater strength sent Althea falling back into her chair and then tumbling over backward, hitting the hardwood floor with a groan. She looked up in horror as McGuire again lowered the knife to Shorty's ear, setting the razor edge against the back of it.

Shorty tried to struggle, grunting, but McGuire held him down hard against the table.

Someone loudly pumped a cartridge into a rifle's action. The tooth-gnashing sound cut through the saloon like a sharp knife through warm flesh.

Silence fell.

Still lying against the floor, Althea turned her head to the right. Ben Stillman stood in the shadows near the bottom of the staircase, aiming his Henry rifle straight out from his right shoulder at Loco McGuire.

McGuire had turned to Stillman, as did every other man in the saloon.

"If you don't want a bullet cored through your crazy brain, Loco," Stillman chewed out, his teeth showing white beneath his thick, salt-and-pepper mustache, "drop that knife and step away from Mr. Skinner. Nice an' easy."

"Stillman," Loco said, keeping Shorty's head pressed against the table, the knife edge taut against the back of the saloon-keeper's left ear. "Well, well..."

"Do it."

"Suppose I don't?"

The rifle roared. Flames stabbed from the barrel.

McGuire lurched away from Shorty, wheeling and dropping the knife and holding a hand to his left ear. The tall killer stood facing the bar now, his back to Shorty, pressing his hand against his ear and glaring fiercely at Stillman, who again pumped a cartridge into the Henry's chamber.

The spent cartridge clanked onto the floor and rolled against the staircase.

"God *damn* you!" Loco bellowed, his voice taut with pain.

"You asked me a question," Stillman said, reasonably, aiming down the rifle again at McGuire. "I answered it."

McGuire groaned in misery, stomped a boot on the floor, and stretched his lips back from his teeth as he glared at the lawman. "God *damn* you!"

Stillman raised his voice to the others in the room. "Anyone else have a question?"

Althea had pushed up onto her elbows. She looked around in shock and surprise. That appeared to be what Conyers' men were feeling, as well. Shorty was hipped around in his chair, looking at the man who had just spared his ear. Everyone in the room stared in hushed silence at the tall lawman in the buckskin coat and gray Stetson, aiming down the barrel of the Henry repeater.

"Stillman, eh?" Conyers said, still sitting in his chair at the table. He was the only one who looked at ease. "That'd be Ben Stillman, then?"

Stillman had never met Conyers, though he'd have liked to. Especially if meeting him would have meant throwing him behind bars or leading him to a gallows. He knew the rancher by his outlaw reputation only. Conyers had come into the country only after the drunk whore had drilled a bullet into Stillman's back, taking him out of commission for a few years.

Stillman said, "I want you fellas to drop your gun rigs. Unbuckle your belts and drop 'em to the floor. Nice an' slow. Anyone gets in a hurry, you'll get worse than what Loco got."

Suddenly fiery, Conyers heaved himself to his feet and thrust his arm and index finger forward, gritting his teeth. "You go to hell, Stillman! This ain't none of your affair!"

Stillman swung the rifle toward the rancher, narrowing one eye as he lined up his sights on Conyers' forehead. He gave a little inward smile when he saw fear pass over the rancher's gaze, making the corners of his eyes twitch.

"Have your men unheel themselves, Conyers, or the next bullet goes through your head."

Conyers studied Stillman skeptically. Calling Stillman's bluff—he sensed that the legendary lawman wouldn't shoot him in cold blood—he smiled crookedly and said, "Fellas, a thousand dollars to the first man who kills this badge-toting son of a goat!"

Stillman slid his rifle back to cover the men standing in a ragged semi-circle fifteen to twenty feet away from him. They were silhouetted against the windows behind them. That wasn't good. At least the sun wasn't shining. Stillman could see them well enough. If any one of the eight so much as flinched, he'd turn him toe-down.

He stared down the Henry's barrel, threatening the room with his flinty stare.

Shorty sat in his chair just ahead of Stillman and on his hard left, six feet away. Althea still lay on the floor, leaning back against her elbows. She and Shorty stared at Stillman, their eyes glazed with shock and cold foreboding.

Loco McGuire stood eight feet away from Stillman, between the sheriff and Conyers' other men. He stared at Stillman with pain in his eyes. Pain mixed with bald rage. Like the others, he wanted to draw his gun, but his gun was under his coat. The only man in the room wearing his guns on the outside of his coat was Conyers.

Some had their coats open, guns exposed. The others would have to dig. And, digging, they would die.

Their wary gazes told Stillman they knew their chances. Still, they were considering their boss's offer. The last thing you wanted to be known as by a boss like John Conyers was a coward. All it would take was one foolish man standing before Stillman to dig for his iron. The others would use that fool's move as a diversion, and dig for their own, and then Stillman would have a firefight on his hands...

That's what happened five seconds later.

A man standing behind Loco McGuire must have thought McGuire blocked Stillman's view of him, for with one hand he reached inside the coat he'd unbuttoned. He was smooth. Stillman didn't detect the move until the man was pulling his gun out of his coat.

Then the Henry roared.

His target screamed and flew backward.

As he did, several others went digging...and dying.

Stillman's sixteen-shot Henry had been fully loaded when he'd entered the saloon from the back door. Now the rifle leaped and roared in Stillman's hands, the spent cartridges arcing over his right shoulder as he pumped the next fresh round into the chamber and dropped the hammer.

Blast after blast crashed around the room.

There was a slight pause as Stillman tried to pick out his next target through the powder smoke billowing in the saloon's heavy shadows. By now, all of Conyers' men were scrambling for cover and digging for iron. A small man beside the bar was aiming his Colt when Stillman planted a hasty bead on him.

Bang!

Two guns flashed in the shadows ahead of Stillman.

Stillman dropped to a knee and silenced both shooters, flipping one backward over a table and throwing the other against the left wall where, yowling and writhing, he triggered a final round into the ceiling before sliding down the wall, dropping to his knees, and falling face down on the floor.

A great bear-like roar sounded from ahead and on Stillman's left. He glanced that way to see John Conyers pushing over his table then dropping to his knees behind it, clawing a pistol from the holster on his right hip and aiming the revolver over the edge of the table.

Stillman cocked the Henry again and fired.

Conyers grunted and triggered his Colt wide, the bullet chunking into the bar behind Stillman. Conyers pulled his head down behind the table. Stillman fired three more rounds into the underside of the table.

Conyers gave a shrill curse then heaved himself to his feet, lifting the table up in front of him. Bellowing like an enraged grizzly, he ran toward Stillman, shoving the table out in front of him so Stillman could see only the man's wild-eyed face above it. Stillman tried to rack another cartridge into the Henry's breech only to find that he'd popped all his caps.

The rifle was bone dry.

He didn't have time to reach for his own Colt before Conyers rammed the table full into him. Stillman hadn't had time to set his boots, and Conyers and the table knocked him backwards.

He fell hard on his back, losing his hat and dropping the Henry, bells tolling in his ears. Still raging, Conyers lifted his head over the edge of the table, and then he raised his second gun as well. He cocked the big piece and started to aim it down at Stillman, who lay flat and helpless beneath him, his arms pinned against the floor.

The lawman felt the devil reach up to tickle his toes.

Conyers had just aimed the Colt at Stillman's forehead when the rancher's head jerked backward suddenly. Stillman stared up in surprise as Althea, crouched over the rancher from behind, lowered the man's big Bowie knife and raked the razor-edged blade across Conyers' throat.

Horror glazed Conyers' eyes. He dropped his gun. He screamed—or tried to. The yell was drowned by blood. Conyers slid off the table to the floor, clutching his laid-open neck as though trying to hold the blood in.

To no avail.

The thick, dark-red fluid bubbled up between his fingers. He lay gasping and kicking as he died. Staring up at Althea standing over him, the bloody knife still in her right hand, he kicked for nearly a minute, turning almost a complete circle there on the blood-washed floor.

"Die, you devil!" Althea cried, bent forward at the waist. "That's for my family! *Die, you devil! Die, die, die!"*

Conyers tried to speak, but only gulps and wheezes issued out with the blood dribbling from between his lips. Gradually, his body relaxed. His hands dropped from his throat to lie in the growing blood pool beneath him.

He gave one last jerk, blinked, opened his eyes, and wheezed out one last breath.

His eyes, raised to the ceiling, grew opaque as isinglass.

Chapter Sixteen

Stillman slid away from the pool of blood widening from John Conyers' bloody carcass.

With a weary grunt, his head still aching from its meeting with the floor, he climbed to his knees. He pushed off one knee and heaved himself to his feet, wincing as his joints popped.

Like the ground, floors had become harder over the years.

He looked at the Jinglebob men lying in bloody piles between him and the front door. None was moving. He slid his gaze back to where Shorty had thrown himself to the floor when the shooting had first erupted. The saloonkeeper had draped himself over Althea, to shield her from a bullet. Althea had climbed out from beneath him to grab the Bowie knife off the floor and cut John Conyers' throat like that of a Thanksgiving hog.

Stillman looked at her. She still stared at

Conyers. Tears dribbled down her cheeks. He remembered what she'd said as she'd watch the devil die. "That's for my family!"

Stillman walked over and took the Bowie knife out of Althea's hand. She looked up at him, her eyes glistened with tears.

"Thanks," Stillman said. He tossed the knife away and raised his hand to slide a crow's wing of his mussed hair back off his forehead.

"Thank *you*, Ben." Shorty had gained his feet and now stood beside Althea, wrapping a thick arm around her shoulders. "Where, uh...where'd you come from, anyways?"

"I glassed the town from a ridge, saw those wolves heading for the saloon, and thought I'd best head back and give you a hand. I had a feelin' Conyers would know Mrs. Coulter had been here. It was the most likely place for her to come. The only place."

He crouched to pluck his hat from the floor. He brushed dust off it, set it on his head. "I figured he'd make you two pay for giving her shelter."

"Sure glad you came back," Shorty said, looking around. "Sure glad you came back."

Peering into the shadows toward the front of the saloon, Stillman frowned. He looked to his left, then to his right. He looked behind him and then he walked several feet along the bar toward the front door.

"What is it?" Althea asked.

Continuing to look around at the dead men strewn around the room, lying in bloody stacks, Stillman said, "I don't see McGuire."

Shorty and Althea cast their gazes around the room.

Stillman wheeled and walked to the front of the Squaw Peak. He pushed out through the front door and onto the boardwalk. He quickly counted the horses tied to the two hitch racks before him, and came up with eight.

One shy of nine.

"He done rode out like a bat outta hell, Loco did..."

Stillman looked at the man standing on the boardwalk fronting the feed store nearly directly across the street. He had a broom in his hand, and he wore an apron around his waist.

He turned to his left, lifting his left hand to point toward the southeast. Stillman turned his head to follow the man's pointing finger to a low, snow-mantled ridge humping a half-mile from Hobbs. As he did, a horse and rider galloped around a pine-studded, snow-dusted knob of granite rising from atop the ridge, and disappeared.

The shopkeeper turned to Stillman, his eyes dark. "Loco McGuire."

Stillman let out a long, wary breath. "I know."

The shopkeeper shook his head and, as he turned toward the open door of his shop, said, "That's one crazy killer..."

He walked inside and closed the door behind him.

"I know." Stillman went back into the Squaw Peak. Shorty stood at the near end of the bar. "He get away?"

Stillman nodded. "He might be back..."

"I'd love that." Shorty raised the long, double-barreled twelve-gauge he was holding in his hands. "Purely I would."

"I would, too." Althea rose from where she'd been kneeling by one of the dead Jinglebob riders. She'd picked up the man's blood-splashed Smith & Wesson New Model 3, broke it open to make sure it was loaded, then snapped it closed. "We might as well finish off the entire pack."

Stillman nodded grimly, glanced around the room. "Can you two take of the mess on your own? I need to get back to my prisoner and Mrs. Coulter. I think Ace's gang might be lookin' for him. No tellin' what Loco might do."

"We got it, Ben."

Stillman began striding toward the back of the room. "I'll send a full report to the county sheriff as soon as I get back to Clantick."

"Buck Reno ain't gonna like it one bit," Shorty called. "He was deep in Conyers' hip pocket!"

Stillman moved out through the back door. Sweets stood where Stillman had ground-reined him. Stillman looked around once more, cautiously. Being involved in two separate lead swaps before noon served to make even an experienced frontier lawman a mite jumpy.

As far as he could tell, there was no one on the lurk out here.

He swung into the saddle and glanced at the sky. The low clouds were breaking up, and a mild breeze was blowing. A Chinook was moving in from over the Highwood Mountains to the west, as they often did this time of year following a squall.

The temperature was still below freezing, but it would climb fast. Stillman knew the warm winds gracing this mountain-studded Great Plains area well enough to know the snow would probably be gone by the end of the day. He'd probably shed his buckskin by noon.

He reined Sweets around, booted the horse south behind the main street business buildings. At the end of town, he turned right, crossing the main trail that became the main street a hundred yards behind him now, and headed southwest toward a jog of buttes rising in the middle distance.

He'd left Ace, Mrs. Coulter, and the boy in a gap between two of those bluffs. He hadn't wanted to do it. Especially knowing that at least some of Ace's gang, apparently having evaded the Winifred posse, were on the scout for him. Like the Jinglebob men who'd split up to search for Mrs. Coulter, Ace's gang must have done the same as they'd searched for one of their own who'd absconded with the loot.

Apprehension touched Stillman now as he loped Sweets through the brome and wheat grass poking up through the snow like blond beard stubble through shaving cream. He'd tied Ace securely, but he'd left the money with the woman. He didn't know Mrs. Coulter. He'd sensed she was the honest, upstanding sort. Still, thirty-four thousand dollars to a woman in her desperate situation was a lot of money to resist.

He rode to the top of one bluff and loped across the cedar-studded crest. He dropped down the far side, weaving through pines and cedars and then booted Sweets into a grove of winter-naked aspens at the bottom. He drew back on the horse's reins, looked around, frowning, his heart quickening.

He could see their tracks in the snow, but they were not here. Their horses were gone. So was were the saddlebags containing the loot.

Stillman cursed, neck-reined Sweets around sharply, looking for the trail they'd taken out of...
No. Wait.

Relief touched him.

This was the first place he'd checked out before deciding it was too exposed. He'd left them farther west, in another crease between bluffs.

He booted Sweets into a gallop, followed a dogleg in the crease, leaped a half-frozen spring run-out, then put the horse into a thick stand of pines peppered with wagon-sized boulders. He smelled the smoke of a cook fire and followed it.

After several more yards, he saw the smoke and the low flames over which his coffee pot hung from his iron tripod. The saddlebags containing the money leaned against a pine near Ace. Stillman hadn't taken the saddlebags with him, because he knew he'd make better time without them, and he'd preferred to trust the three people here than those, most of whom he no longer knew, in town.

The woman and the boy sat huddled together on a blow down pine, to the left of the fire. Ace Darden sat against an aspen to the right. Stillman had left him cuffed and shackled and tied to the aspen with several rounds of hemp. All three watched Stillman enter the slight clearing, which was well protected by rocks and trees. The smoke from the fire was well-filtered by high branches.

The lawman halted Sweets, swung down from the saddle, and dropped his reins.

His relief at finding them here must have shone in his eyes, for Mrs. Coulter regarded him critically, gave an ironic half-smile. "You're surprised we didn't light out for Mexico, Sheriff? Us…" She glanced at the loot. "And the money?"

"It crossed my mind." Stillman walked over to the fire, his shoulders slumped with chagrin. "I apologize, Mrs. Coulter."

"Not at all. I know how the world works. No one can be trusted." She was holding a cup of coffee in her own, mittened hands. Now she sipped it, swallowed, then smiled at Stillman with cold shrewdness. "I'm a desperate woman. On the run with my Indian boy. Homeless. Why wouldn't I think about it?" She shrugged, smiled again, this time with phony chagrin. "In fact, I did. For a few fleeting seconds."

"I don't blame you…under the circumstances. You can stay in Hobbs, if you like, Mrs. Coulter." Stillman poured himself a cup of coffee and glanced over the flames at her. "Conyers is dead."

She raised her brows, impressed. She glanced at the hard bulge beneath his coat, over his left hip. "You must be fast."

"It wasn't their day."

"You took down all those men?" the boy, Daniel, asked. Those were the first words Stillman had heard him speak. He had large brown eyes in a broad, sharply defined face with high, flat cheekbones, a firm broad nose, and resolute chin. Once he grew into his buckteeth, he'd make a handsome man.

"I got lucky, sprout."

Daniel looked up at his mother, who kept her own eyes on Stillman. "You wear your reputation well, Sheriff."

"I told her about you." Ace smiled at Stillman. Oddly, it was a proud smile. "I told her about your younger years. She seemed a mite worried you wouldn't make it out of Hobbs alive." He glanced at Mrs. Coulter. "I told her she had nothin' to worry about."

She turned to Ace. "You weren't worried, though—were you, Mr. Darden?"

Ace compressed one corner of his mouth and shrugged.

Mrs. Coulter turned back to Stillman. "He tried to convince me to untie him."

Stillman chuckled and looked at his one-time friend. "I'd have been surprised if he hadn't."

"He was gonna split the loot with us," Daniel added. His mood had picked up from before. Now he seemed to be enjoying the adventure. "He said we'd split it three ways. I'd get a full third—a man's cut!"

"A man's cut, eh?" Stillman slid his ironic gaze back to Ace. "Leave it to Ace."

"I had to try, Ben."

Stillman blew on his coffee, took another sip. "You keep tryin', Ace. I'll worry when you stop." He turned to Mrs. Coulter. "Loco McGuire got away. He's wounded."

She looked down pensively, then sipped her coffee and returned her gaze to Stillman. "I couldn't return to my saloon even if I wanted to."

"I know they burned it down, but..."

Mrs. Coulter shook her head. "I'm not staying here. I'm not rebuilding. There's nothing for me here. I'd rather take my chances with you, Sher-iff."

Stillman pondered on that. "There's no man, I take it," he asked a little guiltily, hesitant to probe.

"Not anymore. He was a good man. A Pres-byterian minister. Jedediah Coulter. A dashing, red-haired, pious Irish preacher. A warm, friend-ly, genteel man. One of a kind, really." She smiled with warm remembering into her coffee cup. "He came west to spread the gospel to the frontier."

"I'm sorry," Stillman said. "He's passed, I take it?"

She looked at Stillman through the steam rising from her cup. "After service one Sunday, Jedediah was in his office at the church, counting the money from the collection plates. I'd gone home to prepare Sunday dinner. Just as Jedediah was finishing up in his office, two men entered the church and shot him.

"They took the twelve dollars and sixty-seven cents he'd placed in an envelope to be deposited in the bank on Monday morning. They left my beloved husband to die slowly, choking on his own blood. When he didn't come home, I got concerned, hitched the buggy, and drove over to the church. I held him in my arms as he breathed out his last. We prayed together."

Stillman stared at her, surprised by her relative composure. She still smiled into her cup, though the expression was decidedly tighter than before. Bittersweet. Sitting beside her, the boy stood gazing up at her, wide-eyed, his large front teeth poking out from beneath his thick upper lip.

She had one arm around the child, and now she drew him tighter against her. She lifted her clear-eyed, emotionless gaze to Stillman once more. "Don't worry—this is not the first time Daniel has heard this sorry tale. He knows what happened." She looked at the boy huddled up close against her. "He's old enough to know the world is a savage place. By knowing, he'll be all the better prepared to steel himself against it."

She shook him gently. "Right? Won't you, boy?" She pressed her lips to his forehead.

Daniel nodded.

"What's your tribe, son?" Ace asked.

"Blackfoot," Daniel said clearly, with pride. "My ma was half. My pa was full."

Ace smiled and said something in the Blackfoot tongue. Stillman knew enough of the language to know that Ace had asked the boy his age. When the boy started to respond, Mrs. Coulter drew him to her again, hard, with a not-so-subtle reprimand. "You know better, Daniel!"

Ace frowned with incredulity.

So did Stillman.

"His mother taught him the tongue of his people, but I forbid him to use it," Mrs. Coulter explained harshly, holding the boy tight against her, as though protecting him from a physical attack. "I want him to forget every word he learned. Using it would only get him killed." Again, she pressed her lips to the boy's temple—a gesture of both affection and remonstration.

Stillman sipped his coffee. "How did the boy come to be in your charge, Mrs. Coulter?"

"His mother was a whore." The woman drew a deep breath, as though steeling herself against the world's many crimes. She shook loose tendrils of her dark-red hair back from her freckled forehead. "She died when Daniel was seven. He's ten, almost eleven now, but small for his age. Jedediah and I adopted him. We couldn't have any children of our own, as I am barren. But we were more than happy to take Daniel—his name was Three Crows Dancing, but we changed it—into our home and raise him as one of us."

She smiled down at the boy, whose head now rested in her lap, his eyes open, staring at the fire. Almost as though to herself, she said, "I do believe I love this child more than I would have loved one of my own." She smiled and gave the boy's shoulder an affectionate squeeze. "I'll never let anything bad happen to you, my son."

Daniel's expression didn't change. He stared innocently, obliviously, into the fire.

Behind Stillman, Sweets whickered softly. Stillman had opened his coat. Now, dropping his coffee cup, he reached into his coat and shucked his gun from the cross-draw holster on his hip and cocked it.

Stillman glanced over his shoulder. Sweets stood with his head raised, working his nostrils, twitching his ears.

Stillman looked around, trying to scent what the horse scented.

"What is it?" Mrs. Coulter asked quietly.

Stillman rose slowly, looking around.

Ace looked warily up at him. "Loco, you think?"

"I don't know." Stillman kicked dirt on the fire. "Let's get mounted."

Chapter Seventeen

Stillman took a quick look around the camp.

He stirred up nothing more frightening than a couple of squirrels giving him hell from pine boughs. At least, he hoped he was the only one they were giving hell to.

Sweets had spooked at something. The bay was too smart a horse to spook at squirrels. He'd smelled something more dangerous. How far away the danger was, however, was hard to say.

Stillman returned to camp. Ignoring Ace's urgings that he be untied from his tree, Stillman saddled Ace and the woman's horses. He kept his prisoner bound to the tree so he wouldn't have to keep an eye on him while also watching for Loco McGuire or possibly one of Darden's own fellow owlhoots.

He led both horses into the camp. When he'd helped the woman and the boy onto their own mount, Stillman untied Ace and freed his ankles. He left the man's hands cuffed—again despite Ace's urging him to remove the bracelets.

"Come on, Ben," Ace pleaded, miserably, keeping his voice low. He glanced at where Mrs. Coulter and the Indian boy sat the stocky roan. His craggy cheeks reddened above his thin beard. "It's embarrassin'. You know...the boys sees, an'..."

"And what, Ace?" Stillman tossed the loot-stuffed saddlebags over his own pair of bags on Sweets' back, behind the cantle of Stillman's saddle. "He sees what you are?"

Darden bunched his lips in anger. Stillman knew he would have cussed him out good, if not for the presence of the woman and the boy. Ace had enough discretion to hold his tongue, which Stillman was happy to see.

Stillman led Sweets, Ace's steeldust, and the woman's short, solid roan away from the now-cold ashes of the coffee fire. He'd been right about the Chinook. The warm winds were building. The inch or so of snow beneath his boots was turning to slush. He'd removed his coat and wrapped it around his blanket roll, secure behind his saddle with both sets of bags. Nearly all the clouds had been swept away by the mild western winds, and shafts of warm, golden sunlight streamed down through the rustling pine boughs.

As he walked slowly, holding the three sets of reins taut in his gloved hands, he looked around carefully. When he'd led the horses into the open, he peered both ways along the crease between the bluffs.

Nothing.

He walked over and handed Mrs. Coulter the roan's reins. "There you are, ma'am."

"Are we being followed, Sheriff?"

"I haven't seen sign of anyone. If we are being followed, we'll likely lose them once we reach the Buffalo Barrens."

"Near Black Creek?"

Maintaining a firm grip on Darden's reins, Stillman swung up onto Sweets' back. He turned to the woman. "That's right." He nudged Sweets west along the crease, leading Ace's horse. He continued to look around in all directions. Keeping his voice down, he glanced at the woman. "You know the country."

"I've been out here two years," she said. "Most of the men—stockmen, mostly—who frequented my saloon, knew the Black Creek area. I overheard their stories of old Indian fights and bear hunts."

Stillman led the three-horse, four-person procession up a grassy ridge and then over a saddle before dropping down into the valley through which Black Creek meandered between high, rocky ridges. This was wild country—the home of the wolf and grizzly bear.

In fact, Stillman had known market hunters who'd frequented the Buffalo Barrens often, for bear and elk seemed to fancy this remote country with its deep, brush-choked watercourses and the long, gently rising ridges carpeted in the dark-green of lodge-pole pines and firs. He'd once known a man—Melvin Skittle was his name— who'd lost a leg to a grizzly he'd shot. The grizzly had played dead, but when Skittle had walked up to it, and set his rifle down to begin dressing it out, the big bruin had ripped off Skittle's left leg with a single swipe of one of its platter-sized paws wielding claws nearly as long and as sharp as Bowie knives.

Skittle's partner, Junius Friendly, had saved Skittle from certain death by rushing in at the last second with a well-placed Sharps bullet.

Skittle had lived out his last years in the same boarding house Stillman had lived in, in Great Falls, before, like so many frontiersmen of Skittle's time, and who'd suffered the afflictions of a violent and untrammeled life, had drank himself to death, nearly drowning in alcohol sweat in a whore's crib near Stillman favorite watering hole, the Mint Saloon.

The point of Stillman's musings was that this was no country to fool with. He wouldn't have headed this way if he didn't have men on his trail—men he could probably lose in this vast, broken landscape between the Highwood Mountains and the Judiths, with the Little Rockies showing like an isolated gray fog to the northeast. He'd have given it a wide berth, favoring the rolling, butte-pimpled prairie to the east instead. But this badlands country might serve to keep the wolves a good distance behind him. Especially now, with the snow melting, he had a good chance of losing the stalkers' trail in that wild 'n' woolly terrain.

As they rode through a grassy, bowl-shaped open area between haystack buttes, the snow almost gone now, and the warm breeze feeling good on his face, Stillman turned to the woman riding off his right stirrup, and asked, "What brought you out to this Godforsaken country, Mrs. Coulter? If you don't mind me askin', of course. Sounds like a rather abrupt change from the life of a preacher's wife."

Swaying easily in the saddle, Mrs. Coulter studied the wet dun grass they were riding through. "When I was looking for work, I heard that a remote saloon was for sale. It lay in some of the most beautiful country in Montana, so I was told. And it was being sold for a steal. The man who owned it had taken ill—a bad heart or something."

"That would be old Charlie Norman. He ran the Eagle Creek Saloon for many years. I used to stop in there now an' then, when I found myself out that way. Heck, he was old even back then."

"Yes, well, old Mr. Norman turned out to be quite the swindler. He answered my letter inquiring about the saloon with nothing but lies. He said the area around it was as peaceful as paradise. He used those exact words. He said the men who frequented it were mostly market hunters, wood cutters, traveling military contingents from Fort Benton making sure the red men remained on their reserves, and area stock men. In these modern times, they were all tame as sheep and always respectful of the fairer sex."

She glanced at Stillman with one of her trademark cynical grins. "He used those exact words, as well."

Stillman stretched his lips back from his teeth. "Yeah, well...Charlie could gild the lily a tad. He could sure do that."

"Yes, just a tad." Mrs. Coulter removed the hood of her cape, letting it fall down her back. She shook out her hair and the dark-red tresses, hanging free and burnished copper by the lens-clear sun, billowed thickly across her shoulders and down her back.

Stillman found himself studying the woman's patrician profile admiringly. The fine lines of her freckled face, the long clean nose, brown eyes and dark-copper hair, marked her of Irish or Scottish extraction.

She slid her eyes to him, caught his gaze lingering on her a little longer than what was discreet, and arched her brows at him in cold remonstration.

"Sorry," Stillman said, feeling his ears warm as he turned his head forward. "I didn't mean to stare." For some reason, he felt the need to explain himself. "I just...I didn't realize what a pretty woman you are, Mrs. Coulter."

He glanced at her again, smiling. She was having none of it. Her eyes gave him a look of frank chiding.

Again, his ears warmed. "I didn't mean to give offense, ma'am. I'm just yakking, as I tend to do on a long ride."

He'd thought Ace had been asleep on his steeldust, riding off Sweets' left hip. The man's chin had been drooping to his chest. But now Stillman heard Ace give a snort of mocking laughter.

"As I was saying about the saloon," Mrs. Coulter said in a hard, schoolmarm's reproving tone, "and old Mr. Norman..."

"Yeah, yeah," Stillman said, wincing against

the woman's scorn, "as you were saying about old Charlie…"

He was glad to get back to the topic of the old saloon owner.

"He flat out swindled me," she said. "One of the many lies he told was that the saloon was in good repair. Well, I was foolish enough, in my innocence, inexperience, and unfounded faith in my fellow man, to buy the place sight unseen. When Daniel and I rode out there with all of our worldly goods packed into the wagon I'd hired, I couldn't believe what I was looking at."

"It wasn't in all that good of repair the last time I saw it, over ten years ago now. Unless Charlie had something done on it—"

"He hadn't, I assure you." Mrs. Coulter gave Stillman a pointed look. "Unfortunately, he'd left the territory before I got there. I would have hunted him down and hauled him into court if I hadn't spent nearly the last of Jedediah's savings on the freight wagon and the man who drove it. I didn't even have enough money to hire the freighter for a return trip to Billings!"

Speaking up from where he rode the steeldust behind Stillman, Darden said, "You mean you already paid him for the saloon?"

"I sent a bank draft by courier. In return, he sent me the signed deed. He'd made it sound as though he was entertaining several offers, so I felt a desperate need to secure the place for Daniel and me. Mr. Norman also told me he'd stay on for a few weeks and help me get accustomed to the place, so I fully expected to find him out there—*waiting to help me get accustomed to the place!*"

Darden whistled and shook his head.

"I realize now how foolish I was," the woman said, staring down at her saddle horn, her pale freckled cheeks touched with the red of embarrassment. "I was just so desperate to get off on my own, someplace relatively quiet, and run my own small business. A woman has few options, you know."

A fateful glance at Stillman told him that one of her only options would have been what Daniel's blood mother had done, and died for her trouble. "Besides, he gave me such a great price for the place. Or so I thought. The offer he agreed to was right around the amount Jedediah and I had saved over the past couple of years in Billings…and…oh, I just wanted so desperately to succeed!"

She choked back a sob as she rammed the back of her black-gloved hand against her saddle horn. She gritted her teeth, closed her eyes, and shook her head, trying to suppress her emotions. As she did, young Daniel slid his head around her side and looked up at her with concern.

Mrs. Coulter sniffed, smiled, brushed two fingers across the boy's cheek reassuringly, and said, "I'm fine, Daniel. Just fine." She lifted her head to stare out over the roan's ears. "We'll just have to figure out the next leg of this journey called life, is all."

The words themselves would have sounded more optimistic if the tone with which she'd spoken them hadn't been so bitter. Stillman gazed at her as she rode straight in the saddle, her eyes darkly defiant.

She wasn't broken, but she was close.

He felt genuine sympathy for her and the boy. They'd ridden a hard trail together. Her only failing had been trusting a man. Obviously, she'd made a good run at the saloon, or she wouldn't have been out there for two years. She'd been rewarded for her efforts by the goatish Byron Conyers.

He, in turn, had been duly rewarded.

Now the woman had nothing except the boy and a few handfuls of belongings in two carpetbags and a burlap sack.

Stillman was searching around for words that would sound genuinely encouraging, not hollow, but his effort stalled as they approached the crest of a low hogback butte.

"Whoa!"

He drew sharply back on Sweets' reins. Ace's steeldust ran into Sweets from behind, and both horses whickered their indignation. Stillman turned the bay as well as the steeldust, grabbed the cheek strap of Mrs. Coulter's roan's bridle, and hurried back down the side of the butte.

As he passed Darden, who appeared to have been asleep again until a second ago, Stillman said, "Look alive, Ace—we're fallin' back!"

Chapter Eighteen

Clinging to his saddle horn with his cuffed hands, Ace said, "What the hell'd you see, Ben?"

When Stillman had ridden roughly fifty yards below the crest of the ridge, where they couldn't be skylined from the other side, he stopped all three horses and swung down from his saddle. "That's what you're gonna tell me."

"What is it, Sheriff?" Mrs. Coulter looked around fearfully.

Daniel clung to her, also looking frightened.

"That's what Ace is about to tell me."

"*I* am?"

Stillman dug his field glasses out of his saddlebags. "Climb down," he told his prisoner as he opened the case, removed the glasses, and hooked his hat over his saddle horn. He returned the leather case to the saddlebag pouch.

Ace had swung down from the steeldust.

Stillman brushed the man's hat off his head, then said, "Follow me. Mrs. Coulter, you an' the boy wait here."

"I wish you'd tell us what's going on, Sheriff," she said tightly, impatiently. "You're making us both rather anxious."

"In a minute. Come on, Ace."

"I heard ya," Ace grouched.

When he was ten feet from the crest of the ridge, Stillman stopped and motioned for Ace to do likewise. Both men dropped to their knees and, side by side, crawled to within a few feet of the crest. From here they could see down the other side and across a shallow valley between low, timbered ridges. The valley was bisected by a creek and several forks running through the wooded hills.

On the west side of the main watercourse, which wasn't much larger than the tributaries, a half-dozen horseback riders were moving down from the pines capping the western ridge. They moved at an angle toward the creek, generally away from Stillman and Darden's positions.

"Here." Stillman handed Ace the binoculars. "You recognize those men?"

Ace grimaced as he took the glasses in his cuffed hands. "Sure would be easier without these bracelets."

"Quit complaining about your jewelry, and glass those riders."

"I am!" The prisoner's voice was low but peeved.

He raised the glasses, adjusted the focus with the index finger of his right hand. He studied the riders for nearly a minute, scowling. He cursed as he continued staring into the two spheres of magnification.

"Who is it?"

"The big black man is Ralph Rogers. The white man ridin' to his right, in the long wool coat and derby hat, is Otis Strong. I can't make out the other four 'cause they're in shade now and they're too far away, but I can guess who they are."

"I take it Rogers and Strong are members of your elite crew of highwaymen."

"Well, I don't know how elite they are, but"— Ace lowered the glasses, shoved them back at Stillman—"yeah, they're part of my bunch, all right." He glowered at Stillman. "How in the hell did they outfox Sanchez?"

Stillman studied him critically. "You sure don't seem happy your friends think enough of you to come lookin' for you, Ace."

"Yeah, well..." Ace rolled his head, looking sheepish. "I don't always get along so well with my friends, Ben."

"Back at Pogue's barn, one tried to perforate your ugly hide."

"Yeah, well, like I said..."

"Why?"

"Ah, hell, Ben."

"Why?"

"Does it matter?"

"It matters." Stillman wanted to know how badly Ace's gang wanted him dead.

"Ah, hell!" Ace punched the ground. "When we split up, after we lit out of Winifred, Ray Callaghan was carryin' the loot. We didn't have time to divvy it up. The plan was for us all to meet up near Judith Gap. Callaghan has a hideout cabin in the Crazy Mountains. Only...I shot him out of his saddle an' took the money."

Stillman stared at him.

As if in his defense, Darden said, "It wasn't like I planned it out ahead of time! I just seen my opportunity...we'd just split up...the posse was on the heels of the others...and I seen all that money in them saddlebags...and...I shot him!"

Ace shrugged. "I lit out with Billy Three Moccasins an' Kingman. I think one o' the others from the other bunch saw me shoot Callaghan when they were hightailing it up a ridge to the west of us, the posse hot after them. Believe me, Ben—if I'd planned it out ahead of time, I would have planned it a whole lot better than that!"

Stillman glared at him. "A more pathetic excuse for a human being I've rarely seen, Ace. Oh, a few times, but it's been a while, and it's been rare!"

"Dammit, Ben, I was desperate. Desperate poor! Those fellas was all younger than me, and I had me a real good feelin' they were fixin' to cut me out! I'd have ended up with nothin', an' my pockets was already inside out!"

"You're a man without loyalty to anyone, Ace."

"Go to hell, Ben! Just go to—!"

Stillman lunged for him, slapped his hand across his mouth, and drove him back against the ground. Stillman looked out over the ridge. The riders were gone. That didn't mean they hadn't heard Ace's yell. Sound probably traveled well down there in that bowl.

"What in god's name is going on?" Mrs. Coulter stood a few feet down the slope, glaring at them. The boy knelt back where Stillman had left the horses. He was pulling nervously at the blond wheat grass and gazing edgily at Stillman and Darden, who must have cut two ridiculous figures: two aging men roughhousing like schoolboys.

"Nothing." Stillman got to his feet. He hauled Ace up and led him back down the slope by his cuffs, passing the woman as he did.

She fell into step beside Stillman. "How much trouble are we in?"

"Enough."

"I've had enough of your evasive replies to my questions, Sheriff Stillman. If my and my son's lives are in danger, I want to know how *much* danger. I have a right to know that much!"

"You should have stayed in Hobbs."

"What's that supposed to mean?"

Stillman returned the glasses to their case and dropped the case back into his saddlebag pouch. Swinging back to the woman, he said, "Ace double-crossed his bank-robbing pards, and they're out to kill him and take the money. They're close. A half-dozen of them. They must have picked up our trail in Hobbs then, fortunately for us, lost it. For now."

A few miles back, he'd tried to hide their trail by following a creek upstream for half a mile, then leaving the canyon through heavy timber.

Mrs. Coulter turned to Ace, who stood smiling sheepishly nearby, his cuffed hands hanging low before him, like a mourner at a funeral. She regarded him as though looking at an unsightly painting she couldn't believe anyone would have had taste bad enough to hang on a wall.

Turning to Stillman, she said, "Why not just turn him over to them? He'll hang anyway—correct?"

Ace stared at her, aghast. "For a preacher's widder, you sure ain't the forgiving sort, are ya?"

"Not anymore—no!"

"Get mounted, Ace. We're pullin' out." Stillman turned to the woman. "Get mounted, Mrs. Coulter."

"Answer my question. Why risk your life for his?"

Stillman sighed. "It's my job. Besides, they don't just want him. They want the money, too."

"So, you'd endanger your life…and mine and Daniel's…for that man's life and mere *money?*"

Stillman glared at her. He wanted to remind her he'd warned her back in Hobbs that riding with him and his prisoner might not be such a good idea. He resisted the urge. She was only tormented by her own distress, her own bad luck, and her fear for both her own life and the boy's. What she needed now was encouragement. Not harsh words.

"Mrs. Coulter, I will do everything I can to protect you and Daniel. I'm not going to let anything happen to you. Now…please get mounted. It'll be dark soon, and we still have an hour's ride to the cabin."

She glared at him, sulking. "Men." She brushed past him as she walked to Daniel, grabbed his hand, and led him to the roan. She glared at Stillman once more. "Stubborn, unreasoning men!"

Stillman grabbed her around the waist to help her into the saddle. When she was seated, he picked the boy up and set him down behind her, atop the roan's back. The boy didn't say anything. His dark eyes were wide and round with apprehension as he turned to regard Stillman.

Stillman smiled, patted Daniel's thigh, and gave him a wink.

The boy's lips stretched a thin smile.

"Hold on tight to your ma now."

"I will." The boy wrapped his arms around Mrs. Coulter's waist.

Stillman grabbed Sweets' reins as well as those of Ace's steeldust, and swung into the saddle. As he did, he caught the woman studying him.

He held her gaze, trying to decipher her thoughts, but nothing about her gave them away. When she realized he was staring back at her, she turned quickly away and looked down at her saddle horn, the skin above the bridge of her nose wrinkled as though in thought.

"Here we go."

Stillman nudged Sweets around the shoulder of the butte, tugging Ace's mount along behind him. The woman and the boy held back. She maintained her sullen silence. She was angry, and Stillman couldn't blame her. She'd lost everything, and her nerves were understandably shot.

When he reached the main stream threading through the bowl of ground on the south side of the butte he'd glassed the riders from, he followed it for half a mile then turned east to follow a narrow fork of gurgling water turning sand-brown now as the sun began its descent in the west. Small trout, hardly larger than minnows, were black shadows darting among the half-submerged rocks.

Stillman's party followed the narrow stream for a couple of miles before climbing over and dropping down a low divide.

Now Stillman led his sullen charges south and into another canyon. He followed Black Creek to the southeast, then reined up on a low ridge, dismounted, told the others to stay where they were, and grabbed his field glasses from his saddlebags.

He moved, crouching, to within a few feet of the lip of the bluff, then doffed his hat, dropped to his knees, and trained the glasses on the cabin nestled below near the base of the forested northern ridge.

The cabin wasn't much. It was a box roughly ten feet square mounted atop a stone foundation. The old logs the riverboat woodcutters had built the place with had aged to the lusterless gray of ancient granite. The shake roof bowed down in the middle, and was nearly solid green with moss. The stovepipe poking out of the center of the shack was rusted tin; it leaned precariously to the east. Stillman was glad to see a large can overturned on it, keeping out birds, squirrels, and rain.

That meant the place wasn't currently occupied.

No horses milled in the small pine-pole corral and lean-to stable flanking the place. Weeds had grown up around the cabin and corral—thick weeds with wild shrubs and even a few sapling pines and aspens. That meant probably no one had lived here permanently for quite a few years. If the cabin was ever inhabited anymore; probably only by passing wayfarers.

It was an old place, long unoccupied. Chances were slim that any of Ace's gang knew of its presence, especially since they'd been using a cabin in the Crazy Mountains as a hideout, at least a hundred miles as the crow flies from this canyon.

Stillman trained the glasses on the area around the shack.

The canyon trailed off far beyond it, straight out past Stillman, doglegging here and there. As far as he could tell in the dying light, no one was around or had been around for quite some time. A herd of mule deer grazed undisturbed below the tree line on the southern ridge a couple of hundred yards away, their coats showing copper in the fading light.

Stillman rose and walked back to where Ace, the woman, and the boy waited, still mounted.

"All clear," he said, and returned the glasses to his saddlebags.

Chapter Nineteen

Stillman led his dour troop down the ridge and over to the cabin.

He halted his and Ace's mounts out front and saw that, from up close, it appeared even humbler than it had from the ridge. It looked like a derelict old shack more and more imperiled by the forest pushing in around it.

Mrs. Coulter drew a sigh, glanced at Stillman, and pulled her mouth corners down. "Home sweet home."

"Just for tonight."

"Small blessings."

Stillman swung down from Sweets' back and walked onto the rickety front stoop. A backless chair sat against the cabin's front wall, left of the door. He flipped the latch, shoved open the door, having to put his shoulder into it, for the boards had warped, and peered inside.

The cabin looked just as humble inside as it did outside. Like he'd said, it was just for the night.

He moved back down off the stoop and helped Mrs. Coulter and the boy from the roan's back. "Why don't you and Daniel go on inside, ma'am? Getting cold again. Ace and I will tend the horses. Before I forget, I'll climb up on the roof and remove that coffee tin from the chimney, so we don't smoke ourselves out. There's likely enough wood inside so's you can start a fire."

He winked at her, trying to soften her mood.

She wasn't having any of it.

"That would be a good idea," she said tautly, grimly surveying their humble but temporary abode.

"Watch the porch there. Some boards are missing. Don't want you or the boy to turn an ankle."

Just as coldly: "No, I wouldn't like that, either."

Leaving her and the boy standing before the stoop, regarding the place as though they were a little afraid of it, Stillman led Sweets and Ace's horse around behind the cabin to the lean-to stable and corral.

"I've known some sour women in my day," Ace said from his saddle. "But she takes the cake. And her a preacher's widder!"

"Why—because she thinks I should throw you to the wolves?" Stillman chuckled. "I thought that was a pretty fair idea, myself."

"Don't you get no ideas, *Sheriff* Stillman. I know my rights under the law."

Stillman lifted the wire latching loop from a post, releasing the gate, and swung it open. "The only law out here is me, Ace."

"You an' I go back too far back for you to pull any stunts such as that."

Stillman jerked the man out of his saddle, then shoved him against the roan. Grimly, he said, "Our history isn't in play here, Ace. You're a thief and a killer. What you did in Winifred and later, ambushing that posse, pretty much wipes out whatever you were before. Whatever friends we were, too."

"Thanks for the mercy, old friend," Ace said.

"I'm not here to offer you mercy or anything else. I'm here to get you to the judge, plain and simple. And that's exactly what I intend to do."

Stillman hefted the money-laden saddlebags off of Sweets' back, and tossed them over the corral's top peeled-pine pole. "I'm returning this to the bank in Winifred." He gave Ace a hard look. "Now get to work on your horse. I'm gonna go up on top of the cabin and remove that tin from the chimney pipe. Don't try to make a run for it, because I'll have my eye on you, and while you might be able to outrun me, you won't outrun a round from my gun."

"Stillman's gun," Ace spat out on another grunt of sarcasm. "Ben Stillman's famous gun—his trusty, ivory-gripped Frontier .44. Had all the bad men quivering in their boots...at one time. Just keep in mind that was a few years ago, Ben. You're as old as I am."

Stillman had started toward the cabin, but he stopped and turned back to his prisoner. "What does age have to do with it?"

Ace glanced at the bulging saddlebags, and gave a wolfish grin. "Half of that for each of us would give us one hell of a comfortable old-age, Sheriff. It would set your pretty young wife and little boy up right well. And you could finally hang up that gun, Ben. Before it gets buried with you in some lonely grave, maybe out in them bluffs somewhere no one will ever find you."

Ace turned his head slowly to stretch his portentous gaze to the darkening ridges that seemed to press down closer now as the light gave out.

A single coyote yammered a lonesome soliloquy from some rocky ledge to the south.

Stillman glanced around, repressing the urge to shiver. He wasn't sure if it had been Ace's words that had slithered under his collar, or if it was just that damned cooling breeze. He turned back to his old friend and current prisoner, and chuffed. "Just get started on the horses, Ace. I'll be back in a minute."

When Stillman and Ace had finished tending the horses, they closed the corral gate and strode around the cabin to the front. Stillman carried his sheathed rifle, two sets of saddlebags, and the canvas war bag containing his trail supplies.

He and Ace stopped when they saw the boy splitting wood just off the front stoop. Daniel had removed his coat and hat and wore only his plaid flannel shirt over his longhandle top, and the suspenders holding up his broadcloth trousers. Stillman saw that his coal-black hair was cropped short, and shaved close up around the ears, like a white boy's.

Daniel had already split a good-sized pile of firewood. It lay mounded around the oak log he was using to split the softer stuff. He glanced over his right shoulder at Stillman and Ace, then, grinning proudly, swung the splitting maul high over his head. With a deep-throated grunt he wanted very much to sound manly, he slammed the maul through the pine log, splitting it cleanly right down the middle.

It flew apart in four nearly equal pieces.

Stillman whistled his admiration. "You already do a man's work, Daniel. I hope you're paid accordingly."

The boy blushed under his natural tan, then positioned another pine chunk on his splitting log. He'd likely found the wood stacked against the cabin's far wall, as Stillman remembered finding it there when he'd stopped here years ago.

Stillman stepped up onto the stoop, then moved abruptly back, ramming into Ace coming up behind him, when the front door flew open. Mrs. Coulter appeared with a broom in hand.

"Look out!" she warned, and swept a fist-sized clump of dirt, old leaves, dried grass and mouse droppings onto the stoop near Stillman's boots. She followed the rubble over the threshold, elbowing Stillman and Ace aside and giving the debris one more sweep into the yard.

She stopped and looked at Stillman. "Wretched place. But I'm getting it in somewhat respectable condition."

Stillman noticed that her cheeks were touched with more color than he'd yet seen in them, and that her eyes owned a rare glitter. He'd be damned if, despite her customarily chilly tone, she didn't seem to be having fun.

Stillman and Ace followed her inside, and Stillman leaned his rifle against the wall and set his war bag on a chair. There were two lit lamps—one hanging over the eating table to Stillman's right, one on a shelf beside the dry sink running along part of the back wall. Aside from the sagging ceiling, the place appeared in relatively good repair, and now the freshly swept floor fairly shone in the guttering yellow light.

Just ahead of Stillman, the sheet-iron stove fairly roared. He could see the orange confla-gration through the gaps in the closed door. A coffee pot chugged atop the low-slung contrap-tion. Warmth from the stove pushed against him, beating back the chill entering through the open door behind him.

Stillman closed the door. "Well, well," he said, doffing his hat and pegging it on the wall behind him, above his rifle. "You do run a tight ship, Mrs. Coulter."

With a dry cloth, she scrubbed one of the shelves over the counter running along the rear wall. "I cannot abide filth."

"And the boy can wield an axe."

"He had to do the work of a man out at Eagle Creek. Even if I'd been able to find a hard-work-ing man among the louts that people that country, I couldn't have afforded to hire him. After I made the necessary repairs to the building, especially."

Ace gave a wry snort.

"Well," Stillman said, shrugging out of his coat. "He's borne up well under the burden."

Mrs. Coulter made a sour expression as she

scrubbed at a stubborn crusted food lump on the shelf she was cleaning. "Yes, well…I hope he won't have to work so hard in the next chapter of our life. I'm taking him back to St. Louis, where I hope we can live in a little more civilized fashion, though I abhor the idea of running home with my tail between my legs."

Stillman walked around the table and sidled up to her. "Here," he said, nudging her hand from the crusty stain she was scrubbing. He held up his Bowie knife. "Let me give it a shot."

"An airtight tin must have leaked. It's awful."

"I'll get it," Stillman said, scraping at the crusty lump with his knife. "Why do you so resist the notion of returning home, Mrs. Coulter?"

"I dread the judgments of both his and my own families. They thought us foolish for venturing out here. Cork-headed idealists, my father called us. Despite the fact that they were right, I cringe at showing them my flag of surrender."

She looked at the progress Stillman was making on the crusty lump. "That will do." She brushed the crusted bits of food onto the floor, then swept them out the door. "Besides," she added, closing the door behind her and blowing a stray lock of hair away from her eye, "while they know that Jedediah and I adopted an orphan boy, they don't know—" She paused, gave a fateful

sigh. "They don't know the full story of his, uh…
of his lineage."

"Oh." Stillman had pulled three tin cups down
from a shelf and had turned to the table but
paused to glance at the woman sympathetically.
"I see."

She gave an angry groan, shaking her head.
"Damn my life, anyway!"

"I'll drink to that," Ace said, nodding at one of
the empty cups in Stillman's hand. "Fill me up,
there, will you, Ben? And you can pepper mine
with a little who-hit-John, if someone was gra-
cious enough to leave a bottle."

"There was a bottle," said Mrs. Coulter, sneering at him as she returned airtight tins and a
flour sack to the shelf she'd cleaned. "I threw it
out. My son and I will not share a cabin with two
drunk men."

She gave a caustic chuff.

Ace turned to Stillman with an aggrieved look.

Stillman grinned as he poured up three cups
of hot coffee. When he'd set them on the table,
he said, "Let me check my war bag for supplies. I
think I got a couple cans of beans in there."

"Not necessary," the woman said. She glanced
at her two carpetbags and burlap sack sitting on
the floor against the far wall. "Mrs. Skinner gave
me part of a ham and some flour. With what I

found on the shelf here"—she gestured at the several airtight tins she'd returned to the shelf—"I should be able to make a somewhat respectable stew."

"Well...all right, then," Stillman said, smiling at her admiringly.

Flushing, she turned away and set to work on their meal.

───────────

While Mrs. Coulter cooked and Daniel helped, keeping the stove stoked; and the handcuffed and shackled Ace Darden sullenly smoked and sipped his coffee at the table, Stillman slipped back into his coat, picked up his rifle and went outside. He took a slow stroll around the cabin. The sun dropped behind the Highwoods over to the west, near Great Falls, and light faded from the sky as the first stars kindled.

He traced a full circle around the cabin, happy to run across no sign of any possible stalkers, but only scaring up a fox probably hunting rabbits in a brush snag to the east of the shack. The animal gave a mewling cry of disdain for the human interloper, and slinked off through the darkening grass, up the ridge, and into the woods.

Stillman returned to the cabin just as Mrs.

Coulter was serving up her stew, which proved to be right delicious. She'd also made baking powder biscuits, and those did a handy job of soaking up the stew's gravy, and also worked well for swabbing the bowl clean when Stillman had finished.

The woman and the boy cleaned up after the meal.

Stillman poured another cup of coffee for himself and Ace and rolled a quirley. Later, when chores were finished, the woman poured herself a cup of coffee and returned to the table. Daniel begged for his own cup of the mud, for he wanted to drink what the grownups drank, together with the grownups, so Mrs. Coulter splashed a little coffee into a cup for the boy.

While Stillman and Darden sat smoking and indulging in some desultory conversation with Mrs. Coulter, Stillman became aware of Daniel's eyes on Ace. Finally, when the conversation had died, the boy, his big brown eyes fastened on Ace, asked, "Are you bad?"

Ace had just fired a match on the edge of the table. Holding the burning lucifer in one hand, his quirley dangling from a corner of his mouth, he turned to the boy. "What's that, son?"

"Are you bad?" the boy repeated.

"Daniel," Mrs. Coulter softly chided the boy.

The boy kept his eyes on Ace, really wanting to know.

"Nah, nah," Ace said. "I ain't bad. I just ran into a peck of bad luck, is all."

"Ma said you robbed a bank. How is robbing a bank bad luck? Did someone make you do it?"

Ace said, "Ouch!" as the lucifer burned his fingers. He dropped it on the floor, then scowled at the boy before sliding his angry gaze to Mrs. Coulter. "You need to get him under control, ma'am. He needs to mind his manners. I'm his elder, by god, an' I deserve some respect."

"No, no," Stillman said, taking a deep drag off his own cigarette. "I was wondering the same thing, Ace. How is robbing a bank bad luck? Assuming no one made you do it…"

Ace flushed. His scowl deepened, his wiry dark-brown brows hooding his eyes. He looked around at the freshly scrubbed table as though his answer lay somewhere on the scarred surface. He looked at Mrs. Coulter. She studied him with raised brows, as though she, too, were awaiting his response to her son and Stillman's questions.

Ace slid his incredulous gaze to the boy and said, "I had a difficult time of it…findin' work. I was desperate, boy. My dear wife died on me, an' then I got shot in the leg. Not easy for a gimpy man to land a job. No, sir. I had to take to swampin' out saloons after"—he poked both of his thumbs against his chest—"I'd been a respected rancher and a shotgun messenger on a stage line!"

"Ace, you robbed the saloon you were swampin'," Stillman pointed out.

"I had it due me, by god! You know what I was gettin' paid to clean out sandboxes and spittoons and clean the privy? Me—*Ace Darden?*" He blinked as the boy held his gaze, waiting. "He paid me seventy-five cents a day. He owed me that money I stole, by gad!"

"For stealing that money he owed you," Stillman said, "you got two months in the state pen." He switched his gaze to the boy. "Not easy getting a decent job after you've spent time in the pen."

"No, sir—it ain't!" Ace rammed the ends of his cuffed hands against the table, nodding. "That's why I fell in with that pack of curly wolves. You see now how it was? *Bad luck!*"

He dipped his chin as though to both emphasize and punctuate his answer.

Mrs. Coulter looked at Ace, narrowing her eyes pointedly. "The way I see it, Daniel, is that Mr. Darden has made the worst mistake a man can make."

"Oh, really?" Ace said, mockingly. "And what mistake is that, Mrs. High 'n' Mighty?"

"Losing his self-respect."

"I never..." Ace let his rebuttal trail off. He

just stared at her, eyes creased at the corners, lips stretched back from his teeth. He looked at the boy, then at Stillman.

He stared down at the table, letting his head hang in shame.

"Ah, hell," he said. "Ah, hell."

Mrs. Coulter finished her coffee then drew a deep breath. She looked at Stillman. "Sheriff, I'm going to need fifteen minutes of privacy. I'd like to clean up a little. I'd like to tend my toilet, is what I'm saying. Would you mind stepping outside and taking Daniel with you?"

"Sure, sure." Stillman flipped the back of his hand against his prisoner's shoulders. "Come on, Ace. Time to step out. Come on, Daniel. We'll get some air."

"I can't walk around. You got me cuffed an' shackled. All trussed up like some kinda animal." Ace spoke as though in a fog, staring down at the table. He appeared a bitter and broken man. So much so that Stillman almost felt sorry for him.

Stillman reached into his pants pocket. "I have the key right here."

While Stillman dropped to a knee to unlock the man's leg irons, Ace turned to the boy, who still stared at him skeptically, wonderingly. "It ain't like how she says it, boy. I just had a run o' bad luck, is all. I'm still a good man. Deep down, truly I am!"

Chapter Twenty

Stillman spent the night sitting on the backless chair on the stoop, his rifle resting across his thighs.

He needed sleep, but he couldn't let his guard down. He'd had a niggling sensation that they were being followed. This awareness had been sparked by Sweets' warning whicker earlier in the day, when he'd caught up to Ace and the woman and the boy in that crease between bluffs near Hobbs. It had followed him here to the Black Creek cabin, and he felt it even now in the chill, clear night in the Buffalo Barrens.

It was more of a physical sensation than anything else. Two cold fingers seemed to be pressed against the skin behind his ears, a subtle prickling of the fine hairs along the base of his spine.

He'd seen no clear reason for the sensation. He'd glassed his party's back trail several times that day. He'd even ridden back a few times to scour it more closely, looking for sign and also watching his bay for indication that they were being followed.

Nothing.

Still, those two cold fingers remained behind his ears, the prickling at the base of his spine. He'd been a lawman long enough to know the feeling was a sixth sense he couldn't ignore.

He spent a cold, uncomfortable night on the stoop, watching and listening, his veteran lawman's keen senses probing...sensing...forever watching and listening.

He heard the hoot of an owl that, several years ago, might have actually been some Blackfoot or Gros Ventre warrior's signal. He'd heard such signals a few times back when he and Milk River Bill Harmon had first come into this far-flung Montana country in the first years after the war and skirmished with Indians over the buffalo herds.

He'd come to know the difference between a true owl's call from that of a man trying to sound like an owl. The Blackfoot had been great imitators, but there was no mistaking the actual call itself.

Suddenly, the hooting stopped. Stillman heard a whoosh and then the windy creaking of large

beating wings, and the raspy cry as the bird left
its perch to fly up and back toward the forested
ridge to the north.

The unease in Stillman grew.

The owl's final hoot had been abruptly broken.
Its garbled cry had been one of annoyance. Had
something spooked the beast?

Stillman rose slowly, the chair creaking beneath him. His aging knees creaked, as well.
He winced against other sundry pains. He gave
a grunt as he straightened to his full six-two,
thumbed his Stetson up off his forehead, and
took a fresh look around.

Seeing and hearing nothing moving out there,
he moved off the stoop. He held the Henry up
high across his chest in both gloved hands. He
chewed off his right-hand glove, shoved it into
his coat pocket. He wrapped that hand around
the Henry's neck, curving his right index finger
around the trigger.

He considered levering a round into the action.
No point in getting overly eager, he decided. The
owl might have only spied a rabbit and broken off
its cry so suddenly to swoop to the ground for a
late meal.

However, there'd been no shrill, terrified rabbit cry. The owl had apparently merely moved on.

Why?

Stillman walked slowly around the cabin, giving the shack a wide berth and keeping to the shadows of the columnar pines and the secondary shrub growth closing on the cabin and that would, in a few more years, consume the place. He moved around behind the shack, stopped in the shadow of a pine, and looked around.

The night was as quiet as a church on a Friday night. There was no moon, but glittering stars streaked black velvet sky, and the bright light from the firmament lit the night nearly as well as the moon would have.

The lawman held his breath. Above the drumming of his blood in his ears rose the whinny of one of the horses in the corral. The horse's cry was followed by a faint sound ahead and on Stillman's right. The sound came again—that of a twig snapping under a stealthy foot.

Someone was on the lurk out here.

Squeezing the Henry in his hands but keeping his trigger finger relaxed where it curled through the guard, he moved slowly forward, sticking to the dark silhouettes of the trees around him. It was at times like this he wished he moved as quietly as an Indian, but he'd never mastered that feat. He moved as slowly and as quietly as he could, but dead leaves and pine needles still crunched beneath his boots. All he could do was keep close to the trees and hope whoever was out here couldn't draw a bead on him.

He continued to move slowly, weaving between the trees, climbing the gradual slope rising to the northern ridge crest. When he'd walked maybe sixty yards from the cabin, there was another, louder snap from ahead, up the slope maybe another thirty or forty yards.

From the same direction came a man's indignant grunt.

More snaps sounded. Now Stillman heard the thuds of running feet. Whoever had been ahead of him on the slope now moved across the slope on his right. The man was running fast. Stillman heard a louder crunching sound and then a clipped yell, as though the runner had tripped and fallen.

Stillman headed toward the sounds of the man running away from him.

"Hold it!" he shouted, his angry voice echoing loudly on this dark and otherwise silent night.

He stopped beside a lodge-pole pile, dropped to a knee, and aimed in the direction from which he heard the man continuing to run away from him. He considered snapping off a shot.

No.

He had no idea who was out there. It might be one of Ace's gang, but it might also be some innocent soul—a lone hunter, say, from one of the wide-spread ranches dotting this area.

Or, it could be Loco McGuire.

Stillman nixed that idea. Loco wouldn't make as much noise as this fellow. And he wouldn't be skulking around out here without taking decisive action of one sort or another—namely, triggering a well-placed rifle round at where Stillman had been sitting on the cabin's front stoop.

The lawman waited, aiming down the Henry's barrel. The fleeing man's footsteps dwindled to silence.

He was gone.

Stillman lowered the Henry. He looked around, keeping his senses pricked. If there was one man out here, there might be more.

A woman's scream cleaved the night, laying it as widely open as a doctor's scalpel slicing into a man's chest. It had come from the direction of the cabin.

Lightning fired along Stillman's nerves.

Ah, Christ—he'd been baited into leaving the cabin undefended!

He wheeled, lowered the Henry to his side, and broke into as fast a run as he dared, moving downhill through the dark forest, leaping deadfalls and blowdowns, weaving around trees and shrubs. He gained the bottom of the slope, his quick, hot breaths pluming in the starlit air before him.

For a moment, he thought he'd lost the cabin, but there it was ahead and on his right—a pale square object in the darkness.

He dashed past the northeast corner and, raising the Henry in one hand, sprinted toward the stoop. He leaped onto the stoop and stopped suddenly, nearly running into the man standing there, silhouetted in the open doorway.

"Ben, hold on!" Ace cried, raising his cuffed hands defensively.

Stillman stopped, breathing hard. "I heard a scream."

"So did I!"

"Here." The woman's calm voice had sounded behind Stillman.

Stillman whipped around. Mrs. Coulter walked toward him from a patch of brush off the cabin's southwest corner. She wore her cape with the hood up, and a blanket around her shoulders.

Stillman walked out to her, placed his free hand on her arm. "You all right?"

She laughed. "I'm sorry. I went out to tend to nature and something spooked me. Turned out to be a fox. I think I scared it as much as it scared me. I'm sorry if I startled you, too."

Stillman gave a relieved sigh. "Fox, eh?" He

supposed it was the same one he'd spied earlier. It probably shacked up here when no human pests were about. "Well, I'm glad."

Behind him, he heard Ace yawn and then stumble back to where he was bedded down on the floor. The boy must still be asleep. Young folks sleep deeper than older folks.

"Where were you?" Mrs. Coulter asked, frowning up at Stillman.

"I, uh..." He saw no point in worrying her. After all, the man he had run off might not have been anything to worry about. "I was just taking a walk around, checking the place out."

"Any trouble?"

"None. You'd best go back to sleep, Mrs. Coulter. It'll be dawn in an hour, and we've got another long day ahead."

"Oh, yes. I know." She winced as she continued to the cabin, walking rather tenderly and massaging her hip. "Various parts of me are not looking forward to that saddle..."

Stillman didn't say that various parts of him weren't, either.

When she'd gone back into the cabin and closed the door, Stillman walked around the cabin a few more times, trying to convince himself he and his trail partners weren't about to be attacked by men waiting in the brush. The first blush of dawn was always a good time to make such a play, when the light was murky and brains were foggy.

He checked out the area thoroughly, however, and found no indication that human wolves were on the blood scent. He went back to his chair on the stoop, sagged heavily into it, wincing at the ache in his aging behind, and set the Henry across his knees.

He let himself doze for twenty minutes, keeping his ears alert. It was an old trick of the trade, so when he woke to see a brush of pearl and salmon in the east, he felt at least moderately rested.

It was still a tired old lawman, however, who swung up into the leather an hour later, after a Spartan breakfast of coffee and jerky, and led the small procession away from the cabin he and the woman and boy had been sure to leave in at least as good a condition as they'd found it in, right down to the coffee tin overturned on the chimney pipe. They'd consumed some wood and trail supplies; Stillman would stop this way again sometime and replenish what he'd taken. Not that anyone would likely care. Obviously, overnight residents here were few and far between these days.

Still, it was the custom of the country. An important one.

Midmorning found them in rough country—harsh badlands country of deep, ancient watercourses, dry most of the year, as they were now, and high, bullet-shaped bluffs. They followed one such water course littered with ancient, sun-bleached bison bones. Bits of the bones were embedded in the ground and in the embankments on each side of the ravine.

"Why so many?" Mrs. Coulter asked Stillman once he'd told her what all those white things were.

"Jump."

Riding off his left stirrup, she scowled at him, and gave a wry laugh. "What?"

Stillman lifted a gloved finger to indicate a cliff high overhead and on this particular canyon's right side. "That there is an old bison jump. The Indians once ran herds of bison off that cliff and into this canyon."

She shaded her eyes as she stared up at the sandstone bluff, which cast deep shade across the ravine. "Really?"

"An efficient way to kill."

"An awfully cruel one."

"Yeah, well," Ace said, "it's a cruel world, ma'am." He glanced at Daniel riding behind her. "The boy's people were some of the cruelest who ever set foot on this earth." He gave a leering grin. "Hope you thought of that, goin' in." He broadened his mocking smile.

She lowered her hand and glared at him riding behind Stillman. "Go to hell, Mr. Darden!"

Stillman scowled over his shoulder at his prisoner. Ace's feelings were still hurt from last night's post-supper conversation. He blamed the boy for asking the question, one that apparently continued to haunt him. It took a small man to blame a boy for asking a question.

"Shut up, Ace," he warned, "or I'll gag you."

Ace wrinkled a nostril at him.

Stillman turned his head forward and gave an inward groan.

Damn, this trip was getting long.

He'd turned forward a split second too late to see a man pull his head back from the western-most edge of the buffalo jump.

Chapter Twenty-One

Late in the day, Stillman led the three-horse procession out of a narrow gorge in the heart of the badlands and into a relatively open area, the steep chalky walls sliding away from him on both sides. The ancient watercourse he'd been following converged in this large area with another watercourse running perpendicular to the first. It was marked by a broad strip of water-polished gravel and scalloped sand peppered with weathered bits of driftwood.

This second watercourse ran from his left to his right, or east to west.

Or vice versa, depending on the direction the water ran when there was water here.

Stillman paused, trying to decide which way to go—east or west, or continue straight ahead to the south.

He hadn't been in this crazy country for years.

The last time was when he'd been tracking Canadian whiskey runners who'd given him the slip in this isolated devil's playground between mountain ranges. Pondering, he stared absently at the moldering carcass of a coyote that had likely been swept away in some spring flood and deposited here, where it had rotted. It was now little more than dried hide with a small thatch of coarse gray fur, some exposed spine, and a grimacing snout.

It left a musky odor. Sweets shook his head at the stench.

"There but for the grace of god..." Ace commented. Stillman had stopped the prisoner's steeldust off his left stirrup. Mrs. Coulter and the boy still rode behind them, twenty yards away, both looking sun-burned, wind-burned, and weary.

Stillman decided to continue ahead, to the south. If he remembered right, there was a southern outlet to this crazy country. He'd no sooner clucked Sweets ahead than he heard something on his left. He turned to peer that way along the twisting chasm, then gave a startled grunt when he glimpsed the head of a horse coming around a distant bend.

Neck-reining Sweets sharply and tugging on Ace's steeldust's reins, he headed back in the direction from which he'd come.

As he approached Mrs. Coulter, he said, "Back, ma'am. Back, back!"

"Huh?" she said, swinging her head around to follow him with her questioning gaze.

"Back!" he hissed.

When he'd managed to get himself and Ace behind a bend in the narrow canyon, he leaped out of his saddle and ran ahead. Mrs. Coulter was still trying to get the roan turned. The horse, spooked by the musky death smell of the rotting coyote, whickered, stomped, and bobbed its head. Stillman grabbed the bridle's cheek strap, turned the horse, and led it quickly around the bend in the canyon's east wall.

"What the hell's goin' on?" Ace asked, incredulous.

Stillman had shucked his Colt. He laid the barrel across his lips, shushing the man. He gave Mrs. Coulter and the boy, still sitting on their horse, a silent command for quiet. Both returned his gaze with wide-eyed, fearful ones of their own.

Stillman moved over to where the canyon's east wall bulged. He pressed a shoulder against the bulge and, holding his pistol barrel up near his right shoulder, doffed his hat, dropped it, and edged a look up the canyon to the place it opened out where the dry watercourses merged.

Hoof clomps sounded, the iron shoes clattering

on the rocks. A shadow slipped onto the ground where Stillman's canyon merged with the open area, and then the horse's head appeared from behind the slope on Stillman's left. As the horse continued clomping from Stillman's left to his right, the horse's head and neck were followed into view by the man straddling the animal.

Stillman began to jerk his head behind the bulge but stopped when the rider, not turning toward him, drew back on the reins of his brown and white pinto. "Whoa, whoa," he said softly.

The man turned to his left, gazing down canyon to the south. He gave a soft, inquiring whistle through his teeth. He waited, staring away from Stillman. The pinto lowered its head to sniff the dead coyote then jerked its head up, whickering distastefully. It stomped one front foot.

"Whoa, now," the man said, turning his head forward.

A second later, he turned his head toward Stillman. Stillman drew back behind the bulge, gritting his teeth.

He'd only caught a brief glimpse of the rider's face. However, he'd seen enough to know the man was Loco McGuire—complete with black bear fur hat and coat. Loco had wrapped a white bandage across his head, angling it down over his left ear, the one Stillman had shredded with his Henry.

Stillman pressed his shoulder against the sandstone bulge in the slope to his left. His heart beat an anxious rhythm. No sounds issued from Loco's direction. Had the man seen him?

Stillman considered killing him, thought better of it. He didn't want to take the shot and risk alerting Ace's former friends, if they were in the same general area.

He waited.

A soft, raspy, inquiring whistle came from Loco's direction.

Stillman tightened his jaws, waiting.

The seconds ticked by. He looked at Mrs. Coulter and the boy and Ace, all staring at him anxiously. Ace furled one brow and started to open his mouth to say something, but Stillman shushed him by pressing his Colt's barrel to his lips again.

Silence.

Stillman held his breath, pressed his thumb taut against the Colt's hammer, ready to cock and fire.

"Pee-YOU!" Loco said. "That dead ole thing is sure whiffy on the lee side—ain't he, hoss?"

The pinto gave a soft, corroboratory whicker.

Stillman looked at Sweets and the other two horses, willing them not to make any sounds. The steeldust twitched an ear. Sweets gave his head a slight shake but did not whicker.

"Come on, hoss," Loco said from the other side of the sandstone bulge. "My ear's hurtin' an' it's gettin' late. Let's find a place to hole up fer the night, have me some whiskey."

The man kept talking to himself and his horse in a desultory way, but his voice trailed off to silence as horse and rider rode on along the intersecting watercourse to the west, on Stillman's right.

Relieved, Stillman released the breath he'd been holding.

So, he thought, it must have been McGuire outside the cabin last night. Wonder why he didn't make a play...

Stillman holstered his Colt.

"Wait here till I signal you," he told the others, then swung up onto Sweets' back and rode to the intersecting watercourses. He peered cautiously to the west, the direction McGuire had ridden.

There was no sign of the man. He'd ridden around a bend in the narrow canyon, out of sight.

Stillman gestured for the others to come, then he led them straight south, hoping McGuire didn't backtrack and pick up their trail. Again, Stillman wondered how, if it had been McGuire on the lurk outside the shack last night, he hadn't made a play by now but had let his quarry get ahead and away from him here in the Barrens.

If it were Stillman tracking someone in this devil's playground, and he had them sighted, he wouldn't let them out of his field of vision before making a play.

Of course, he knew from experience how hard it was to track man or beast through the rugged Barrens. Maybe Loco didn't.

Anyway, there was no point dwelling on it. Stillman had eluded the crazy, one-eared killer, and now he had to keep it that way, and stay wide of Ace's gang, as well.

He figured they were nearing the south end of the Barrens when he stopped to make camp. It would be dark soon. You didn't want to be moving through the Barrens at night.

Stillman chose a bivouac spot on a gentle, grassy hillside peppered with rocks and cedars and concealed by a horseshoe dyke of what appeared granite or limestone. A spring-fed steam cut through the area, and it was near the sandy shoreline of the stream Stillman chose to camp.

The stone dyke would conceal their fire from three sides, while a long, low, cedar-stippled hill on the other side of the stream would conceal it from the south. It was a large but self-contained area. He scouted it thoroughly, making sure they were the only ones here, before he stopped the horses and began stripping tack from their backs.

They were the only ones here now. However, when there was still enough light in the sky, he saw clearly the many circular indentations of tipi rings. The place had apparently offered prime shelter to Indians many years ago as they'd followed the buffalo herds. Maybe the people who'd once camped here had been the same ones who'd operated the jump.

Seeing such things as ancient buffalo jumps and the indentations of old tipi rings, both of which he'd seen plenty on his travels around this vast and varied territory, had never failed to make him appreciate the passing of time and his own very small, ephemeral place in a vast and mysterious universe.

He was sitting on a rock and sipping a cup of coffee after supper when he saw Mrs. Coulter step away from the small fire they'd built, and walk toward him through the long, straw-colored grass. She was a slender silhouette against the dark green of the sky in which the first stars winked.

The air was still relatively mild; she clutched only a light blanket around her arms. She wasn't wearing her hat, and her long, dark-red hair tumbled messily about her shoulders.

She held a cup of coffee in her hands.

"Mind if I sit down?"

"Please do."

He used his gloves to brush off the rock a few feet away on his left.

"Why, thank you, sir."

"Not all, my lady," he said with a courtly bow of his head.

She smoothed her skirt against the backs of her thighs and sat. She drew her legs together, leaned forward, and once again held her coffee cup in both hands.

Facing the stream, the same direction Stillman was facing, she stared at the stream for a time, the breeze rustling her hair. She seemed deep in thought for a while, and Stillman did nothing to interrupt. It was a nice evening. Maybe she just wanted to enjoy it with him in silence.

That was fine with him. Despite her often sour moods, which were understandable, he'd grown to like her. And he felt a soft spot for the boy, as well. He just hoped he'd get them both to safety.

She glanced at him with a sidelong smile. "You're a good man, Sheriff Stillman."

The compliment took him off guard. It hadn't been the conversation starter he'd expected. "Well…I thank you for saying so, Mrs. Coulter."

"It's just that a good man is hard to find these days," she said with a sigh, staring off again through the brush toward the creek.

"Out here, maybe. You'll find a good man once you get back east."

"You think so?"

"You're a good woman. Pretty to boot," he added with an admiring smile. "I know you will."

She slid her pensive gaze to him again and said with an almost devilish curl of her mouth. "I suppose you're married…"

It had almost been a question. But only almost.

"Yes, I am," Stillman said. "Very happily."

"Is she a good woman?"

"Better than I deserve."

"Children?"

"A little boy. Too young for me. But, then, Fay is quite a few years younger, as well. She does most of the raising while I'm off collecting taxes, issuing court summons, or chasing owlhoots."

Mrs. Coulter smiled and stared down at her coffee again with a pensive furl of the skin above her nose. After a time, she turned to him and said, "I'm sorry, Sheriff. For being such a pain in the behind with all my complaining. You don't deserve that. After all, I sort of fell into your lap. Daniel and I did."

"Not at all, Mrs. Coulter."

With what almost seemed genuine anger, she said, "Would you please call me Olivia? I mean, we've been together for a couple of days now, out in the middle of nowhere. I think we know each other well enough, don't you?" She paused. "May I call you Ben?"

"Of course, you may...Olivia." He smiled.

She smiled back at him. "There. I like the sound of that much better than Mrs. Coulter."

"I gotta admit I do, too." She looked away again, and her smile became another brow-furrowing frown. She sighed heavily.

"What's the matter?"

"By the time you reach my age, all the good men are taken."

"I don't think that's true."

She turned to him, gave him a tolerant smile, and blinked. "Tell me about your wife."

Stillman looked around, trying to keep an eye on the terrain around him, fading quickly as the light died, but in his mind's eye he saw his wife as she would be now, working in the kitchen, cooking a meal only she and little Ben would enjoy together.

He said, "She's a beautiful woman. A loving wife, and a great mother. She comes from a French ranching family down along the Powder River, near Milestown. A few years older than you, most likely." He drew a breath, smiling reflectively. "She's way too good for me. I don't deserve her. Not a bit."

"How old would you say I am, Ben?"

"Oh, maybe…twenty-four, twenty-five."

"Twenty-eight."

"No!" He really didn't think she looked twenty-eight.

"Yes. An old widow already."

"Hardly."

She scowled off again toward the creek and rammed the end of her fist against her right thigh. "Damn Jedediah for dying on me, anyway!" She shook her head, her cheeks touched red with frustration. "Everything had been going so well. We had a growing congregation in Billings. We had a nice home. We were deep in love, and we were enjoying raising our beloved Daniel."

She turned her head to stare at the fire. The flames shimmered in her tear-filled eyes. Her lips quivered.

Stillman set his cup on the ground and lifted himself off his rock. He dropped to a knee before her, and wrapped his hand around wrist. "Life kicks sometimes. It kicks hard. We just have to set ourselves strong against those kicks, keep putting one foot in front of the other."

She turned to face him, drawing her mouth corners down. A tear rolled out from her left eye and dribbled down her cheek. He reached out to wipe it away with his thumb. She stared into his eyes, and then suddenly her arms were around him. She pressed her lips to his.

He was so startled by the woman's obviously impulsive move that he didn't know what to do, until he found his hands on her shoulders. Gently, he eased her away.

"Oh, god," she said, turning her head away in embarrassment and scrubbing tears from a cheek with the back of her hand. "Now I have just added humiliation to my list of indignities!"

She climbed to her feet, sniffing.

Stillman remained on one knee, staring up at her in shock.

"I truly am sorry, Ben!"

She wheeled and hurried back to the fire, leaving her coffee cup on the ground beside her rock.

Later, he was dozing against a tree well out from the fire, his empty cup in his hand, when her scream woke him again.

Chapter Twenty-Two

Stillman poked his hat brim off his forehead and reached for the Henry, which had been leaning against the tree behind him. He pumped a cartridge into the action and stared out into the night, toward the cedars and the creek murmuring beyond them.

Again, Mrs. Coulter's scream sent electricity sparking along his nerve endings.

He heaved himself to his feet and went running straight south through the brush.

"What the hell's that?" he heard Darden exclaim behind him.

"Ma?" called Daniel.

The boy's voice was nearly drowned by another scream. Stillman saw two figures silhouetted against the starlight-speckled stream behind them, struggling together violently. Stillman could tell one was a man, the other a woman.

"No!" she yelled angrily as she lunged at her assailant, swiping a hand at the man's face. "No!"

Her assailant cursed and drew back.

Mrs. Coulter twisted away from the man, tripped, fell to a knee, then, sobbing, regained her feet and ran toward where Stillman was running up on her from the north. As Stillman approached, the man disappeared into the brush lining the creek. Stillman heard the man's rasping breaths and thudding footsteps as he fled.

Mrs. Coulter lifted her head to see Stillman before her, the Henry in his left hand. She gave a startled cry.

"It's me!" he said. "It's Ben."

"Ben!" She threw herself against him, wrapped her arms around him, buried her face in his chest. "He...he came out of *nowhere!*"

"Are you all right?"

She nodded. "He jumped me, tried to drag me away...!"

"Who?"

"I don't know." She shook her head, drew a breath. She trembled in Stillman's arms. "I've never seen him before. There might have been two, but I'm not sure. The other one, if there was another one and not just a shadow, disappeared after I started screaming."

Stillman cast his gaze toward where the man

or men had disappeared in the brush. He couldn't see them now. Could hear no running footsteps.

"What were you doing down here?"

She cast him an incredulous look. "You have to ask?"

"Come on," Stillman said, turning himself and the woman toward where the fire flickered beyond the cedars. "Let's get you back to camp."

"Oh, god, I was scared!" she sobbed as they moved back through the tall grass and the cedars.

"You're fine now. You're fine."

"Ma!" Daniel cried as Stillman and Mrs. Coulter reached the edge of the flickering firelight. He ran out and threw himself against his mother, who wrapped her arms around him and held him tightly, rocking him gently.

"I'm fine, Daniel. I'm fine, boy." She gave another sob, sniffed.

The boy wrapped his arms more tightly around her waist.

"Ben!"

Stillman turned to where he'd tied the cuffed and shackled Ace Darden against a scraggly cottonwood on the other side of the fire. "Who was it?"

Stillman walked over to him, shook his head. "She didn't get a good look at him. Maybe Loco."

"Ah, hell!"

"I'm gonna take a look around, see if I can find where he's camped."

"Untie me!"

"No."

"Ben, what if somethin' happens to you out there?" Ace's eyes were bright with fear beneath the brim of his battered Stetson. "You can't just leave me here all trussed up, defenseless!"

Stillman walked over to where Mrs. Coulter now stood by the fire, one arm wrapped around Daniel's slender shoulders. He dug two sets of keys out of his pants pocket and held them out to her.

"What are those?" she asked.

"Keys for his cuffs and leg irons. In case I don't come back. Release him only if I'm not back by dawn." Stillman looked at Ace, scowled. "I don't trust him."

"Come on, Ben!" Ace pleaded, kicking his legs, which were extended straight out before him. "You can't leave me here like this."

"Watch me." Stillman shouldered the Henry and started walking away from the fire.

"Ben!"

Mrs. Coulter hurried toward him, leaving Daniel by the fire. "You can't go after that man in the dark. It's too dangerous."

"I'm gonna stay after him while he's on the

run. If it's the man I think it is, he's slippery. We might not see him again until it's too late." Stillman offered a reassuring smile, and gave her arm a gentle squeeze. "Don't worry. I'll be careful. I'll be back. Those keys are just in case. Remember, don't free Ace unless I'm not back by dawn. I will be, but..."

"Yes, I know," she said grimly, looking down at the keys in her hand. "Just in case."

Stillman pinched his hat brim, then swung around and strode back toward the creek. When he reached the star-dappled water, he followed it downstream to where he'd seen Olivia struggling with her assailant.

He picked up only a single pair of boot prints angling away from the scuff marks that showed the spot where the man had attacked Olivia. At the edge of the brush he thought the one set of boot prints became mixed with another set. The night was too dark to tell for sure, and there were several sets of deer tracks here, mixing up the message, as well.

Stillman lowered the Henry, levered a cartridge into the action, off-cocked the hammer, and walked into the brush. He moved slowly, cautiously, wary of an ambush.

When he'd walked a few feet, stepping around a blowdown cottonwood, he saw what he be-

lieved to be two sets of boot prints in the sand
and gravel between larger rocks, brush clumps,
cottonwoods, and cedars. Soon the faint tracks
led him into a ravine. Turning northwest, he followed the ravine to where it gave out at the base
of a steep bluff.

Because of the deep darkness inside the ravine, he'd lost the prints of the two men he was
tracking. He'd hoped to pick them up again, but
it didn't look like...

Wait.

He lifted his gaze to the side of the bluff. In the
starlight he saw what appeared two faint swaths
of disturbed grass and brush.

Olivia's assailants must have climbed the bluff.

Stillman did likewise, tracing a switch-back-
ing course to save his legs and lungs, not to mention his thudding heart. *Too much office work. Too
much beer, too many cigarettes.* He made a mental
note to banish the latter two habits, knowing he
wouldn't. He'd given up the hard stuff. That was
enough.

By the time he'd gained the crest of the bluff,
he was sweating inside his coat. The chill air
quickly turned his sweat cold. He walked generally north along the relatively flat, forested top of
the bluff, again moving slowly, weaving among
the trees, sticking as much to their shadows as
possible.

Every few yards, he stopped and peered around.

There were no sounds except for the soft rushing of the slight breeze in the tree tops, the scuttling sounds of burrowing creatures, and the intermittent yammers of distant coyotes.

The top of the slope fell away gradually. Just as gradually, the trees thinned and fell back behind Stillman.

He continued down the gentle decline until he saw what could only be the glow of a fire maybe a hundred yards farther down the slope, sort of where the declivity bottomed out to form a low saddle, with more woods farther along the saddle to the northeast.

The fire was just inside those trees, slightly to Stillman's left. He thought it might be in a shallow cut of some kind, because he seemed to be seeing only the very tops of the flames and their guttering glow.

He studied the fire from one knee for a time, considering his options. If the two men he'd been following were part of Ace's bunch, then the others might be at that camp, as well. *Why, though, would only two have paid a visit to Stillman's camp earlier, when they'd attacked Olivia when she'd been tending to nature?*

Stillman wasn't going to get any answers here.

He straightened and continued walking down the slope, grateful to have the forested top of the bluff behind him now. Its darkness would conceal his own silhouette. At least, he hoped it would. There was no other cover out here. Not even rocks. Just knee-high grass and a few small, widely scattered cedars, most of which appeared charred from a fire that must have burned through here a few years ago. There were still patches of burned brush and charred ground where the flames had burned down through the thin soil to bare rock.

Moving slowly, it took Stillman nearly twenty minutes to reach the edge of the next forest. When he did, he dropped to a knee to study the campsite pitched in a low area just beyond the edge of the pines, maybe sixty feet away from him now. Two men milled around the fire—one stirring the flames with one stick while holding what looked like a skinned rabbit over the flames with another stick.

The second man was going through his gear on the other side of the fire from the first man, whose face Stillman couldn't see, since his back was to him. The other man, the one going through his gear, lifted his head, throwing back his long, thin, red hair and glaring at the other one with his wide-set jade-green eyes. "Where in the hell is my Dr. Noble's Bear Salve? That bitch scratched me damn near to the bone, and I need that salve, dammit!"

The firelight glistened in the long line of blood marking a scratch on the red-haired gent's left cheek, near his scraggly side whisker.

"I told you, Pinto!" said the man roasting the rabbit at the fire. "I didn't do nothin' with your consarned Dr. Noble's Bear Salve!"

Stillman felt a scowl cloud his features.

Sure enough, the tall, lean man with the green eyes, long red hair and the nasty scratch was Pinto. That meant the man roasting the rabbit was Pug.

Pug and Pinto—the two grubline riders from the Squaw Peak Saloon & Gambling Parlor, one of whom—Pug—Stillman had tattooed with his Colt's barrel.

What in the hell...?

They must have been trying to sneak into his camp, but got distracted by the woman. The two dunderheaded louts must have been so overcome by their goatish desires that they grabbed her and tried to drag her back to their camp for some fun.

Anger burning high in his chest, Stillman strode forward, raised the Henry, ratcheting the hammer back, and stopped on the lip of the slight depression the two men were in.

"Hold it!"

Both men froze—Pug by the fire, his back to Stillman. Pinto still crouched over his gear.

Pinto lifted his head to Stillman, and cursed, stomping one foot in anger.

"Is that...is that who I think it is?" Pug asked, his voice quivering as he turned his head to one side, trying to get a look at the man behind him.

"Dammit!" Pinto bellowed, stomping his boot again.

"You two idiots," Stillman said. "What the hell are you doing out here?"

Pug kept turning his head until both he and Pinto gazed at the sheriff guiltily.

"I see," Stillman said, nodding grimly. "You got sore about the tattoo I gave you." He'd addressed that sentence to Pug. "So, being down on your heels as well as your luck, and not having anything else to do, and both being as dumb as hammers, you decided to trail me for the bank loot. Maybe even the woman. Only you got a little too daring as well as distracted when you saw the woman. You tried to drag her off to your lair. I doubt either of you two cork heads thought through your little chivaree—did you?"

Their bodies frozen, tense, Pug and Pinto shared a conferring look. His voice thin and reedy, Pug said, "What're we gonna do, Pinto? I can't go to jail. No, sir—I just can't. Three times is plumb enough for ole Pu—"

He cut himself off as he dropped both sticks and wheeled, reaching for the Schofield on his right hip. Stillman's Henry spoke twice from his hip, the rifle leaping and roaring, flames lapping from the barrel.

As Pug was punched back onto the fire, Pinto gave a squeal and reached for his pearl-gripped Bisley. He was a little faster than his partner. He got the gun clear of the holster and was leveling the barrel while starting to ratchet the hammer back before Stillman's Henry spoke again... again...and again, sending Pinto sashaying off into the brush behind him, dragging the toes of his boots and triggering his Bisley into the ground three times.

The bullets blew up dirt and pine needles, sent a pinecone flying high and away.

Pinto fell in the darkness beyond the firelight, and shivered out his soul.

Meanwhile, Pug lay in the fire, screaming and burning, trying to gain his feet, but with Stillman's lead weighing him down, he couldn't manage it. Rather than put up with anymore of the dunderhead's infernal caterwauling, Stillman blew two more well-placed bullets through the man's skull, silencing him.

Pug fell still in the flames leaping around him.

Stillman sighed. He walked over, leaned the

Henry against a tree, grabbed Pug's boots, and pulled him out of the fire. Pug continued to burn, flames enshrouding him. Stillman grabbed a blanket and threw it on top of the man, snuffing the flames.

Smoke rose from the man's inert, charred body, giving off a foul-smelling stench.

Chapter Twenty-Three

Olivia gasped as a gun cracked in the distance.

Even muffled, the shots sounded like especially loud firecrackers detonated at a Fourth of July parade.

Daniel, who'd been poking a stick around in the fire, jerked his head up with a start and turned his wide, dark eyes to his adoptive mother. On the other side of the fire from Olivia, Ace Darden had nodded off. Now he gave a snort and drew a deep, phlegmy breath as he lifted his chin from his chest and moved his legs, trying to sit up a little straighter in spite of the ropes securing him to the tree.

He turned his head to stare across his left shoulder, toward the creek.

The gunfire continued.

There was a paused before a couple of more shots sounded, each one making Olivia tense, as though the bullets were threatening her own flesh.

Another pause, then there were three more pops. Those pops were not quite as loud as the previous ones. They were followed by two more slightly louder hammering crashes.

Silence fell over the night like a giant, unseen ocean wave, pinning Olivia against the tree she'd been resting against, blankets drawn up to her neck.

Daniel's eyes stayed on hers—inquiring, fearful.

Darden turned his faintly amused gaze to Olivia. "Exchange of gunfire."

"What does that mean?"

"Someone fired and someone fired back."

"Yes, I know, but..."

Darden curled his thin-lipped mouth. "It wasn't easy."

"He'll be all right. He's a seasoned lawman."

The outlaw gave a noncommittal grunt, shrugging. He turned to stare toward the stream again.

Daniel tossed his stick in the fire and then sat on a large, flat-topped rock. He drew his knees up and rested his chin on them, nervously lifting and lowering his boot soles in the dirt, gazing into the fire. The orange flames danced light and shadows across his sharp-boned, cherry-brown, coffee-eyed face.

His body looked especially small in his over-sized wool coat, a coat Olivia had bought sec-ond-hand from the same ranch wife she'd bought her eggs from, in hopes that Daniel would grow into it, saving her from having to buy more coats than she could afford, now that she'd been left on her own and trying to run a saloon she'd had to put more money into than she'd expected.

She frowned, not sure why those thoughts were on her mind now. She was just trying to get mind off her anxiety over the sheriff...

"Now we wait, I guess—huh?"

She looked across the fire to see Darden re-garding her again, an inexplicable humor touch-ing his eyes.

"Yes," Olivia said, drawing the blankets up higher, shivering against the cold, or her jangled nerves, maybe both. "Now we wait for him to return."

"Just hope it's him who comes."

Olivia frowned at the prisoner. "What do you mean?"

"Well, if he didn't make it..." Darden shrugged a shoulder. "I mean...on the off-chance he walked into a nest of the men after the money...I reck-on...I don't know, I reckon it would be them that came." He smiled shrewdly. "Wouldn't it?"

"If that's who he ran in to, I suppose. And if they got the upper hand."

"Who else you suppose would be out there? That wasn't one man firing back at him. That wasn't Loco McGuire. That was more than one man firing back."

Olivia was starting to get annoyed at the man's blather. He was fishing around for something, and Olivia didn't like it. "Look, Mr. Darden, I don't know what you're getting at, but..."

"What I'm getting at, Mrs. Coulter, is that you're a pretty young woman with your whole life ahead of you. Do you really want to risk it not bein' Stillman who comes waltzing up to this fire?"

He cemented those words on her brain with a hard, level look from the other side of the fire. She glanced at Daniel. The boy had turned his head so that his left cheek rested atop his knees, his gaze directed at Olivia.

She shook her head and spoke to her son. "Don't listen to him. He's trying to frighten us." She looked at Darden and raised her voice a little: "I don't know why you're trying to scare us, Mr. Darden, but—"

"We could take the money and ride out of here." Darden grinned, showing tobacco-stained teeth, two of which were badly chipped. "We could split it up and light a shuck...before they came."

He paused, staring at her darkly.

"If it's my gang who comes, Mrs. Coulter..." His eyes dropped slightly from her face, roaming goatishly across her body. His voice was low and dark with portent.

Fury flared in her. "Mr. Darden, if you're trying to—"

"And the boy." He'd switched his gaze to Daniel, still sitting as before, his attention on his mother. Darden drew a deep, fateful breath. "Well, I don't know..." He gave a wicked chuckle as he turned his head again to gaze off toward the creek.

When he turned his head back to her, he found her own gaze on the bulging saddlebags. A flush rose in her cheeks. She turned her face away.

Darden laughed, winked. "You were thinkin' about it."

"No, I wasn't." she objected, cheeks burning. "I would never. I am not that kind of person, Mr. Darden."

Darden laughed louder, squirming around where he was tied against the tree. When his laughter died, he pitched his voice low and soft again, with sharp accusation. "Lady, you're more like me that you'd like to think." He winked.

Olivia looked at Daniel. The boy's attention still rested on her, making her even more uncomfortable.

"That's ridiculous," she said, lowering her gaze to the ground.

"Just mull it over...is all I'm sayin'," Darden said. "Personally, I feel like...after all you been through...you deserve a cut of that money. A fresh start."

"Please, be quiet."

"Seventeen-thousand dollars."

"I said be quiet, Mr. Darden."

"Seventeen-thousand dollars would give you and the boy one hell of a nice stake—oh, do please forgive my farm talk, Mrs. Coult—"

"I told you to be quiet! You're frightening my son!" She stretched her arms out to the boy. "Come here, Daniel. You look cold."

The boy crawled over to her, huddled down beside her. She wrapped her around him, holding him close against her.

She tried to relax, but of course that was impossible. Darden's words had wormed their way under her skin. What if Stillman didn't return? What if, instead, the outlaw gang came? Stillman had told her they wanted Darden dead. Then they would take the money and anything else they wanted.

She'd lived on the frontier amongst unwashed men just like Ace Darden himself, long enough to know what that would include. She remembered the lusty glitter in his eyes only a moment ago, and her skin crawled beneath all the clothes she wore.

Also, there was Daniel. Her native son. How would they treat him?

She cast a quick glance at the stuffed saddlebags. The firelight played across them. Her heart quickened. She slid her glance guiltily at Darden. Thankfully, he appeared to be asleep again. At least, his eyes were closed. But his head was up. He couldn't be asleep. His own life was in just as much peril as was hers.

She waited.

Time slowed. The fire burned down. Daniel had fallen asleep, so she eased him back against the tree while she moved to build the fire back up. She reached for a broken branch, then stopped.

No. Why build up the fire? If Darden's gang was after them, the fire would only draw them in. If Stillman wasn't back by morning, then she would take Daniel and leave.

Again, she glanced at the saddlebags.

Again, guiltily, she fired a look over to Darden. This time the man's eyes weren't closed. His gaze met hers. He smiled.

Smugly, he closed his eyes again and rested back against the tree. "You let me know when you're ready to pull out, Mrs. Coulter. I don't think he's comin' back. If anyone's gonna come, we both know who it is. I say we pull out now, give ourselves a good head start. I'll take half...

you'll take half. You'll be in Winifred by tomorrow night, waitin' for the stagecoach to start you on your new journey. I hear San Francisco's a nice city. Good weather all year long…"

He smiled again, mockingly.

Olivia's heart thudded. She couldn't believe the next words she heard leaving her mouth: "How do I know you'd give me half?"

She stared at him, her heart beating fast. He opened his eyes. "My word is good, Mrs. Coulter." There'd been a crispness to his tone. The question offended him.

"No, it isn't."

He glared at her. He glanced at Stillman's gear piled beside the fire, to Olivia's right. "In Ben's saddlebags you'll find my gun. You can hold it on me, make sure I keep my word."

She studied him. Her heart ached now, beating so fast and erratically. She glanced quickly at Daniel. Curled on his side against the tree, he was fast asleep. "You maybe don't think I'd kill you. A preacher's widow. You'd be wrong, Darden."

"No, no." He gave her a cold, knowing smile. "You'd kill me, all right." He paused, and his smile broadened, his eyes alive with mockery. "You an' me, Mrs. Coulter? We ain't all that unalike." He gave his head a wag. "No, sir."

She didn't respond to that. What he'd said

was ludicrous. Still, what was the point in arguing with such a deluded and lowly man as Ace Darden?

"We wait," she said. "We wait another hour."

"It'll be gettin' light by then," Darden warned. "Might be too late."

"We wait," she said, more firmly. "We wait one hour. If he's not back by then, I'll release you."

"We'll go our own separate ways?"

She nodded. "We'll go our own separate ways."

"With the loot." It wasn't a question. He was just drilling it home for her. Into her consciousness. What they would do. And what that would make her.

Only, it wasn't true. She was desperate. What she would do in an act of desperation, she wouldn't do for herself alone. She had the boy to think about.

What she would do, she would do for Daniel.

"One hour," she said, and tossed one small branch on the fire, so they wouldn't freeze to death while they waited.

Again, time passed slowly. It was like waiting for an overloaded, underpowered train to chug its way up a steep hill. She wasn't sure she wanted it to arrive at the station.

Still, she couldn't help imaging the life she and Daniel could have with the help of that seventeen-thousand dollars. With that money, she wouldn't have to return home with her tail between her legs, with an Indian child to explain to her parents, to Jedediah's parents.

No, it was not her money. But didn't she deserve it as much as anyone, including those it rightfully belonged to?

Of course, she did. She'd done her best. She'd been married to a good man. A Presbyterian minister. They'd adopted a needy orphan boy. An *Indian* orphan, no less. Her husband had been taken from her too soon, and then came the debacle at Eagle Creek. On top of that, some human goat had tried to rape her, and she'd been forced to kill him to protect herself.

She and the boy were on the run for their lives.

There was no one on God's green earth who deserved that money more than she did.

She kept track of the time on Jedediah's old, gold-washed Waltham pocket watch, which was one of the few things she'd managed to grab in her haste to leave the saloon. It was all she had to remember her beloved husband by—the watch he'd been given upon his graduation from the seminary in St. Louis.

Unfortunately, her buggy horse had foundered and died the week before the horrific incident involving Byron Conyers, and she and Daniel had to make a run for it. They'd each carried one carpetbag filled with only a few of their precious belongings—mostly clothes to help stave off the late-autumn cold.

When she checked the watch for maybe the eighth or ninth time, her heart fluttered. She looked over the open lid at Darden, who stared at her across the glowing coals of their dwindling fire. "All right," she said, softly snapping the watch closed, returning it to the carpet bag then closing her hand around the keys in her coat pocket. "It's ti—"

"Hello the camp!"

Stillman's voice made her jump, nearly caused her to scream. "Ben!" she said, horrified when she realized the smile on her face was stiff and manufactured.

She glanced across the fire at Darden. He grinned coldly at her, his eyes as black as coals.

Chapter Twenty-Four

Stillman dozed by the fire for twenty minutes while the woman and the boy kept watch.

He knew he was taking a chance. Loco Mc-Guire or Ace's gang might have heard the shots he'd fired into Pug and Pinto, the shots Pinto had triggered into the ground as he'd danced off into the brush. They could be headed this way. But Stillman would be no good against them unless he had at least a few minutes of forced sleep.

He'd been tired even before he'd tramped over to Pug and Pinto's camp. When he'd returned, he was naturally even more worn out. Worn out and cold. Too worn out to pay much attention to the odd reaction he'd noted in Olivia Coulter when he'd stumbled into camp.

The strange feeling he'd experienced had been nothing he'd been able to put a finger on. Still, something foul had been in the air. It had slipped in and out of his mind like a beaver sliding into a lake and pulling its head under water. He'd just needed to sit down against a tree and close his eyes.

"Ben?"

A hand shook him. He'd been so solidly out in even that brief time that when he opened his eyes, he expected to find himself in his own bed in Clantick, looking up into his wife's chocolate brown eyes, framed by the lustrous waves of her thick, chestnut hair. He had to admit the face looking down at him out here in the Barrens was a pretty one, indeed, if drawn and pale with exhaustion and worry. But not his wife's.

Disappointment was a raw ache in him.

"It's time," Mrs. Coulter said quietly, with a guilty air, almost as though she felt responsible for not being Fay.

Softly, she closed the gold-washed time piece in her hand.

"Thanks," Stillman said, poking his hat brim onto his forehead and heaving himself to his feet with a grunt.

He glanced at Ace. The man hacked up phlegm and spat it into the fire. He cast a quick look at the woman. Just as quickly, she glanced back at him.

Yes, there was definitely a foul tinge to the air around the camp. Something had happened while Stillman had been away, but there was no time to ponder on it. Ace and the woman were still here. So was the bank loot.

"Let's get the horses rigged, and mount up," he said, shucking his Bowie knife and cutting Darden free of the tree.

Later, when the others were mounted and they were ready to pull out, Stillman heaved his weary body onto Sweets' back. The sun was not quite up, but there was enough light to see the dour faces of his trail mates, obscured by hats and mufflers, their breath pluming in the purple air around their heads.

"Grim group this morning," he commented. "Just tired of the trail, or did something happen while I was away?"

Ace gazed back at him obliquely, his customary ironic smile quirking the corners of his mouth. He slid his gaze to the woman. She slid her gaze from Ace to Stillman and flashed a too-bright smile. "No. Nothing. I'm relieved you came back, Ben."

"All right, then," he said, and booted Sweets ahead, tugging on Ace's lead. "We should be in Winifred by nightfall, if all goes to plan. We'll get you on the next stage headed for Billings."

"That will be wonderful," Olivia said, booting the roan up beside Stillman. "I'm going to feel like a fish out of water in the big city...after two years on Eagle Creek." She chuckled. "Why, I'm going to have to brush up my manners!"

Stillman glanced at her. Her tone had been overly jovial.

They rode a few paces and then Stillman said, "Mrs. Coulter...Olivia...he didn't try anything on you, did he? Ace? While I was gone?"

"What?" She looked at Stillman, startled. Then she glanced at the prisoner riding behind him. "Oh, no. No...nothing like that. I mean, he was all trussed up. How could he?"

"All right," Stillman said.

They were following a shallow creek now as they made their way between rocky dykes. They'd ridden in silence for about ten minutes before Ace piped up with, "You know what really happened, Ben? While you were away giving ole Pug an' Pinto a deadly case of lead poisonin'?"

Stillman hipped around in his saddle to stare back at the outlaw. "What?"

Olivia cast Ace a withering scowl. "Hold your tongue, Mr. Darden!"

Ace grinned. "We was plannin' how if you didn't come back, she was gonna turn me loose and we was gonna split the loot." He spat to one side then grinned again at Stillman.

"Oh?" Stillman glanced at Olivia. Her cheeks were red as she stared down at her saddle horn.

She shot a defiant look at the sheriff. "Don't listen to him, Ben! That was his plan. He was just talking, and I let him talk because I couldn't get him to shut up."

"Hah!" Ace laughed.

"I never would have taken that money," Olivia assured Stillman. "I am not that kind of woman."

"Hah!" Ace laughed again.

Stillman turned his head forward, swaying with the movements of the bay. "Tell me, Mrs. Coulter...er, I mean, Olivia...what would you have done if I hadn't returned?"

She shook her head. "I honestly don't know." She looked at Stillman. "What should I have done?"

Stillman looked across his shoulder at her. "Whatever you'd have needed to do to survive." He turned his head forward, let Sweets walk a few more paces, then added in a flat, level tone, "The loot, however, belongs to the bank in Winifred."

———————

An hour later, they climbed up out of the Barrens, the deeply scored and twisted land dropping back behind them. A broad, bowl-shaped valley swept ahead of them, carpeted in straw-yellow

grass and rising gently to low, separate mountain
ranges and bluffs towering in nearly all directions. Stillman knew that, beyond a pass in the
next jog of bluffs maybe three miles to the south,
he'd pick up the old army supply trail, which now
served as a stage trail that would take them into
Winifred.

They rested their horses, watering them at a
spring. As the day was heating up, they shrugged
out of their coats and secured them behind their
saddles. Stillman even rolled his shirtsleeves up
his corded forearms.

He passed around a bag of jerky, for they
hadn't taken time for breakfast earlier. Then
they mounted up again and continued riding for
another hour before, reaching the rim of a long
line of low bluffs, Stillman halted his party once
more. He stared down the south side of the ridge
and silently cursed.

Olivia rode hers and the boy's roan up beside
Stillman, to his right. She looked into the next
valley and slapped her hand to her mouth in a
futile attempt to squelch a gasp.

"Ah, hell," Ace said, riding up to Stillman's left.
"Hell, hell, hell, hell!"

"Easy, now."

Stillman's command was as much to himself
as to the others. His own ticker had picked up its

pace as he stared at the line of seven riders spread out in the valley below, maybe a hundred yards away from Stillman's group and on the other side of a twisting, narrow creek.

The riders sat stirrup to stirrup with maybe ten to fifteen feet between them. Their horses switched their tails and tried to lower their heads to pull at the grass, but the riders drew their mounts' heads up sharply by the ribbons.

All seven men were staring toward Stillman from beneath the brims of their battered hats, limned brightly by the clear, midday sun and nibbled at by the warm Chinook breeze blowing down from the western mountains.

That the seven were from Ace's gang there was no doubt.

They were a hard, raggedly attired lot prominently displaying pistols and rifles. Heavy fur coats tied behind their saddles, a couple wore wooly chaps. Others wore buckskins or faded denim or black broadcloth. One man, a thickset fellow with a thick red beard, wore a pair of Bowie knives in sheaths across his chest.

All held rifles either on their shoulders or across their saddlebows.

A member of the group lifted a hand to the side of his mouth, and yelled, "Send our man down here, Stillman, and we'll let you an' the woman an' the boy go!"

The speaker was a tall gent second from left, sitting a buckskin horse. He had long hair—as long and yellow as Custer's. He wore butterscotch doeskin trousers, a white shirt, red neckerchief, and three pistols holstered around his waist. He wore a hat with one of the widest brims Stillman had ever seen.

"Earl Davis," Stillman muttered to himself, going through the file of Montana outlaws in his mind. He glanced at Ace sitting the steeldust beside him. "Is that Earl Davis?"

Ace grimaced. "Yep." He turned to the sheriff. "You, uh…you ain't gonna send me down there, are ya?"

"What's the matter, Ace?" Stillman said, keeping his gaze on the seven men below. "You don't think your pards would welcome you with open arms?"

Ace didn't say anything. He just stared warily down the slope at the seven men glowering back at him.

Again Earl Davis raised his hand to his mouth and shouted, "You got one minute to think about it, Stillman! Then we're gonna come, an' we're gonna come hard, an' we're gonna shoot you!… shoot your prisoner!…shoot that Injun kid the woman's got clingin' to her like a red-skinned louse!…an' then we're gonna the take woman and the money!"

Davis canted his head to one side, and even from this distance, Stillman could see the lewd smile on his face.

Olivia's voice trembled a little as she said, "What are you going to do, Ben?"

Stillman gazed back at Davis. "I'm thinkin' on it."

"I don't see that you have much choice," she said, her tone rising, brittle with fear. She turned to Stillman, her eyes wide with desperation. "I don't see that you have much choice!"

"Take it easy, Olivia."

"You heard what they said they would do to Daniel...to me!"

"To me, too, don't forget!" Ace put in.

"Be quiet, both of you."

Stillman swung down from Sweets' back. He walked to the bay's left hip, and dug Ace's shell belt and holster containing the man's Merwin & Hulbert revolver from his saddlebag pouch. The belt was wrapped around the gun and the holster. Stillman shook the belt out, draped it over his shoulder then walked up to Ace's left stirrup.

He dug his handcuff keys out of his pocket.

Ace stared down at him, brows arched hopefully. "What're you doing?"

"Making the lesser of two mistakes, most likely."

Stillman unlocked Ace's handcuffs.

"What are you doing, Sheriff?" Olivia gazed at him apprehensively, keeping one nervous eye on the seven men below.

"Yeah," Ace said, a smile growing on his mouth. "What are you doing, Sheriff?"

Stillman handed the man his gun and holster.

Ace studied him skeptically, one eye narrowed, as he grabbed the nickel-washed revolver bristling from the black leather holster.

"I don't...I don't get it..."

"I want you to take Mrs. Coulter and Daniel off this butte and into those rocks up yonder."

Stillman pointed to a large mesa roughly half a mile to the west. Its near side wasn't too steep for horses and peppered with cedars and large, black rocks likely blown out by some ancient volcano. Pines studded the top of the mesa, which appeared three hundred feet from its base, set atop a high, grassy pedestal rising from the broad, bowl-shaped valley.

"Head for the crest of that mountain," Stillman said.

"What are you going to do, Ben?" Olivia asked.

Stillman slid his Henry from his saddle sheath. "I'm gonna hold 'em off, buy you some time." He pumped a cartridge into the sixteen-shooter's action, then off-cocked the hammer. "Try to whittle their numbers down a little." He glanced at Ace. "By the time they get to you, I'm hopin' there will be few enough for you to hold off with your pistol."

Ace quickly wrapped the gun and cartridge belt around his waist. He slid the M&H from its holster and broke open the nickel-washed popper at the breech to make sure it was loaded. "You got it, Ben," he said, snapping the gun closed. His mood had improved noticeably. He spun the cylinder and said, "No problem at all." He glanced at the mesa to the west. "We'll make it!"

Stillman walked over and lifted young Daniel off his mother's horse. He set the boy on Sweets' back, then tossed the reins to Olivia. "You'll have a better chance with three horses."

Glancing at Daniel, he said, "Hold on tight, son."

The boy leaned forward and wrapped his gloved hands around the saddle horn.

"Ben, please," Olivia said. "Listen to reason. It would be so much easier just to…" She let her voice trail off as she cast her desperate gaze to Ace, who sat smiling at her and twirling the Merwin & Hulbert on his finger.

"I love you, too, honey," Ace said, and winked.

Stillman leveled a hard, commanding look at the outlaw, and arched a brow. "Get them to safety, Ace."

Ace's suddenly hopeful gaze darted to the bulging saddlebags on Sweets' back.

"Their lives are more important than the money," Stillman said. "Get them to safety. I'll meet you on top of that ridge just as soon as I can."

Ace leveled his own tart gaze on Stillman. "And if you don't?"

Stillman glanced at Olivia, staring at him worriedly. He turned back to Ace and said, "Just get her and the boy to safety. You were a decent man once. I'm trusting you have enough decency left in you to do that much." He wasn't sure he could trust the outlaw, but he thought he could. It was worth the risk, anyway, since there really didn't seem another way out.

Regarding the money, however—there was no point in worrying about it. Like he'd said, the woman and the boy were worth more than thirty-four thousand dollars.

If he was still alive when this was over, he'd track Ace down all over again if he had to. Which he probably would. It wouldn't be hard.

"Well, don't sit there grinning like the cat that ate the canary," Stillman told Ace, jerking his rifle toward the mesa. "Hightail it for that ridge!"

Ace grinned and turned to the woman. "Lady... boy...if you're comin' with me, let's powder some sage!"

He gave a loud whoop, swung his horse around, and put the spurs to it.

The steeldust lunged into an instant gallop to the west.

Olivia stared hesitantly at Stillman. So did the boy.

"What the hell are you two waiting for?" Stillman said, jerking both of their horses around by their bridles, pointing them west. "We don't have all day!"

He stepped back and triggered the Henry skyward.

Both Sweets and Olivia's roan lunged down the slope and off to where Ace was galloping across the bottom of the bowl, heading for the mesa.

Stillman turned to the seven riders.

They'd seen what was happening up here, and now they were riding hell for leather toward the sheriff, triggering lead.

Stillman got down on one knee, pressed the Henry's butt to his shoulder, took aim, and yelled, "All right, pilgrims—let's dance!"

Chapter Twenty-Five

The Henry bucked in Stillman's hands, punching his shoulder.

His first two shots flew wide, tearing into the sod beyond the oncoming riders. The men rode hard and fast, spreading out slightly, making for hard targets. What was good for the goose was good for the gander. Their hard riding wasn't doing anything for their accuracy, either.

Their bullets tore into the ground well short of or well over and beyond their target.

At least for now. That was changing fast, the more ground they tore up between them and Stillman.

Wincing as one bullet buzzed through the air a couple of feet over his head, Stillman cocked another round, pressed the Henry's brass butt plate against his shoulder, drew a bead on a rider now hammering toward him within fifty yards, and fired.

The man jerked in the saddle. He pulled back so sharply on his horse's reins that the horse's head came up hard. The mount fell back and to one side, rolling on top of its rider, who gave a shrill cry. Stillman ejected the spent cartridge casing, seated a fresh one, lined up his sights, and stretched his lips back from his teeth as he again pulled the Henry's trigger.

The bullet plowed into the lower chest of the next-nearest rider—a chunky, bespectacled man in a shabby broadcloth coat and bowler hat. He gave a guttural yell, falling back in his saddle, then slumping forward as the horse continued toward Stillman. As the horse pounded up the ridge in front of the lawman, quickly gaining the saddle on which the sheriff knelt, its rider tumbled off its back, striking the ground to Stillman's left, only a few feet away, and rolling as the horse gave a frightened whinny and bounded past Stillman and off down the slope behind him.

The man's wire-framed glasses, one lens cracked, plopped into the dirt only three feet away from Stillman's left knee.

The sheriff glanced at the unseated rider, seven feet beyond the glasses. Seeing blood bibbing the man's blue shirt, the sheriff returned his attention to the other five riders.

One more came fast while four others, having

watched the demise of the other two, were either slowing their pace or stopping and dismounting. The one still coming fast moved up the slope on Stillman's right, below a field of honeycombed black volcanic rocks. He was levering a carbine from his right shoulder, his reins in his teeth.

One round blew up dirt and grass just inches in front of Stillman, throwing the sod over his right boot. Another bullet curled the air off the sheriff's left ear.

Stillman took quick aim and loosed a shot.

The shooter cried out as the bullet puffed dust from his bib-front shirt, high on his left side. He dropped his rifle and then turned to his left, sagged out of his saddle, hit the ground, and rolled.

His still-galloping coyote dun nearly kicked his lost rider in the head as it continued up the ridge at a slant, crossing in front of Stillman from the sheriff's right to his left, ten feet in front of him, and then lunged on over the ridge in the tracks of the previous mount.

Stillman's view of the man he'd just shot had been obscured for a second by the man's horse. Now Stillman saw the man scrambling on hands and knees into the rocks littering the side of the ridge to Stillman's right, peering up at Stillman, wide-eyed and holding a revolver in his hand.

Stillman threw a .44 round at him, but the man

ducked behind a rock, and the bullet smacked another rock just beyond it, tearing the air in which the son of a bitch's head had been an eye blink before. Ejecting the spent round, the sheriff turned his attention to the other four outlaws.

They'd all dismounted and were scrambling on foot up the ridge, widely spaced and crouched low, looking for cover. The only real cover, however, was in the rocks peppering the ridge to Stillman's left or to his right. To the right, the spine of the ridge rose sharply to join another higher, shelving ridge to the southwest.

Stillman dropped a few feet farther down the ridge he was on, to the west, as the four cut-throats triggered lead at him from where they crouched behind weed tufts and small shrubs or in small depressions. He knew the man he'd shot off the coyote dun was trying to work up through the rocks on the right, where the ridge rose sharply. If he did, he would not only have the higher ground, but he and the others would have Stillman in a whipsaw.

The sheriff rose to his feet and ran, crouching low, along the side of the ridge, rising as the ridge rose to the southwest. Here there were more rocks for cover. He kept moving fast, the Henry held at port arms across his chest, until he'd gained ground at least a hundred feet higher than where he'd just been.

He positioned himself in a nook in the black volcanic rock and quickly tripped the tab to open the loading tube beneath the rifle's main barrel. He dropped fifteen shells into the tube from his shell belt, then, securing the tab against the steel housing, he pumped a fresh round into the chamber.

Taking advantage of this higher perch, he scanned the slope falling away more steeply below him.

The four other cutthroats had seen what was doing, and they were scrambling through the rocks down there, weaving and ducking, occasionally pausing to trigger a shot at him. One of them was Earl Davis. Stillman recognized him by his Custer-like long flowing yellow locks and mustache.

The fifth man, the man Stillman had blown out of his saddle, was out of sight.

That was worrisome. Stillman had to assume the man was still alive. If so, he was likely trying to worm his way in close, using the rocks for cover, to take Stillman out with his six-shooter.

Stillman angled the Henry over his covering rock, snapped a shot off at Davis, who was thirty feet nearly straight below him. Davis cursed as he jerked his head down, Stillman's slug hammering the rock he was using for cover. Stillman moved out from behind his own covering rock and worked his way higher up the ridge, weaving among the rocks, which were larger here—privy- and wagon-sized.

He moved around behind one that was not only the size of a privy but shaped like one. As he stepped around its left side, one of his stalkers froze in his tracks six feet down the rocky slope. He'd just moved out from behind a rock and had been about to rush toward Stillman's position.

But now the sheriff had him dead to rights.

The man cursed wickedly as he crouched and slid his Colt's revolving rifle toward Stillman. The Colt rifle cracked off a shot skyward as the Henry ground two slugs into the man's chest and sent him pin-wheeling over the rocks behind him.

Movement on Stillman's right.

Davis and one other man were trying to rush Stillman from fifteen feet down the rub- ble-strewn slope, firing their carbines. The slugs peppered the rocks to each side of the lawman. He felt a sudden burn in his left side, then low- ered the Henry to his hip and triggered several shots quickly, firing and levering, the ejected cartridges arcing over his right shoulder to clank against the rock wall behind him.

One man screamed and flew backwards.

Davis cursed and dove behind a rock on his

left, Stillman's right. Davis's blond head reappeared, poking out from behind the rock on its far right side.

The man's face was pinched with pain and rage as he raised a Smith & Wesson and cocked the hammer. Stillman raised the Henry to his shoulder, took quick but careful aim, and drilled a .44-caliber hole in nearly the dead center of Davis's freckled forehead.

Davis dropped the Smithy as though it were a hot potato. His head jerked back to smack the rock behind him with a solid thud. "He fell to the dirt and lay still..." His dead eyes stared at the gravel which the blood from his forehead painted red.

Stillman stepped back into a nook in the rocks, the wall to his left formed by the privy-sized boulder. He brushed a hand against his left side, felt the oily wetness of blood. He felt as though he'd been punched by a brute wielding brass knuckles that had been heated to glowing in a smithy's forge.

A gun thundered to his left. The sound was so loud in the close, rock-walled confines, the report itself felt like a punch to Stillman's head. Church bells tolled above a high scream in his ears.

Stillman's left arm went numb as the bullet that had just plowed into it twisted him around and punched him back against another boulder. The man he'd blown out of his saddle was a crouched silhouette staggering toward him now, a smoking Colt in his right hand. The man gritted his teeth and thumbed the Colt's hammer back for a kill shot.

Stillman raised the Henry one-handed. He blew the cutthroat back out of the niche in the rocks and into the sunlight on the other end, triggering the Colt into a rock beside him. The man wailed and writhed and tried to rise. Stillman fired two more rounds into him, silencing the man's foul-mouthed death dirge.

The sheriff leaned back against the rock wall behind him. He looked at his arm. It hurt like a son of a buck, but he didn't think the bullet had clipped the bone or an artery. It was bleeding, but not as badly as it might be.

He wasn't sure about the wound in his left side. That appeared a flesh wound, as well. He removed his dark-green neckerchief and tied it, cursing a blue streak against the pain himself, around the wound, stemming the blood flow. Using his teeth to tug on one end of the wrap, he jerked the knot tight, grunting against the pain searing up and down his arm.

He pulled a handkerchief from his back denims pocket, wadded it tightly, and, reciting several ancient oaths as well as a few he'd manufactured here and now for the grisly occasion, shoved the wadded cloth into the wound in his side. The pain from those two maneuvers so weakened him, he dropped to his knees, shaking. He lowered his head, trying to shove the pain to the back of his brain, groaning with the effort.

Now would be a great time for a shot of the ole busthead, certain past promises be damned...

Finally, hoisting himself to his feet with the aid of the Henry, he staggered out from behind the privy-sized boulder and started down the spine of the ridge, heading for the saddle below. As he did, using the Henry as a cane—albeit gently, not wanting to damage the prized piece—he looked around for a horse. Both mounts that had galloped over the saddle, heading west, were grazing relatively contentedly a couple of hundred feet below.

Fortunately, while one was skittish and ran away as the stranger approached, the other—the coyote dun—was not. It backed away a few steps, whickering softly with apprehension, and even shook its head so hard it nearly lost its bridle. But Stillman was holding out his right hand into which he'd deposited one of Sweets' favorite treats, a sugar cube. Apparently, the dun had a sweet tooth of its own.

Unable to fight off its desire for the cube, the dun allowed Stillman to come close enough to step on the mount's reins as the dun closed its bristling, rubbery lips around the cube, plucking it from Stillman's hand.

Stillman reached down and grabbed the reins just as the mount wheeled and started to flee.

Cursing the burning pain in his side and arm, Stillman managed to get the horse under a tight rein. He slid the Henry into the dun's empty saddle boot, then cursed and grunted his way into the saddle.

"All right," he said. He sucked sharp breath through gritted teeth. He let his butt settle into the leather and turned toward the slanting mesa to the west. "Now we just got a little climbing to do, is all." He grunted spat, and spurred the dun to the west. "Piece of cake..."

Chapter Twenty-Six

Olivia huddled with Daniel against a tree near the edge of the mesa.

They were up a slight rise from where Olivia watched Ace Darden kneeling near a rock at the very lip of the formation, a perch from which he could look down and out across the valley toward the spine-like ridge to the east. That was where the shots had been coming from for the past half hour—sporadic but angry gun reports punctuated by shouted epithets and wails, all muffled by distance.

Still, each one had made Olivia give a slight start.

Now, however, there hadn't been the crackle of a gun report for the past five minutes.

With each second that passed, Olivia felt a large fist of cold apprehension squeeze her more tightly.

"All right," Darden said, rising from his knee, fatefully shaking his head.

Swinging around, he walked to Olivia and the boy, holstering the big, silver revolver he'd been holding, as though making sure it would never be taken from him again. "All right, all right," the outlaw repeated. "That tears it. I ain't waitin' up here no longer. It's too damn quiet down there."

He stomped past the woman and the boy. Olivia turned her head to watch him, more fear rushing at her. "Where are you going?"

"Ole Ace is done with this parade."

Olivia gentled the worry-eyed boy away from her, then heaved herself to her feet. Holding Daniel's hand, she walked to Darden, who was headed to where they'd tied the two horses in a thin stand of pines.

She said, "What is that supposed to mean?"

Ace gave her a cold glance. "You're a smart woman, Mrs. Coulter. You figure it out."

He walked to Stillman's bay and lifted the swollen set of saddlebags off the horse's rump. He carried them to his steeldust.

"What on earth do you think you're doing?" Olivia asked, a wash of dark emotions flooding her.

"Pullin' out." Ace tossed the loot-filled saddlebags over his own horse's rump.

"With the money?" She hated the shrillness and terror she heard in her voice.

"Of course, with the money." Ace swung toward her. "Look lady, Stillman's dead."

"You don't know that."

Ace picked his reins up off the ground. "I know that."

"He could be lying over there badly injured… dying."

"So, what—you want me to ride over there and check? And likely ride into those men from my gang? *Oh, no!*" Ace shook his head, gritting his teeth, his eyes bright with fear, greed and unbridled eagerness to get the hell away from here with the money. "That's suicide, lady. Ole Ace— he knows when the cards done all been played, all the tricks done all laid out. He knows when the game's over, when to cash in his chips…" He swung up onto the steeldust's back. "When to head south to Ole *Mejico!*"

Olivia left Daniel and strode quickly to the rear of Ace's horse. "Not with the money, you don't!" She grabbed the saddlebags off the horse's rump before Ace, hipped around in his saddle and reaching for the bags, could stop her.

"Hey, there! Getaway from there, dammit! Gimme back them bags!"

She backed up with the saddlebags. "You said we'd split it."

"Hah!" Ace slapped his thigh. "So much for your distress over dear old Ben. You're a piece of work, lady. You know that?"

Olivia was amazed at how easily she shrugged off her shame. "Just the same...you said we'd split it."

"That was last night. You don't have as much leverage as you did then." Ace showed her his cuff-free wrists. "Now, toss those bags on my hoss, or I'll come down there an'..." He stopped and glanced at the boy standing wide of both horses, regarding Ace and his mother with anxiousness glistening in his wide, dark eyes.

"No!" Olivia said, backing toward her own horse. "We split it!"

Ace cursed and swung down from his horse's back. He strode at Olivia, saying, "We ain't gonna split, but...I'll let you ride along with me."

"Why would I ride along with you if we don't split the money?"

"Because I'm a rich man, Mrs. Coulter. All women...especially them down on their luck... always set their hats for rich men." Ace stopped a few feet away from her and laughed. "Besides, I can get you out of this country clean. I bet you don't even know which way you'd ride. Well, I do. I can get us out of here, but we're gonna have to do it quick, before those cutthroats down there pick up our trail."

He thrust out his hand. "Now, hand over the bags. Let's mount up and get out of here."

Olivia stared at him, dazed by her racing thoughts.

She knew she couldn't trust this man. But what choice did she have? She'd never be able to keep the money away from him, and she couldn't avoid his gang members by herself. They'd run her down. Besides, he was also right that she had no idea the route to Winifred from here.

"All right." She drew the bags back sharply, defiantly, behind her left shoulder. "But we share the money. What's yours is mine, and..." She stopped, hesitating, her mind recoiling at the implication.

Darden's lusty mind didn't recoil at it. Not a bit. He grinned broadly, raking his gaze across her, and said, "...what's yours is mine." He cut his eyes toward Daniel, and a frown erased the grin on his face. "Except the kid. It's a no-go with the kid. Any kid is a ball and chain, but a redskin is like an anchor around the neck. Forget it." He slid his pistol from its holster, cocked it, and aimed it at Daniel. "Let me take care of it. Real painless this way."

"No!" Olivia dropped the saddlebags and lunged at Ace.

She tried to grab the gun but he jerked it up and away from her. With his other hand, he shoved her hard. She stumbled backward, tripping over the saddlebags, and fell.

"We'll have us a much better time without the shaver." Grinning, Ace extended his pistol toward where Daniel stood frozen in horror.

"No!" Olivia screamed.

The gun barked.

She gasped. Horror froze the blood in her veins.

She frowned as she slid her gaze from Daniel, who remained standing as before, to Ace. The man staggered backward, stopped, fell to his knees. The gun in his hand barked once. The bullet drilled into the ground near his left knee.

He looked down in amazement at the hole in the center of his chest, right where his open shirt exposed his grimy red longhandle top. Blood geysered from the hole.

"What the...hell?" were his last words before he fell forward, striking the ground with a solid smack.

He shivered as though chilled.

Numb with shock, Olivia looked around. The horses had scattered when they'd heard the gunshot. Another horse came into view—a horse and rider just now leaving the pines to the north and entering the clearing in which Olivia sat, staring in shock at the black-bearded stranger in the bear fur coat and hat. The man rode a rangy brown and white pinto horse. He wore a bandage over his left ear. The white bandage glinted in the high-country sun.

As he approached at a trot, the pinto's hooves thudding and crunching the autumn-cured grass capping the mesa, Olivia saw the rifle resting across his saddlebows. Her heart quickened again when she recognized the rangy, bearded man with amber eyes slightly drawn up at the corners, giving him an especially menacing appearance.

John Conyers' *segundo*—Loco McGuire.

A smile grew on his bearded mouth, and his eyes narrowed wolfishly.

He drew the pinto up in front of Olivia and gazed down at her. The pinto stretched its neck to sniff the dead man and shook its head.

"Stillman?" McGuire asked.

Olivia shook her head and was about to speak when another voice said, "Right here."

———

Gaining the top of the mesa, Stillman had followed the pines fringing the formation's northwestern edge, not wanting his presence to be known in the clearing until he was ready. He'd seen and heard Ace and the woman arguing. He'd seen Ace go down when he'd been about to shoot the boy.

He'd seen Loco McGuire ride out of the trees to the north.

Now, as Stillman rode the borrowed coyote dun into the clearing, he kept his Henry trained on McGuire. It wasn't an easy task. He'd lost some blood, and it had been a stiff climb in his wounded condition. He tried desperately to keep his hands from shaking.

Stillman drew the dun to a halt. He kept the Henry aimed straight out from his right hip, angled over the dun's right wither.

"Drop the rifle," he told McGuire. "Climb down off the horse."

McGuire looked Stillman over with his wolfish gaze. His amber eyes went to the wound in the sheriff's side, to the one in his arm. He smiled.

"Now!" Stillman barked.

"Sure, sure." McGuire threw himself off the right side of his horse. That was the side opposite the one Stillman was on. In half a second, he'd gone from sitting the pinto to gone.

"Dammit!" Stillman raked out, trying to draw a bead on the man, whom he could see only parts of as he scrambled to his feet on the other side of the pinto.

McGuire dashed from behind the horse, which

wheeled toward Stillman and gave a startled
whinny. Stillman fired the Henry, but the bullet
flew wide and plumed dirt well beyond the killer.

He cocked the rifle quickly, but held fire.

McGuire had grabbed Olivia. He jerked her to
her feet and held her in front of him.

He dropped his rifle, grabbed his Colt Lightning, and held it to her head.

"Throw away the Henry or the woman's crow
bait, Stillman." He showed his teeth inside his
bearded, thin-lipped mouth as he barked, "You
blew my ear off, you old devil! You killed my *em-
ployer!* For that, I'm gonna kill you, old man! I'm
gonna take the loot you been tryin' so hard to get
back to Winifred, and I'm gonna take the woman
in the bargain. An' there ain't a damn thing you
can do about it, less'n you wanna see her get her
head blowed off right here!"

"Ma!" Daniel cried, and came running.

"Stay there, boy!" Stillman yelled.

Olivia gave a fierce wailing cry and slammed
her left heel down on Loco's right boot toe.

McGuire cursed and staggered backward,
triggering his pistol into the air.

As Olivia dropped, Stillman drew a bead on
Loco's chest, and fired.

Loco screamed. So did Stillman's dun.

The horse reared suddenly, violently. Stillman

in his weakened state was too slow to grab the horn. Suddenly, he was flying over the horse's arched tail. He hit the ground hard and rolled. A war lance of sharp pain lashed through his brain, and then everything went black for a while.

When he opened his eyes, he groaned against the sunlight assaulting them. He wasn't sure how much time had passed. All he could see before him were two dead men—Ace and Loco McGuire. Stillman's bay, the pinto, and the steeldust stood a way off, grazing, idling switching their tails.

The roan was gone.

Hearing distant hoof thuds, Stillman stretched his gaze to the south. A horse just then galloped up a far slope. The roan dragged a dust plume behind it. Stillman saw the woman and her dark-red hair streaming out behind her and over the boy clinging to her back. He saw the lumpy saddlebags atop which the boy sat.

The roan and the two riders galloped up and over the rise and out of sight, their hoof thuds dwindling quickly.

"Damn," Stillman said, then dropped his weary head to the ground.

He lifted it again. More hoof thuds had reached his ears. They seemed to be growing louder.

He squinted against the bright sunlight, staring south. A horse and rider were galloping toward him. The woman and the boy atop the roan. They'd just crested the ridge and were making a bee-line for Stillman.

He heaved himself onto his knees, then sank back against his heels.

She approached at a hard gallop, reined in sharply, the roan skidding to a halt before the lawman. She swung down from the saddle, lifted the boy down, and strode over to Stillman. Tears ran down her cheeks.

She dropped to her knees before him and hung her head in shame. "I'm sorry!"

She wrapped her arms around his neck, pressed her cheek to his chest.

"I'm sorry!" she wailed.

A Look at: Stillman's Wrath

ROBBERS AND COLD BLOODED KILLERS WON'T STOP STILLMAN

Sheriff Ben Stillman's wife, Fay, and the Clantick town doctor, Clyde Evans, are riding the stage back to Clantick from Rocky Ford when the coach is hit by Dutch Wayne's outlaw gang, including Dutch's simple-minded son, Waylon. Waylon is badly injured during the robbery, so Dutch forces the doctor and Fay to ride with his gang as they head to their outlaw hideout in the Highwood Mountains.

Back in Clantick, Ben Stillman gets word of the robbery via the telegraph, and rides off in hard pursuit. His task is made more difficult when rancher Phil Triber leads his own men after the outlaws. Dutch Wayne's gang stole the coach's strongbox carrying fifty thousand dollars belonging to Triber, and Triber wants it back. Stillman demands Triber and his men turn back. The sheriff is afraid that in their zealousness they'll get the hostages killed.

Stillman doesn't give a damn about the money. He's desperate to overtake the robbers and cold-blooded killers before they murder his wife and the doctor. He doesn't realize just how badly Triber wants that money returned to him…nor what it is for.

AVAILABLE ON AMAZON OCTOBER 2019 FROM PETER BRANDVOLD AND WOLF-PACK PUBLISHING.

About the Author

PETER BRANDVOLD grew up in the great state of North Dakota in the 1960's and '70s, when television westerns were as popular as shows about hoarders and shark tanks are now, and western paperbacks were as popular as *Game of Thrones.*

Brandvold watched every western series on television at the time. He grew up riding horses and herding cows on the farms of his grandfather and many friends who owned livestock.

Brandvold's imagination has always lived and will always live in the West. He is the author of over a hundred lightning-fast action westerns under his own name and his pen name, Frank Leslie.